LILY'S STORY, BOOK THREE

Love AT LAST

This is a work of fiction. Any resemblance it bears to reality is entirely coincidental.

Love At Last (Lily's Story, Book 3)

Visit Christine's website: christinekersey.com

LILY'S STORY, BOOK THREE

Love AT LAST

CHRISTINE KERSEY

SAPPHIRE CREEK PRESS

Books by Christine Kersey

Lily's Story Series
He Loves Me Not (Lily's Story, Book 1)
Don't Look Back (Lily's Story, Book 2)
Love At Last (Lily's Story, Book 3)
Life Imperfect (Lily's Story, Book 4)

Parallel Trilogy
Gone (Parallel Trilogy, Book 1)
Imprisoned (Parallel Trilogy, Book 2)
Hunted (Parallel Trilogy, Book 3)
After (a parallel story)
The Other Morgan (a parallel story)

Over You — 2 book series
Over You
Second Chances (sequel to *Over You)*

Standalone Books
Suspicions
No Way Out

Chapter One

Four months after my husband nearly strangled me to death, I received a letter from his mother. Standing next to the mailbox, I stared at Marcy Caldwell's neat handwriting on the envelope, and recalled the lie Trevor had told her about me after our wedding when she'd discovered a bottle of vodka had been stolen from her house. *Lily has a drinking problem.* When I'd tried to explain to her that it was actually her son who had the problem, she hadn't believed me.

I hadn't spoken to her since I'd gone into hiding from Trevor. And I certainly hadn't been in contact with her since my dog had saved my life by crushing Trevor's windpipe. Adrenaline pulsed through me as the unpleasant memories assaulted me.

What does she want?

With shaking hands, I tore open the envelope and read the letter as

I stood in the street.

Dear Lily,

It has taken me a long time to gather the courage to write to you. I don't know all the details of what happened between you and Trevor, but regardless, John and I would really like to get to know Trevor's child—our grandchild.

On the Fourth of July we will be having our annual family get-together and we would like to invite you and your baby to join us. It will be John and me, along with Trevor's brothers and their families. I've included a check to cover the cost of your flight. Please let me know when your flight will be arriving and we will meet you at the airport.

Looking forward to seeing you and the baby,

Marcy

I looked in the envelope and pulled out the check, then felt guilt lance through me. In the six months since I'd had Natalie, I'd never so much as sent Trevor's parents a picture of their grandchild. In truth, I'd hardly thought about them at all. I'd only met them twice—on the Christmas I'd accepted Trevor's proposal, and at the wedding. They'd been kind to me when they'd seen me, and I'd had hopes Trevor's parents could become my surrogate parents. But I'd left Trevor and gone into hiding so soon after the wedding that I'd never had the chance to spend time with them.

I walked back up the gravel driveway to the house and thought about the invitation. The get-together was only a few weeks away, so I needed to decide soon if I would go. I pictured myself and Natalie arriving at the airport, and then seeing the faces of Trevor's parents. Would they truly be happy to see me? Did they blame me for their youngest son's death? What if things got uncomfortable and I wanted to leave?

"I could just drive there," I muttered as I walked into the house, pausing to listen for the sound of Natalie waking from her nap. All was quiet, and I closed the door and locked it—a habit I'd developed since moving there—then sat on the couch. I reread the letter, visualizing Natalie playing with her grandparents, aunts, uncles, and cousins, and knew I had to go. John and Marcy Caldwell were Natalie's only living grandparents and it wasn't fair to them or Natalie to keep them apart. I had fond memories of my grandparents, and I wanted Natalie to have the same kinds of memories.

I grabbed my laptop and pulled up Google maps. It was a seven hour drive to their house in Las Vegas. Not too bad, although with Natalie being only six months old it might be a little more difficult, but hopefully she'd sleep for much of the drive. My decision made, I needed to let Marcy know I would be coming and that she wouldn't have to pick me up from the airport. I didn't have the Caldwell's phone number or an email address, so I decided to write a letter, using the return address on the letter she'd sent me. I would have to buy stamps before I could mail it as I rarely sent anything through snail mail, and decided to drive to the post office after Natalie woke from her nap.

I went into the kitchen to straighten up, and moments later Greta, my sweet German-Shepherd, came bounding through her dog door and into the room. With her tail wagging, she rushed over to me, looking for attention.

I squatted next to her and gave her a good scratching. "Hi there, you good girl."

She seemed to smile at me as her tail wagged even harder.

"You're such a good girl, aren't you?" I cooed to her. "I'll have to see if Marcus will take care of you while I'm gone." Thinking of Marcus made me smile. Over the last few months he'd grown to mean so much to me and Natalie, but when I thought about the day I'd met him, I felt my face heat with remembrance.

I'd gone next door to see if Trish's husband could help me carry in the crib I'd just bought, but a man with the most incredible green eyes answered her door. It turned out that Trish's son, Marcus, had just come home from Afghanistan. He'd carried the crib into the house, then set it up for me. Since I wasn't obviously pregnant yet, it had been a bit embarrassing for me to have him discover my pregnancy that way.

After a bumpy start to our friendship, recently we'd become closer. I still regretted that I'd had to lie to him about my real name and the fact that I'd been in hiding from my husband, but I hoped he'd truly forgiven me. We hadn't taken our relationship past friendship yet, but I felt like we were on the verge of that next step, and I was eager for Marcus to feel the same way.

Greta perked up her ears and I heard sounds coming from Natalie's room upstairs. I stood, listening to her baby sounds, and smiled, then headed toward the stairs. I paused at the bottom, suddenly recalling the horrible day four months before when Trevor had knocked me unconscious and taken Natalie with the intention of letting his girlfriend, Amanda, become Natalie's mother. My heart contracted in anger and terror at the memory. That day had been the worst day of my life.

Why am I thinking about that now? Then I realized it must be due to the letter from Trevor's mother. Ever since Trevor's death, I'd tried very hard to put the events of that day behind me, but hearing from Trevor's mother had dredged up many of the bad memories, broadcasting them in vivid high definition pictures in my mind.

Closing my eyes, I shook my head, forcing the images away, then I opened them and hurried up the stairs to my baby girl's room. When I opened the door my gaze went directly to Natalie, who lay on her back, her little fingers wrapped around her toes as she watched the bright colors on the mobile above her head.

"Hi, baby," I murmured to her as I approached her crib.

Her head turned in my direction and her face lit up with a smile. Every time she did that, my heart brimmed with love—my baby girl knew *I* was her mommy, and once again gratitude flooded my body that Trevor had failed in his attempt to take her away from me.

I reached down and lifted her from her crib and held her close, breathing in her precious baby scent. "My sweet, sweet, Natalie," I whispered in her ear.

She giggled and I kissed her soft neck, bringing on more peals of laughter. I gazed into her vivid blue eyes—one trait she inherited from Trevor—and smiled. "I love you so much." Warm tears filled my eyes as I gazed at her. This little baby was my absolute world and I'd do anything for her. I blinked the tears away, then changed Natalie and fed her.

A short time later I carried her out to the car and set her car seat in its base. "In a few weeks you're going to meet your grandparents, cousins, aunts, and uncles." As I said the words, I realized that without Trevor's family, the number of people in Natalie's life was tiny—just me and Marcus. And Marcus was just a good friend.

I stroked Natalie's cheek—she deserved to have lots of people in her life who loved her—then climbed into the car and drove to the post office. After mailing the letter, we went to the park and I pushed her on a baby swing for a while, pushing her from the front. She smiled brightly as the swing brought her closer to me, then giggled loudly as the wind blew across her face.

There were very few people at this park and it felt like I had the place to myself. Across town was another park, one that was much more popular, but I hadn't been able to make myself go there. It was the park where I'd met Trevor to make an exchange: He would give me Natalie if I gave him the money I'd found buried in the Nevada desert.

Against all odds, I'd managed to get Natalie back that night, but I'd had to fight for my very life, and would have died if Greta hadn't intervened. Pushing the painful memories aside, I focused on my baby, who smiled with innocent joy, completely unaware that she'd been at the center of such a dramatic event.

After a while the heat of the June day became uncomfortable, and we headed home. When we pulled up to the house, I was pleased to see Marcus's Jeep parked out front, although I didn't see Marcus. I brought

Natalie into the house, and when Greta didn't meet me at the door, I knew where Marcus must be. Holding Natalie on my hip, I smiled as I went to the kitchen door and out into the backyard. My smile widened as I watched Marcus playing with Greta. His back was to me, but when Greta ignored him to race over to Natalie and me, he turned around and saw us.

"Hi, Lily." He strode toward us, smiling. "I hope you don't mind that I let myself into the backyard."

I smiled in return. "You know I'm fine with that." I sat on the porch steps with Natalie balanced on my lap.

Marcus squatted in front of me and put his finger in Natalie's hand, then gazed into her face. "Hi, baby girl. Were you out with your mommy?"

Natalie squealed with happiness, kicking her feet, and held on to his finger. I watched Marcus's face and felt my attraction to him grow. He'd been there when Natalie had been born—the most important moment of my life—and after he'd gotten past the lies I'd told him about my true identity, he'd been part of our lives ever since. For all intents and purposes, he was the closest thing to a father Natalie had.

As I watched him watching my baby, my heart filled with warmth. He was a good man and my feelings were deepening all the time. A couple of months before I'd thought he was feeling the same thing, but then he'd seemed to back away into the friend zone. I knew he'd been hurt by an old girlfriend, but I thought he should be over that by now.

His gaze shifted from Natalie's face to mine, and the intensity of his gorgeous green eyes drew me in. "How's your day going?" he asked.

"It's been . . . interesting."

His eyebrows went up in question. "Yeah? How so?"

On the night Greta killed Trevor, Marcus had arrived at my house just after the awful event had happened. He'd seen the aftermath of Trevor's attack and had stayed by my side as the police had questioned me, but in all that time we'd never talked about Trevor. I had no desire to talk about my late husband with Marcus—there were too many painful memories—and Marcus had never brought it up either, so it was with hesitation that I broached the subject of the letter I received.

"Today I got a letter from Marcy Caldwell."

Marcus looked at me blankly. "Who?"

I bit my lip, realizing he wouldn't know who the Caldwell's were—I'd never told him Trevor's last name. "She's Trevor's mother."

His eyes widened slightly, then settled back to normal. "What did she want?"

"She wants to meet Natalie."

His gaze went to the baby on my lap, then back to me. "What are you going to do?" He moved from his squatting position to sit next to me on the porch step.

"I'm going to go."

He pressed his lips together and slowly nodded. "Where do they live?"

"Las Vegas."

"So you're going there? To Vegas?"

"Yes. They're having a family get-together over the Fourth of July and she invited me to come."

"Do you really think that's a good idea?"

My brows pulled together. "Why wouldn't it be? They're Natalie's family."

"I know that. It's just . . ." He shook his head. "Never mind."

"What? What were you going to say?"

He shook his head again. "It's really not my place to say anything."

I disagreed. Marcus was very important to both Natalie and me and his opinion mattered greatly. "Please, Marcus. Tell me."

He sighed. "From the little you've told me about Natalie's father, well, I just wonder what his family is really like."

I relaxed. "They're nice people."

"How much time have you spent with them?"

"Some. Not a lot."

He nodded. "Okay." Then he smiled, but it seemed forced. "Good. It will be good."

His hesitation in my decision made me rethink it, but I'd already told Marcy I was coming. "Can you take care of Greta while I'm gone?"

"Sure, of course."

"Thank you."

He looked at me with sudden intensity. "You know you can always count on me, don't you, Lily?"

I nodded, taken aback by the emotion in his eyes. It was at moments like this that he confused me the most. One moment he was advising me as a friend, and the next his eyes seemed to convey that his feelings ran deeper than mere friendship. "Yes." I looked at him and tried to express with my eyes that I cared for him as well. I debated whether the time was right to tell him exactly how I felt, but something held me back.

"Marcus?" a voice called from the gate. "Marcus, are you back there?"

I recognized the voice of Trish, my neighbor and Marcus's mother, and held back a frown. She'd been a good neighbor, but I'd felt a strain between us ever since the truth of my situation had come out. Even before that though, she'd asked me not to encourage Marcus's attention. But once she found out I'd lied about being widowed—although it was true now—she'd been even more standoffish.

"Yeah, Mom. I'm back here."

"Can you stop by the house, please?" She stayed on the other side of the gate, never coming in to the backyard.

"Sure."

Then all was quiet, and I assumed she'd walked back to her house, which was a short distance away.

Marcus smiled at me and I could tell he felt embarrassed by the behavior of his mother—she hadn't even said hello to me.

"It's okay," I said in response to his unspoken message. "I can't blame her for being upset with me."

"It's not her place to judge you, Lily. She has no idea what you've been through."

Though I appreciated his support, I didn't want to come between him and his family. "You'd better go see what she wants."

He sighed. "I already know what she wants."

I raised my eyebrows in question.

"She's going to tell me I shouldn't spend so much time with you and Natalie," he said. "But I've already told her that we're just good friends."

I felt my heart break a little at his words and was glad I'd held back from telling him that I thought I was falling in love with him.

Chapter Two

The weeks leading up to the get-together at John and Marcy's house passed uneventfully. Marcus stopped by when he could, brightening my day each time I saw him, but our relationship didn't show any signs of progressing beyond friendship. When the day came for me to drive to Las Vegas, Marcus came by to get the key so he could take care of Greta.

"It would be a lot easier if I could just take her to my apartment," he said. "But they don't allow pets."

An idea occurred to me. "Why don't you just stay here while I'm gone?"

"Are you sure?"

I completely trusted Marcus. "Yes. It makes sense, don't you think?"

"Yeah, I suppose it does."

I smiled. "It's settled then."

"Okay. I'll bring over a sleeping bag and sleep on the couch."

"Don't be ridiculous. You can use my bed. I just washed the sheets this morning, so you'll be all set."

His face reddened a bit. "If you're sure."

I nodded. "I am."

He finally agreed and a short time later Natalie and I were driving south. We stopped a few times so I could stretch my legs, as well as give her a break from her car seat, but by evening we arrived in Las Vegas. The last two times I'd been to the Caldwell's house, Trevor's parents had picked us up from the airport and I hadn't paid much attention to where they lived. Fortunately, I was able to use the GPS app on my phone to guide me there.

As their house came into view, happy memories of Trevor filled my mind, making my heart ache with what could have been. I'd loved him so much, and wished with all my heart that things had worked out differently and for the better. If only he'd been the person he'd led me to believe, we'd still be happily married and we'd be enjoying our daughter together.

I pulled up to the house and turned off the engine, then realized tears were streaming down my face. I'd really never properly grieved for Trevor, and now, being here, the grief overwhelmed me. Not wanting Trevor's parents to see me like this, I turned the car back on and drove away, hoping they hadn't seen me arrive.

With Natalie sleeping, I drove around until my emotions were under control, then I parked on a street not far from the Caldwell's house and used a baby wipe to erase all traces of my tears. When I pulled up to the Caldwell's house the second time, even though I felt sad, I was able to keep the tears at bay. I took Natalie out of her car seat, along with her diaper bag, and walked to the front door.

Nervous to see Trevor's parents face to face, I pressed the doorbell and waited, my heart pounding. They must have been devastated when they'd learned of their son's death, and I feared that on some level they blamed me. I heard footsteps approaching and I took a deep breath, then slowly released it. A moment later the door swung open.

"You made it," Marcy said, her gaze skimming over me and going to Natalie, who was starting to wake up in my arms.

"Hi, Marcy."

Her gaze came back to me and she smiled as she held the door open. "Please come in."

As I walked into the house, memories assaulted me—Trevor showing me around his childhood home, Trevor's ecstatic joy when I accepted his proposal, me getting ready for our wedding. I forced myself to breathe slowly, doing all I could to keep the tears away.

"Are you okay, Lily?"

When my eyes met hers, I didn't feel any animosity from her, just sincere concern, and I had to swallow around the lump that formed in my throat. My chin quivered as I spoke. "I'm just thinking about Trevor."

Her eyes filled with tears and I worried that I'd made her sad. "I think about him all the time," she whispered. Then she pulled me and Natalie into a warm embrace. "That's why I wanted to meet his baby so much." After a moment she released us.

"Would you like to hold her?"

Her face lit up. "Yes. Very much."

I handed Natalie to her, and she pressed her cheek against Natalie's head.

"She's so beautiful."

I smiled. "Thank you."

She held the baby away from her and gazed at her face, then looked at me with wonderment. "She has Trevor's eyes."

I nodded. "Yes. I always loved his eyes."

"Come and sit down, Lily. We need to catch up."

I followed her into the living room and sat on the couch. She sat in a plush chair nearby. Natalie was such a momma's girl, I was afraid she'd start crying when she realized a stranger was holding her, but thankfully she seemed content.

"Is John home?" I asked.

"No, just me."

I had to admit that I was glad about that. I wasn't ready to face everyone just yet. And Marcy's reaction to seeing me had been much more positive than I could have hoped. "She usually takes a little time to warm up to people she doesn't know, but she seems to like you just fine."

Marcy smiled at Natalie. "That's because I'm her grandma."

"You know, you're her only grandma."

Marcy looked at me with surprise. "Oh. I guess I hadn't thought about that." Then her eyebrows drew together. "How are you doing, Lily?"

I was completely unused to having anyone show me such motherly concern. The only person who'd been involved in my life lately was Marcus, and though he'd been attentive to me as a friend, it wasn't the same as having the love of a parent. My mother had died when I was a child—killed by a drunk driver—so I had only a vague memory of what it felt like to have a mother worry about me. But I liked the way it made me feel—loved and cared for—and felt fresh emotion welling up.

I swallowed several times to force down the tears that seemed to insist on coming. After a moment I got my emotions under control. "We're doing fine."

She nodded, then looked at Natalie for a moment. Finally she looked at me again. "Do you still have that dog?"

I felt my heart lurch as I imagined where she was going with her question. "Yes."

"Do you really think that's a good idea? You know, with Natalie being so little and helpless?"

Greta had literally saved my life. Trevor had been strangling me and

I'd begun to black out—I *knew* I was about to die. And then Greta had seemed to appear out of nowhere. She'd knocked Trevor off of me and crushed his windpipe. She had killed him, but she had saved me. How could I explain that to Marcy without hurting her? My dog had saved me, but she had killed Marcy's son. "Greta protects us."

Marcy's lips compressed into a thin line, then she said, "There are other ways to protect yourself."

I wasn't sure where she was going with this. "What do you mean?"

"Isn't your house kind of far from any neighbors?"

I wondered how she knew that, but since she had gotten my address, it wouldn't have been difficult for her to discover that my house was somewhat isolated. "My neighbors aren't too far."

She sighed softly. "But wouldn't it be safer for both you and Natalie if your neighbors were closer?"

I didn't want to argue with my former mother-in-law—our visit had been so friendly up to this point—but I also didn't like her telling me what to do. I was an adult and no one had the right to tell me what to do. "Are you suggesting that I move?"

Her face softened. "John and I would like to invite you to move in with us."

My eyes widened at the unexpected invitation, but I quickly settled down. "That's very generous of you, Marcy, but Natalie and I are quite happy where we are."

"You said it yourself, Lily. John and I are Natalie's only grandparents. And my other two boys, Scott and Chris, and their families, are the only other family you have. Don't you think it would be wonderful if Natalie could be raised among family?"

What she said was true, and the thought of Natalie not knowing her cousins, grandparents, aunts, and uncles very well made me feel selfish and guilty, but I'd made a life for us in the little house that we rented. Plus there was Marcus. Inwardly, I smiled as I thought about the man I was falling in love with. I couldn't leave him. If I did, then I was certain our relationship would progress no further than friendship—and even that would be in jeopardy if I moved over seven hours away.

"Of course I want Natalie to know her family," I said, wanting to prove to Marcy that I was a good mother, that I considered what was best for my child. "But I can't ask you to house us."

She held one hand out to encompass the room. "We have plenty of space here. And then you could save your money."

How could I convince her that I didn't want to move there without hurting her feelings? She'd been through enough heartache with the loss of Trevor. I didn't want to add to it. "I have enough money to support us. I've started a web design business and I already have a few clients in my town."

She smiled. "I'm glad to hear that. You could run your business from here though, couldn't you?" She paused. "What if you just moved to this area? You wouldn't have to live with us."

I held back a frown.

"What's keeping you where you are, Lily?"

Marcus. But of course I couldn't tell her that. I was certain she would disapprove of me having a male friend so soon after Trevor's death. Not only that, I felt confident she would feel hurt to think of another man being like a father to Natalie. My voice came out in a whisper. "I like where we live."

Marcy's brow furrowed. "Doesn't it bother you to live in the house where Trevor was . . . killed?" Her eyes filled with tears on the last word.

That house had been my refuge long before Trevor showed up, and soon after his death I'd determined not to let the bad things he'd brought with him keep me from loving my little home. "I try not to think about that night, Marcy."

Tears spilled over her lashes and cascaded down her face. "I think about it all the time."

Seeing her tears made the tears I'd held back push their way into my eyes. Nothing I could do would stop them and soon I was sniffling along with her. "I'm so sorry about the way things turned out," I cried.

Natalie must have sensed the sad feelings in the room because she began fussing. I took her from Marcy and snuggled her close, which settled her down.

"Lily, I want you to know that I don't blame you for what happened."

Relief swept over me at her words. "Thank you." I took a tissue out of my purse and wiped my eyes and nose.

Marcy's tears had slowed and she took a handkerchief out of her pocket and wiped her face. "But I think it's only fair to warn you that not everyone agrees with me."

My heart began to pound. "What do you mean?"

"Trevor's brothers are still feeling pretty angry about everything that happened."

"Do they think it's my fault?"

She frowned. "I'm not sure exactly. I think they're just having a hard time knowing their brother was killed." She hesitated. "By your dog." She quickly went on. "And I worry about that dog around Natalie. Do you really think that's the best idea? She could be dangerous."

"Greta was protecting me. Trevor was strangling me and I would have *died*." As soon as the words left my mouth, I wished I hadn't said them. Marcy's face had gone pale—even the rosy red of her lips had turned white. "I'm sorry," I said, my voice softer. "But it's true."

She stood, and shaking her head, she fled the room.

Stricken to know my words had cut her to the bone, I felt paralyzed. I hugged Natalie as my mind raced. Should I go to her? Should I flee this house and this town and never come back? And if things had started out so nice, and turned bad so quickly, what would it be like with the rest of Trevor's family? Especially his brothers who apparently held me responsible for their brother's death?

"We should go," I whispered in Natalie's ear. I picked up her diaper bag and slung it over my shoulder, then headed for the door.

"Wait," Marcy said from the hallway. "Please don't go."

I spun around, my heart racing. "It was a mistake to come here. It's too soon."

Marcy hurried over to me and grabbed my arm. "No. Please. Give us a chance."

I turned to her, and when I saw the pleading in her eyes, my resolve slipped. How would I feel if I was her? Of course I'd want to get to know my grandchild, especially if my own child was dead. My shoulders slumped in acquiescence. "Okay."

She put her arm around me and led me back to the living room. "Thank you, Lily. You have no idea what this means to me. To our family."

I let her lead me back to the couch and I sat down and Natalie began fussing again. "I think she's getting hungry."

"Okay. What do you need?"

I smiled. "I just need to nurse her."

Marcy smiled back. "I'll give you some privacy then."

I watched her leave, then I nursed Natalie and soon she fell asleep. I gazed at my precious daughter and watched her eyelids flutter and wondered what she was dreaming about.

"I borrowed a port-a-crib from a friend," Marcy said as she walked in the room. "Do you want to put her down?"

I nodded and followed her to the room where I'd stayed before. I placed Natalie in the crib and tucked her favorite blanket around her, then tiptoed out of the room and closed the door.

A short time later John came home, and he was as nice as Marcy had been, and I felt better about my decision to stay. When I went to bed that night, I thought about the last time I'd slept in that bed. It had been the night before Trevor and I had married—which was less than a year and a half earlier. If I had known then what I knew now, would I have gone through with it? As I listened to the soft breathing of my sweet baby in the crib nearby, I had to admit that all I'd been through was worth it because I had her.

The next day Trevor's brothers and their families would be coming over and I was worried about how the day would go. Would they be friendly to me, or would they be openly hostile? I had a hard time falling asleep as my mind conjured up ugly scenes with Chris and Scott. I'd spent so little time with them that they'd never gotten the chance to know me in happy circumstances. Would that keep them from giving me a chance now? And if so, would that keep Natalie from getting to know her cousins?

Chapter Three

Shortly before lunch Scott arrived with his family. His wife, Deena, gave me a warm hug.

"It's so good to see you again," she said as she smiled at me. Then she looked at Natalie, who I held in my arms. "Can I hold her?"

"Sure." I handed her over and Deena held her close.

"Oooh, I just love babies," she cooed.

"Uh oh," Scott said. "Don't get any ideas now." I looked at Trevor's oldest brother and saw a slight resemblance, but remembered that Chris looked more like Trevor than Scott did.

I smiled at him and was surprised by the friendliness he showed me. Maybe Marcy had been exaggerating a bit.

He pulled me into a hug, then released me. "It's been a while."

I nodded. "Yeah."

"Well, I'm glad you could come."

I smiled. "Thanks."

Scott went to help his Dad with the barbecue while the kids played in the pool. The temperature was well over a hundred degrees—closer to a hundred and ten—and I decided to keep Natalie in the air-conditioned house. I helped Marcy with the side dishes while Deena held Natalie, and we all chatted companionably.

Just before the barbecue was ready, Chris and Melody and their two boys arrived. The boys raced out to the pool, but when I saw Chris I nearly gasped. For some reason I hadn't remembered how much Chris and Trevor looked alike—maybe because when I'd been here before I'd only had eyes for Trevor. But now, seeing Chris, my emotions were in a whirl as memories of Trevor—good and bad—rushed through my mind, and my heartache at all that had happened intensified.

How I wish Trevor was here now, and we were a happy family.

I watched as Chris greeted his mother, then hugged Deena. When he completely ignored me, I felt hurt—everyone else had been so kind.

"You remember Lily, don't you, Chris?" Marcy said.

How could he forget me? He probably blames me for Trevor's death. "Hi." I smiled, trying to thaw the air that now felt frozen.

He glanced at me, then looked at his mother. "Where's Dad and Scott?"

Marcy frowned. "Outside."

He walked past me and out the door to the backyard.

Melody walked up to me and gave me a hug. "Hi, Lily."

I hugged her back, wondering if she felt the same as her husband. Of course it wasn't her baby brother who had died. "It's good to see you, Melody."

She pulled back and smiled. "You, too." Then she turned to Deena and held out her arms toward Natalie. "My turn."

Deena laughed and handed Natalie over, and the tension in the room dissipated.

I glanced at Marcy and she looked sad, but I didn't know what to say, so I kept quiet. A few minutes later John called everyone outside to eat. Deena and I helped Marcy carry out the side dishes, then we all sat around a table with a large shade over it. I looked at Chris and noticed him staring at me, but when our eyes met, he looked away. Sadness and guilt washed over me, but then Natalie started fussing in Melody's arms.

I walked over to Melody, who sat next to Chris, and took Natalie from her. As I walked away I heard Chris murmur to Melody, "Why did she have to come anyway?"

Then I heard Melody shush him.

I just have to get through today, I told myself. Then I'll leave first thing in the morning. I sat down and ate as best as I could while holding a baby, and listened to the conversation around me.

"Let me take her," Marcy offered halfway through the meal. "I'm finished eating."

I handed Natalie off and continued eating.

"So, Lily," Scott said.

I looked at him, my fork halfway to my mouth.

"Mom tells me you're considering moving to Vegas."

Before I could even answer, Chris shouted, "What?!"

My face reddened at Chris's obvious unhappiness with such an idea. I set my fork down. "No, I'm not moving anywhere."

"That's good," Chris said under his breath, but loud enough for everyone to hear.

"Chris," his dad warned.

"Come on, Dad," Chris said. "We talked about this. No one wants her living here, reminding us every day of what she did."

Melody put her hand on Chris's shoulder and whispered something to him, but he just pushed her hand away and shook his head.

Mortified, I pushed back from the table, grabbed Natalie from Marcy's arms, and rushed inside. I hurried into the room where I'd slept, lay Natalie on the bed, and shoved my things into my suitcase.

"Not everyone feels like that, Lily." John stood in the doorway with Marcy by his side.

I turned and looked at them. I shook my head and continued gathering our things, not able to speak through a throat swollen with unshed tears. Then I slung Natalie's diaper bag over one shoulder, along with my purse, scooped up my baby, then stood there with my back to the door, knowing I couldn't carry everything by myself.

I coughed to clear my throat and turned around to face Trevor's parents. "I appreciate your hospitality, but it's time for me to go."

Marcy stepped toward me. "Please, don't leave."

I shook my head. "No. I need to go."

She must have seen the look of determination on my face, because she stared at me a moment, then nodded. "I understand."

"Thank you."

She looked at her husband. "John, can you get the suitcase?"

"Of course." He grabbed the handle and lifted the bag.

"May I hold Natalie again?" Marcy asked.

I let her take Natalie and we walked toward the front door. As we passed through the kitchen, I could hear the conversation outside—someone had left the sliding glass door open—and I clearly heard Chris say, "She's leaving, huh? Things get too tough, so she just leaves. Typical."

I pretended like I didn't hear and walked to the front door, then out to my car. John helped me load my things into my car, then I took Natalie from Marcy.

"I hope you'll come visit again," Marcy said.

"Maybe." John and Marcy had been nothing but kind, so maybe if it was just them it would be okay.

Marcy pulled me into a hug. When she let me go, John hugged me too. I put Natalie in her car seat and turned back to them. "Bye."

They waved and I climbed into the hot car and turned on the

engine, turning the air-conditioner on full-blast, then we pulled away from the curb. As we drove away, I glanced in my rear-view mirror and saw Marcy wiping a tear off of her cheek, and felt guilt slice through me that I was leaving so soon. But Chris clearly didn't want me there and I felt like I was intruding on their family party. It was better if I left, I told myself, and I was just glad I'd decided to drive so that I could leave when I needed to.

By the time Natalie and I reached home, it was late, but I was thrilled to see my house as I pulled up the gravel driveway. Then I saw Marcus's jeep parked out front and remembered that, at my insistence, he'd agreed to stay at the house while I was away.

Natalie stayed asleep as I lifted her from her car seat and carried her to the front door. Just as I reached the door, it opened and I saw a smiling Marcus there to greet me. His welcoming face was just what I needed after the long day I'd had, and I felt warmth toward him surge within me. He held the door open and I walked in. Greta came right to me, but he held her back as my hands were full with Natalie.

"Let me put her down," I whispered as I walked past him and toward the stairs. After I put her in her crib, I came back downstairs to talk to Marcus. Greta rushed over to me and I gave her some attention, then looked at Marcus.

His face clouded with worry. "You're back a little earlier than I expected. How did it go?"

I grimaced. "Not so great."

"Do you want to talk about it?"

I looked at the earnest expression on his face, then remembered the way I'd felt when Chris—who looked so much like Trevor—had announced that they'd all talked about me before, and had decided they really didn't want me there. I shook my head. "Not really."

He smiled in understanding. "Okay." Then he paused. "Since you're back there's no reason for me to stay. Let me just get my things."

As much as I enjoyed his company, I was exhausted, so I didn't try to convince him to stay. "Thank you for taking care of Greta for me."

He smiled. "Anytime." He went upstairs, and I went out to the car to get my suitcase and the diaper bag. I carried my things up to my room and set them on the floor, then watched Marcus as he finished packing his toiletries.

"Were you able to go see any fireworks tonight?" I asked.

He shook his head. "It's not as much fun unless you go with someone you care about."

I wasn't sure if he was implying that he would have liked to go with me, or if he was just speaking generally. Most of the time it was hard to know how he was feeling, which I found frustrating, so I just nodded.

He zipped his duffel bag closed and tossed it onto his shoulder. "I'd better get going."

I followed him downstairs, then to the front door. "Thanks again, Marcus."

He smiled at me as he reached for the doorknob. "Anytime."

I watched him walk to his car, then locked the door behind him and turned on the alarm. After getting ready for bed, I slipped between the covers and immediately noticed the familiar scent of Marcus. He'd slept in my bed the night before and the unmistakable aroma of his cologne lingered on the pillow. Feeling suddenly lonely, I snuggled into the pillow and breathed his scent.

Tears filled my eyes as I allowed self-pity to wash over me. My relationship with Marcus didn't seem to be going anywhere, yet he was my only friend.

"Wait a minute," I whispered. "What about Alyssa?"

I hadn't talked to my friend from Reno in ages. What was wrong with me? How could I have forgotten about her? I'd been so wrapped up in being a new mom, and then after Trevor died I'd kind of cocooned myself from the world. It was time to break out of that cocoon.

My tears stopped as a smile spread onto my face. The last time I'd heard from her, she'd been planning her wedding. She'd never emailed me about the date and I hoped I hadn't missed it. I picked my phone up from my bedside and pulled up my email account, then composed an email.

Alyssa,

I'm sorry I haven't talked to you in forever. So much has happened since I last emailed you! We need to get together and catch up. When is your wedding? Are you at home for the summer?

Take care!

Lily

Feeling better, I set the phone on the nightstand and closed my eyes. Marcus's scent filled my nostrils, and as I drifted to sleep, his face filled my mind.

Chapter Four

After I fed Natalie a breakfast of baby rice cereal, then nursed her, I put her on a large blanket on the floor for tummy time. I'd folded the blanket several times to make it thick and soft since I was placing it on the hardwood floor, and she cooed and giggled as she watched Greta walk around the blanket. Greta knew to stay off the blanket and I smiled as I watched my little family.

But when I remembered Marcy's comment on the day I'd arrived in Vegas, about the family's concern with Greta being around Natalie, I frowned. Greta would never hurt my baby—if anything she was very protective of Natalie and who was around her. And I resented the implication that I was a bad mother for letting my sweet German-Shepard be around my baby girl.

I pushed the thoughts away. They could think whatever they wanted

—when it came to my family, I would do whatever I thought best.

My phone chimed, indicating an email had arrived. I didn't get many emails and hoped it was from Alyssa. I tapped the email app on the phone and saw a new email from my friend.

Lily -

What a wonderful surprise to hear from you! I've been thinking about you these last few days. My wedding is August 14th and we've decided to do something kind of wild. A shipboard wedding! I've always wanted to visit Alaska, so we decided to take a cruise there and have whatever family and friends come that can, and then get married on the ship! I don't know if you'd be able to come, especially with such late notice, but I would love, love, love it if you could!

Let me know as soon as you can as we have to let the cruise people know who's coming.

Take care!

Alyssa

She'd put the cruise ship information in the email, as well as the specific dates she was going.

"Wow," I said to Natalie and Greta. "Wouldn't that be fun?" I considered the idea of going on a cruise as I absently watched Natalie and Greta. I'd never done anything like a cruise before—the idea had never even crossed my mind—but it sounded like a lot of fun.

The more I thought about it, the more I wanted to go. I hadn't seen Alyssa in a long time and it would be a wonderful opportunity for us to catch up. Not only that, but it would be good for me to get away for a while. I'd been so busy learning how to be a mother, as well as focusing on myself after the trauma I'd been through, I felt like going on a trip like this would be a great way to step outside of my normal life—see new places, meet new people.

I grabbed my laptop and pulled up the website for the cruise company. After a little research I found it was kind of pricey, even if I got an interior room, but oh, how I wanted to go. With the money from the sale of Dad's house, plus the large amount remaining from his life insurance policy, not to mention the little bit of money I was making by designing and maintaining the website for *Billi's,* as well as some other small businesses in town, I could afford this splurge.

"I'm going to do it," I said out loud, a wide grin on my face.

I pulled up the email program on my laptop and replied to Alyssa's email. As I started writing, it occurred to me that she didn't know I had a baby. The last time I'd seen her was before Trevor had locked me up, and when I'd seen her last I hadn't known yet that I was pregnant. And once I'd gone into hiding, I hadn't told her because I hadn't wanted to worry her.

My smile grew as I wrote the email.

Alyssa,

I'm so excited for you! That sounds like a blast! And guess what??? I'm going to come!! I'm going to book the cruise right now. I'm super excited to go on this cruise, especially since I'll be able to see you and meet your fiancé.

I'll be bringing a guest with me—but don't worry, she won't require anything from you—because she's only six months old! Yes, I have a baby! Her name is Natalie and she is gorgeous. I have so much to tell you and I can hardly wait until I see you.

Can't wait!

Lily and Natalie

I pressed Send, and a few minutes later I received a reply from Alyssa.

Lily,

I can't believe you're a mother! Wow—you do have a lot to tell me and I'm super stoked that you're coming on this cruise. The wedding is on the third day after we leave Seattle, so that should give us plenty of time to catch up before the wedding and honeymoon. Make sure to bring a pair of binoculars because I understand there's a good chance you'll be able to see whales from the ship.

Anyway, I'll see you in just a few weeks. Having you there will make my day that much more special!

Alyssa

We emailed back a forth a few more times, which just emphasized my desire to go on this trip. I was eager to catch up with her, but we decided we'd wait until we saw each other in person. Next, I went to the cruise website and booked the room that Natalie and I would stay in. As I selected my room and my other choices, I felt my excitement growing. The last year had been so difficult, I really needed this break.

As I considered the distance to Seattle, I decided I would rather fly than drive, so I booked a flight that would arrive the morning of the departure date. I could hardly believe how quickly I'd made the decision to go and then made the arrangements, but I was thrilled to have something so fun to look forward to.

I looked at Natalie and Greta and realized I would have to ask Marcus if he'd be willing to take care of Greta for me again. He'd said he'd be willing to do it anytime and I hoped he'd meant it. I decided to invite him over for dinner and ask him then. Even though I was sure he'd be willing to do it without me giving him dinner, it made me feel better to do something for him in return.

I called his cell phone and he answered on the second ring.

"Hello?"

I smiled when I heard his voice. "Hi, Marcus. This is Lily."

"Hey, how are you?"

"Great. I was wondering if you'd like to come over for dinner tonight."

"I have another commitment tonight. Is there another night that would work?"

"What about tomorrow night?"

He paused, like he was checking his calendar. "Yeah, that would work."

"Great. I'll see you then."

The next night before he arrived, I set the table with the remains of my mother's china, and created a delicious meal. As I looked over my preparations, I flashed back to the night I had planned to tell Trevor I was pregnant with Natalie. He'd promised to come home by six o'clock for a special dinner, but he hadn't shown up until nearly one o'clock in the morning, and he'd been drunk. That was the night he pushed me, making me fall over the coffee table and onto the floor. And that was the night I'd first left him.

I shook my head, trying to dislodge the distressing memories, and instead focused on the happy news I was planning on sharing with Marcus. Right on time, he knocked on the door, and with Natalie in my arms and Greta by my side, I opened the door.

"Hi, Lily." His green eyes seemed to sparkle as he smiled.

"Thanks for coming over."

"As if I'd turn down a free meal. Especially when it's cooked by such a beautiful woman."

I blushed at his words, but also felt myself glowing with the compliment. "Come in. Dinner's just about ready."

He walked inside and I shut the door behind him. "Do you want me to take Natalie?" he asked.

"That would be great." I handed her over, smiling as I watched him look at my daughter. He was so good to her, and to us, and I felt my feelings of attraction grow as I looked at him. *Maybe tonight I should tell him how I really feel about him.* Nervousness at the thought made my heart pound. I pushed aside my anxiety and focused on the tasks I needed to complete to get dinner on the table.

A short time later I invited Marcus to sit at the table. "You can put Natalie in the swing while we eat."

He did as I directed, then joined me at the table. He looked over the spread I'd laid out. "This smells great." He looked at me and smiled. "I barely had time to eat lunch, so I'm really hungry."

After we served ourselves and started eating, I said, "How are things at your work?"

He swallowed the bite he'd been chewing. "Really good. I like it there and the people I work with are great." He took a sip of water. "How about you? How's your website business going?"

"Besides Billi's boutique, I have four other clients, so it's enough to keep me busy right now. Natalie takes most of my time, so the amount of work is perfect for me."

"I think it's fantastic that you were able to start that business. The timing couldn't have been any better."

"I know. I'm thrilled with the way it worked out."

He took another bite of his casserole. "What else do you have going on?"

A slow smile spread across my face.

He obviously sensed my excitement. "What?"

"A friend of mine from Reno is getting married next month and I'm going to go to her wedding."

"That's great." He paused. "Did you need me to take care of Greta while you're gone?"

"That would be wonderful." I smiled with a hint of guilt. "That's kind of why I made dinner for you. I appreciate it so much when you watch her for me."

"You don't have to make dinner for me. You know I don't mind."

"I know. But it's the least I can do to say thank you."

"So when is it?"

I told him the date I would be leaving. "I'll be gone for just over a week."

His eyebrows went up. "I thought weddings were usually a weekend kind of thing."

I couldn't hold back my grin. "This wedding is going to take place on an Alaskan cruise."

He returned my smile. "Ah. Now I see why you're so excited. That sounds really fun."

"I've never been on a cruise, so I'm super excited to go. Have you ever been on a cruise?"

"A few years ago I went with some friends on a cruise to Mexico. It was a blast."

"Do you have any pointers for me on cruising?"

"Well, going to Alaska is probably quite different than going to Mexico. Do you know what the temperature will be at that time of year?"

"It should get in the sixties during the day, so I think it will be nice."

We talked about cruises in general, which made me even more excited about going. Marcus helped me clean up, then we sat on the couch. I had put Natalie on a blanket on the floor and she was content.

"She has such an easy disposition," Marcus said.

"I know. I feel really lucky."

He looked at me. "She takes after her mother."

I smiled and looked away from him and over to Natalie, and wondered if this was the right moment to tell him how I felt. When I looked back at him, he was watching me. "What?"

He grinned. "I just like to look at you."

I decided to go for it. "I like to look at you too."

His grin widened. "Is that right?"

I suddenly felt shy. "Yes." I hesitated. "I really like you, Marcus."

A mix of emotions swept across his face, then he bit his lip. He looked at Natalie, then across the room, then finally at me. "I have to be honest, Lily. I'm not sure exactly how I feel."

My heart sank. I had told him my feelings too soon.

He glanced at his hands in his lap before looking back at me. "Don't get me wrong, you mean a lot to me, but . . . I'm just not sure if we can be more than friends."

Devastated, but also confused, I shook my head. "Then why do you say those things?"

"What things?"

"Like a minute ago, when you said you like to look at me. What was that?"

His face reddened. "I guess I like to flirt with you."

"Is that what 'just friends' do? They flirt?" I shook my head and turned away, then looked at him. "I just feel like you're sending me mixed signals, Marcus."

"Maybe I am." He shook his head. "I don't know." He looked at Natalie for a moment, then back at me. "It's just that I don't feel ready to be in a relationship yet. After Marissa . . . well, ever since we broke up, I just don't want to put myself out there like that." He gazed at me, and his brows pulled together. "To be one hundred percent honest, I'm not sure *you're* ready. I mean, a few months ago you were still married. Yeah, you were separated, but . . . I don't think I even want to go in to how complicated all of that was." He looked away again, then back at me. "Right now I think it's best if we're just friends."

His comments sent me reeling. Who was he to say what I was and wasn't ready for? Or was he right, and I wasn't ready for anything more than mere friendship? Either way, he clearly didn't want to move beyond friendship with me. Disappointment shot through me, which surprised me. I hadn't realized how much I'd been hoping he would respond with feelings similar to mine.

I tried to hide my dismay as I forced a smile on my face. "I understand."

He looked relieved. "Do you still want me to take care of Greta while you're on your cruise?"

I nodded. "If you don't mind."

"No, I don't mind at all."

"You can stay here, if it would be easier."

"Okay."

We chatted a little while longer, then he announced that he needed to get going. I walked him to the door and he opened it.

"Thanks again for dinner, Lily. It was delicious."

"You're welcome. Thanks for being willing to take care of Greta."

He left a moment later and I locked the door behind him. Natalie started fussing and I picked her up. "Are you getting hungry, baby girl?" Her crying got louder and tears sprang to my eyes. "I know, sweetheart. I know. I wish he felt towards me like I feel towards him, but there's nothing I can do about it."

Before I knew it, tears were cascading down my face. I held Natalie close and patted her back and she began to quiet, then I took her into the kitchen and placed her in her baby seat. My tears stopped and I wiped my face, then fixed her something to eat.

That night as I lay in bed and breathed in Marcus's fading scent from the pillow, loneliness washed over me, making me cold. I pulled the blankets up to my chin and snuggled into the warmth of the bedding. I missed having strong arms around me, and longed for Marcus to return the feelings I had for him. I remembered the close physical contact I'd had with him before Natalie had been born, when he'd taught me self-defense moves.

Maybe it's time for a brush-up course, I thought as I drifted off to sleep, a smile growing on my face.

Chapter Five

I waited two days to call Marcus to ask him if he'd be willing to teach me a refresher course on self-defense. He said he would have to check his schedule and get back to me, which I found surprising. Before, he'd always seemed available to come over whenever I asked. He called back a short time later and said he could come over on Saturday.

Bright and early Saturday morning he appeared on my door step. It was early in July and very hot, so we had agreed to have the lesson first thing in the morning while it was still relatively cool.

"Good morning," I said as I let him into the house.

He wore a pair of sweats, along with a t-shirt that hugged his biceps. "You sure you want to do this today? It's already pretty hot."

"Are you wimping out on me, Marcus?"

He grinned. "I was only thinking of you."

"Uh-huh. Well, I'm fine, so unless it's too hot for *you*, I'm ready to go."

He laughed. "Okay then."

We brought Natalie's swing outside and set it in the shade of the porch, and I placed her in it, then locked Greta in the house. The first time Marcus had given me self-defense lessons, she'd gotten upset and growled at him.

"I think we're all set." I walked out into the middle of the backyard and waited for Marcus to join me.

A moment later he stood in front of me. "What brought on this sudden desire to review your self-defense moves?" A look of concern filled his face. "Is someone bothering you, Lily?"

His sincere worry touched me deeply, and I smiled. There was no way I would admit the truth. I wanted these lessons for two reasons: One, an excuse to spend time with him, and two, a good reason to have physical contact with him. The more I thought about how little touch I got in my life—besides Natalie, but that was different—the more I wanted it. "No. It's just been a while and I, well, I do live alone out here."

Relief spread across his face. "Okay." His eyebrows pulled together. "You would tell me if someone was bothering you, wouldn't you?"

"Of course." Although in reality, I didn't know if I would. What would he do about it if there was? Not that there was any great likelihood of anyone stalking me—I hardly interacted with anyone lately.

"Good. Let's get started then."

I smiled, ready for this.

"Turn around and try to forget I'm behind you. I want to see how much you remember."

"Okay." I turned my back to him and tried to forget he was about to grab me, which was nearly impossible as I was eager to feel his touch. Trying to be a good student, I ran through the moves in my mind, preparing to respond to his 'attack'. A moment later it came, catching me off-guard. For a moment I froze as I flashed back to Trevor's attacks only a few months before, then I went into action, running through the steps I'd learned. A moment later I was free.

Marcus faced me, a wide smile on his face. "Very good."

Pleased by his compliment, I beamed. As I looked into his striking green eyes, my body warmed and I was glad I had thought of this reason to invite him over.

"Let's try an attack from the front," he said.

I glanced at Natalie and made sure she was okay, then nodded to Marcus. He moved toward me and grabbed one of my arms, but I immediately went through the moves I knew, and broke free. We went through a few more attacks from the front and I was able to break free from all of his attempts.

"I don't think you need a refresher course, Lily. You seem pretty solid."

"Thanks. After what happened with . . . well, a few months ago, I run through the different defensive moves in my mind from time to time."

"That's great."

"But it's nice to actually go through the steps once in a while too. I don't want to get rusty."

"True." He paused. "Let's try one more. Turn around."

I did as he said, wondering what attack move he was going to try next. Suddenly his arm wrapped around my throat. This time I froze as I had a vivid flashback to the night a few months before when Trevor had nearly strangled me to death. Panic pumped through me, and my heart began to race. I squeezed my eyes closed for a moment, then opened them and focused on the row of flowers planted along the fence, anchoring myself in the here and now, which calmed me. I grabbed Marcus's arm, then I went through my moves to break free. He dropped his arm to his side as I turned to look at him for approval.

"You hesitated that time. Is everything okay?"

We were standing just a few inches apart and I gazed up at him. "For a moment I remembered that night, and I froze."

Worry and sadness filled his eyes. "I wish I'd gotten to your house sooner that night. I feel so guilty that I didn't answer your phone call right away. If only I'd been there, things might have turned out different." He looked past me and frowned, then looked at me. "I should have been there for you, Lily."

I shook my head. "It's not your fault. You had no idea what he was capable of." I smiled. "Anyway, Greta saved the day and I'm okay now."

He gazed at me and his eyes sparkled with unshed tears. "I can't even allow myself to imagine what would have happened if Greta hadn't come in at that moment. You would have *died*, Lily."

Our eyes locked and an overwhelming feeling of love swept over me, and without thinking, I threw my arms around his neck and pressed my cheek against his chest. After a brief hesitation, his arms went around me, pulling me close. I relished the moment, memorizing the feel of his body pressed against mine. I didn't move, never wanting for him to let go, but a moment later Natalie started fussing, and reluctantly, I pulled out of his embrace.

I looked at his face and saw the same mix of feelings I'd seen the night I'd told him I really liked him, and I wondered how firmly he wanted to stay in the friend zone.

"Motherhood calls," he said, his expression smoothing out.

"Yep." I walked over to Natalie and took her out of her swing. "Are you getting too hot, baby girl?"

"I think we've done enough today, don't you?" Marcus asked as he stepped onto the porch.

"Yeah, I suppose I should bring her back inside. Do you want something cold to drink?"

"Sure."

We went into the house, and with Natalie on my hip, I poured a cold glass of lemonade for both Marcus and myself. "Here you go." I handed him the glass and he gulped it down.

"That was exactly what I needed. Thanks."

"Help yourself to more." I drank mine and watched as he poured himself another. I wondered what he was thinking—had he enjoyed our embrace as much as I had? Had it made him reconsider our relationship status as only friends? Or had it confirmed to him that he wasn't ready to go beyond friendship?

He acted like he always did—as if nothing unusual had happened—and I decided I must be the only one who felt something. Sharp disappointment flooded my heart, but I forced it away, focusing on the fun time we'd had. I fixed a bottle of water for Natalie, worried she might be thirsty after being outside in the summer heat, but she didn't seem interested in drinking it. I smiled at Marcus. "Thanks for running through those moves with me. I'm glad to know I still remember how to do them."

"Anytime, Lily. I had fun."

I tried to read between the lines, but decided to just accept his comment on its face. "Me too."

"I'd better get going. I promised my parents I'd help them with some things around the house today."

I nodded. "Tell them I said hi."

He tilted his head to one side. "Why don't you tell them yourself? They just live next door."

"I don't think your mom approves of me, Marcus."

His eyebrows pulled together. "Why do you think that?"

I gave him a look like, *Isn't it obvious?*

He shook his head. "What?"

I wasn't sure if he was being dense on purpose, or if he really had no clue. "Don't you think she was just a little . . . I don't know . . . disappointed in me, when she found out I'd been lying about myself for all those months?"

"I'm sure she understands why you did it. You had a crazy husband trying to find you."

"I don't know. And to be honest, I'm kind of embarrassed about the whole thing. I mean, your parents were so nice to me and I lied to them about my marital status, even my name."

He laughed. "I'm sure they're over it by now, Lily."

I wasn't so sure, but I shrugged to show that there was nothing left to discuss. "Thanks again for coming over."

He grinned. "Like I said. Anytime."

I felt a rush of desire as I looked at his smile, then heat spread across my body as I thought about being in his arms only moments before. I walked him to the door, then waved to him as he backed out of my driveway and drove away.

The next morning Marcus's mother, Trish, called. "How are you, Ka . . . uh, Lily?"

I cringed at her near-use of my alias, embarrassed about the lies I'd told her. "Good, Trish. How about you?"

"I'm fine. I was calling to invite you over to lunch today. I haven't really spent any time with you since your baby arrived and I'd love to see you and to get to know her."

I wondered if Marcus had put her up to this after the conversation we'd had the day before. Though I feared the lunch would be uncomfortable, Trish was my neighbor as well as Marcus's mother, and I decided it was better to break the ice now, rather than put it off. "Sure, that sounds great. What time would you like me to come over?"

"Would twelve thirty work?"

"Yes. Natalie will be between her morning and afternoon naps then, so that will work fine. Would you like me to bring anything?"

"No, no. I'll take care of it. See you then."

I set my phone down and looked at Greta, who lay on the floor at my feet. "Well, girl, this should be interesting."

She looked up at me, her tongue hanging out, then stood and

pressed her nose against my hand.

"You want to play? I think we have a little while before Natalie wakes up from her nap." Greta followed me as I went out back, then I picked up her favorite ball and threw it for her. She ran to pick it up, then trotted back to me and dropped it at my feet.

"You're such a good girl." I scratched her head and she seemed to smile in her doggy way. I threw the ball for her over and over until my arm was tired and I knew she needed to take a break. "Let's go inside and cool off."

I made sure her bowl had plenty of water, then cleaned up and checked on Natalie, who was awake, but happy. As I changed and fed her, I thought about the lunch I would be having with Trish in another hour, and imagined myself explaining why I'd had to lie to her and her husband. I pictured Trish's reaction going one of two ways. Either she'd forgive everything and it wouldn't be a big deal, or she'd lecture me on why I should have told her the truth from the start.

As the time to go next door drew near, I found myself becoming more and more nervous. If it weren't for my interest in Marcus, I really wouldn't care what Trish thought, but because I cared for her son so much, her opinion mattered to me. A lot.

"Time to go, baby girl," I said to Natalie as I put her in her stroller and wheeled her out the door. We walked the short distance to Trish's house, but by the time I reached her porch, I was sweating. I thought it was due to the heat of the day, but in the back of my mind I wondered if it was also due to my worry about how this meeting would go.

Trish must have seen me coming, because she opened the front door before I had a chance to knock. She immediately knelt in front of the stroller. "Oh, you are a pretty little thing, aren't you?" She looked up at me. "What a beautiful baby."

I smiled, feeling more comfortable. "Thank you."

"Please come in."

I took Natalie out of her stroller and held her on my hip, then slung her diaper bag over my shoulder and followed Trish inside. I admired her immaculate home and the beautiful way she'd decorated. I hadn't been there since before Natalie was born, and realized how much had happened since I'd had dinner with Marcus and his parents.

"May I hold her?" Trish asked as she and I stood in the middle of the living room.

"Sure." I let her take Natalie from my arms, and Natalie frowned like she was going to cry. "It's okay," I murmured to her.

Trish held her facing out, so that she could see me. "I know sometimes at this age they don't like to be away from Mom."

I laughed. "She is definitely a momma's girl."

"Please, sit."

I sat on a nearby chair and she sat on the couch. "I'm glad you invited me over," I said, wanting to get the awkward part of this over with.

She smiled. "I haven't really talked to you since everything happened and I just felt it was time to clear the air."

I nodded, grateful for her honesty. "I don't know what Marcus told you about my . . . well, my circumstances. But I had to conceal my identity to keep myself and Natalie safe."

"He told me about your husband." She glanced at Natalie, who sat on her lap, then back at me. "To tell you the truth, after he told me about what you went through, I felt really bad that I had basically turned my back on you after Natalie was born and I found out your husband was actually alive and well."

The blood rushed to my face as I remembered the mortification I'd felt when Marcus had walked into the hospital room and Trevor had been there and had announced that he was my husband. "I didn't tell him where I was. He tracked me down and found me."

"I know you were doing what you could and I feel bad I wasn't more understanding."

I shook my head. "It's not your fault, Trish. Please don't feel bad. *I'm* the one who should feel bad for lying to you about who I was. But I just couldn't take the chance of Trevor finding me." I paused. "Not that it mattered. He found me anyway."

She smiled. "Well, I hope we can put it behind us and move forward."

"I'd like that."

"Good." She stood. "Why don't we eat some lunch?"

I nodded and followed her into the dining room, where she'd set out a plate of chicken-salad sandwiches on croissants, along with a fruit salad, and a pasta salad. "This looks delicious."

"Thank you."

"Let me put a blanket on the floor and we can lay Natalie on it." I took a blanket out of the diaper bag and lay it out on Trish's thick carpet, then took Natalie from her and placed her on the floor, along with a couple of toys.

We sat at the table and Trish invited me to serve myself. "I'd love to get the recipe for this chicken-salad from you," I said as I set a sandwich on my plate.

"Sure. It's a recipe I've been using for years and it's a family favorite."

"Those are the best kind."

As we ate and chatted, I felt completely relaxed and happy that Trish and I were back on friendly terms. That is, until she made an off-hand comment toward the end of lunch.

Trish spooned a serving of fresh fruit on her plate and smiled at me. "Did Marcus tell you about his new girlfriend?"

Chapter Six

The fork I held in my hand froze as I stared at her, but after only a moment I was able to wipe the shock off of my face. I used all of my self-control to keep my voice from betraying my feelings. "No. Tell me about her."

"She's worked at his firm for quite some time, but they only started working together a couple of months ago." Trish seemed oblivious to my consternation as she spoke. "He's told me so much about her, I'm surprised he hasn't told you. I know what good friends you are."

I nodded, unable to speak as I felt my hopes in a relationship with Marcus slipping away. "I haven't spent a lot of time with him lately. He's been working a lot." My words trailed off as I made the connection between the time he'd been spending at work with this new girlfriend, and his hesitation in coming over to see me. Of course he'd been spending more time at work—that's where she was. "What did you say her name is?"

"Chelsea." Trish took a bite of cantaloupe. "She's quite lovely."

"So you've met her?"

"Oh yes. We've gone out to dinner with her and Marcus several times."

I felt my heart sink even further. It sounded serious. "I'm glad he's found someone. I know he had a hard time after he broke things off with Marissa."

Trish frowned. "Yes, I'm glad he was able to move past her. I didn't like her at all." She smiled at me. "Would you like some dessert? I made some chocolate mousse."

Normally I would have loved some, but my appetite had vanished and I'd only eaten half of my sandwich. "I'm completely full, thank you."

Trish glanced at my plate. "Okay."

Natalie started fussing then, which gave me a good excuse to head home. I picked her up from the floor and held her on my lap. "I'd probably better take her home and feed her. I really enjoyed talking with you." That was true up until the last five minutes, so I didn't feel like I was lying. "Thank you so much for having me over."

"We'll have to do this more often."

I nodded.

"Let me send some of this food home with you. Jeff's out of town and I can't eat all of this."

"Thank you."

A short time later Natalie and I were walking home, loaded down with containers of salad, along with a couple of sandwiches. When we reached our house I brought Natalie and the food inside. After I put the food in the fridge, I sat on the couch and nursed Natalie and thought about the revelation about Marcus having a girlfriend.

Is that why he'd seemed so ambivalent about my confession that I liked him more than a friend? He'd told me he wasn't ready to be in a relationship—clearly untrue. Did he think it was okay to lie to me because I had lied to him in the past? I'd only lied to keep myself safe—I'd never lied about the way I felt about him. Did he think he was protecting me by not telling me the truth? Did he really believe I was so weak that I would fall apart if I knew he had another woman in his life?

Confused and hurt, I held Natalie close and tried to think about happy things—like the cruise I would be leaving on in just a few weeks. I didn't have time to get passports for Natalie and me, but I'd learned that since we were leaving and returning to a U.S. Port, we could use our birth certificates instead, so that was one less thing to worry about.

After I finished feeding Natalie, I looked at the list I'd created of the things I needed to do before the cruise. All that I had left was to pack up and go. My excitement helped to push aside my sadness over Marcus, and I tried to stay focused on the positive.

One evening, a week after my lunch with Trish, Marcus stopped by.

"I was over at my parents' house and I wanted to come see how you're doing."

I stared at him a moment, picturing him with his new girlfriend, Chelsea, then pushed the thought aside and invited him in. Natalie had fallen asleep in her swing, and Greta lay on her pet bed in the corner of the living room. "I'm doing fine." *Except for missing you.* We sat on opposite ends of the couch. "Your mom had me over for lunch last week."

"Yeah, she told me."

"We had a nice talk." Except for the news she delivered about you, I wanted to add. "I think you're right and she's over what happened in the past."

He smiled. "Told you so."

I laughed. "Tell me the truth. Was it your idea for her to have me over for lunch?"

He crinkled his nose. "I may have mentioned that you were feeling bad about everything. So technically no, it wasn't my idea."

"You just planted the seed."

"Okay. Yes."

"It's okay. I'm not mad about it. I'm glad we cleared the air."

He nodded. "Good. Hey, are there any projects you need help with around here?"

Is that why he'd come by? Just to see if I needed any help? Not that that was a bad thing, but I would have preferred it if he'd come over just to see me. I shook my head. "No, we're okay."

"Will you tell me if you need anything?"

If my expectations for our relationship had to be reduced to us just being friends, I would need some time to adjust to that before I could allow myself to spend time with him. Otherwise I would just be torturing myself. "Of course," I said in answer to his question, but in reality I wasn't sure I would call him.

I really wanted to ask him about his new girlfriend and ask why he hadn't told me about her, but I wasn't sure how to go about it. He'd obviously made a conscious decision to keep me in the dark about her, but why? Was he afraid of hurting me? Did he want to keep me on the back burner in case things didn't work out with her?

That last thought made me angry and reminded me of Trevor and Amanda. After Trevor had taken Natalie, he'd admitted that he'd been waiting to see if I'd agree to come back to him, and if I didn't, he was going to 'give' Natalie to Amanda. Evidently she couldn't have children of her own, but really wanted to be a mother, so he'd promised her he'd get his baby for her.

The memory drew my gaze to my baby and I felt a jolt of adrenaline as I remembered that night only a few months before when I'd literally had to fight Trevor to get my baby back.

"What are you thinking about, Lily?"

I looked at Marcus, who was watching me. "I was just remembering how I almost lost Natalie."

A look of regret came over his face. "That was a terrible night." He looked thoughtful. "You never told me what happened when you went to see Trevor's parents on the Fourth of July."

It had been two weeks, so the sting of Chris's comments weren't quite as sharp now that a little bit of time had passed. "It started okay—his parents were really nice to me. But one of his brothers hates me and blames me for what happened."

Marcus seemed to bristle at the idea. "Does he know his brother tried to kill you?"

I shrugged. "I don't know how he wouldn't know that, but that doesn't mean he doesn't think it's my fault for bringing Trevor to that point."

He shook his head. "That's just crazy. You did nothing wrong. You were only trying to protect yourself and your child."

I smiled at the anger in his voice. "I know that and you know that, but his brother must still be in denial."

"Sounds like it." Marcus looked at me with a question. "Is that why you came back early?"

I recalled Chris's comment that no one wanted me there. "Yeah. Things were getting uncomfortable, so I decided it would be best if I left."

"I don't blame you."

Natalie woke up and started fussing. "I think she's getting hungry."

"I need to get going anyway, but I wanted to check up on you."

What are friends for? "I appreciate it."

"I'm going to be pretty busy at work for the next couple of weeks," he said. "But I'll be sure to stop by and pick up your key before you leave for your trip." He hesitated. "And I've decided not to stay here while you're gone."

That didn't surprise me. Not with his new girlfriend in the picture. "You know, now that your mom and I are talking again, why don't I just have her take care of Greta? It would be a lot easier since she just lives next door."

His brow furrowed. “Are you sure? I don’t mind.”

“No. I’m sure you have better things to do then drive over to my place every day.” *Like spend time with Chelsea.*

“Okay. I guess that would work. Let me know if my mom can’t do it and I’ll be happy to.”

I smiled, but it was forced. I felt him slipping further away and I didn’t like it. “Thanks, Marcus.”

“No problem.”

I walked him to the door, and as I watched him get in his jeep, I wondered when I’d see him again.

Chapter Seven

The next morning Natalie and I walked over to Trish's house. She seemed surprised to see me on her porch. "Would you like to come in?"

"That's okay," I said. "I just stopped by to ask you a favor."

"What is it?"

"I'm going on a cruise in a couple of weeks to see my friend get married."

"That sounds like a lot of fun."

I smiled. "Yes. I'm really excited about it. Anyway, Marcus was going to take care of Greta, but I know he's busy at work and with . . . other things, so I was wondering if you'd be willing to keep an eye on her and feed her."

She hesitated. "I have to be honest. After what she did to your . . . husband . . . I'm a little nervous about being alone with her."

Though I understood her concern, I felt a need to defend Greta. "She was just trying to protect me. Trevor was on top of me, strangling me."

Trish recoiled slightly at my description and I wondered if it was too graphic—but it was the truth.

"Oh." Her hand touched her throat. "I'm just not sure."

"If you're not comfortable, I understand. Marcus said he'd do it if you weren't able to."

A funny look crossed her face, but was quickly gone. "I suppose it does make more sense for me to do it since I live right next door." She paused. "Would it be okay if I came over a few times before you left so I can see how she reacts to me?"

I smiled, pleased she was willing to try. "I think that's a great idea. Stop by anytime. I'm usually around."

She returned my smile. "I'll do that."

"Thanks, Trish."

She nodded and closed the door. I pushed Natalie's stroller back down the driveway and continued further down the street, enjoying the relative cool of the morning. In the spring I'd taken Natalie on frequent walks, but lately it had been so hot that I'd mainly stayed inside. I decided I should start getting out early in the morning and enjoying fresh air and sunshine with my baby girl.

We walked for half an hour before turning around and heading back home. As I passed Trish's house, I smiled, grateful for a good neighbor who was willing to help out when asked.

A few days later she stopped by while Natalie was napping, and I brought her to the backyard to play with Greta. I showed her which ball was Greta's favorite and handed it to her to throw.

"That's okay," she said. "I'll just watch you for a few minutes first."

"Okay." I threw the ball for Greta and she raced after it, then picked it up and dropped it at my feet. I scratched her head as I told her what a good girl she was. We did this several times, then I held the ball out to

Trish. "Do you want to try it?"

She took the ball from me. "Okay." She held it out for Greta to sniff, and when Greta sniffed her hand, then licked it, she smiled. Then she threw it and Greta ran after it, then brought it back and set it at her feet. "She's a smart dog."

I nodded, proud of my Greta. "I know. I'm so glad I got her. She's a great companion."

Trish threw the ball a few more times, then I suggested we sit on the porch to give Greta a break from the heat.

"She'll keep playing even when she should stop, just to please me, so I need to make sure and stop when I think she's had enough." I made sure her bowl was full of water, and sat on the porch step. Trish sat next to me.

"You didn't tell me where your cruise is going."

I grinned. "Alaska. Have you ever been there?"

She smiled. "Yes. That is beautiful country, and it should be nice when you're there."

"That's what I understand."

Trish came over two more times before my trip, and decided that she felt comfortable enough with Greta that she was willing to take care of her. The day before Natalie and I left, I brought the key over to her house. "Thank you so much for taking care of Greta for me. I really appreciate it."

"I'm happy to do it. I'm glad she got to know me—she really is a good dog and I feel much more comfortable with her now."

"Good. I'll let you know when I'm back."

"Have a fantastic time, Lily."

That was the first time she'd called me that—she'd always known me as Kate before, although lately she hadn't said my name at all. I felt pleased that our friendship had progressed over the previous few weeks.

I stopped by the mailbox on my way home and was surprised to find a letter from Trevor's mother, Marcy. It had been over a month since I'd been to see her in Las Vegas and I was curious what she had written. I wheeled the stroller up to the front porch and brought Natalie inside, then sat on the couch and opened the letter.

"It's from your grandma," I said to Natalie as she reached for the paper in my hand. I held it just out of her grasp as I read it.

Dear Lily,

I wanted to take a moment and let you know how much I enjoyed seeing you and Natalie last month. I'm sorry you felt the need to leave early, and I'm even more sorry about the things Chris said. Like I told you before you left, the rest of the family doesn't feel the same way he does and we'd like you to come visit again.

I felt like I hardly got to know Natalie at all and I would really like to get to know her better—and I'd like to make sure she knows me. Please consider coming for a visit. If it would make you more comfortable, I won't invite Chris over while you're here. I know his wife, Melody, would like to see you though—as would the rest of the family.

I'd also like you to know that the invitation to move here is still open. I know you are on your own, and as you know, I don't have any daughters, just daughters-in-law. I'd like to have the chance to get to know you better.

I don't want to pressure you, but please let me know what I can do to persuade you to come spend time in our home.

Love,

Marcy

As I reread the letter I felt her sincerity, and tears filled my eyes. She was right. I had no one. "Except you, baby girl," I whispered as I snuggled Natalie closer. Even my friendship with Marcus seemed to be in jeopardy. At least his mother, Trish, had warmed to me.

I decided to give Marcy another chance. After putting Natalie in her swing, I wrote a letter to Marcy letting her know that I would come for a visit in a few weeks. I didn't tell her I was going on a cruise—I figured she'd worry about Natalie going and I didn't feel the need to explain myself—then I put the envelope in the mailbox and flipped up the flag.

The next morning I woke early, eager to get going on our big trip.

Chapter Eight

Natalie and I arrived at the Sacramento airport early and I dropped our luggage off with a curbside porter, then parked in the long-term parking lot. We caught a shuttle to the terminal, made our way through security, and walked to the gate. I was glad I'd been able to print off our boarding passes at home. I kept Natalie entertained as I waited for our flight to be called.

With Natalie on my hip, and the diaper bag over my shoulder, I made my way onto the airplane. The airline didn't have assigned seats, so I chose the first empty seat I came to. I sat Natalie in the seat while I placed her diaper bag in the overhead compartment, then I sat in the window seat and put Natalie on my lap.

I watched as the other travelers got on the plane, and smiled inwardly as people glanced at Natalie, then passed by the empty seat next to me. I couldn't blame them for not wanting to sit next to a baby, but as more and more people streamed onboard, I knew someone would have to eventually sit next to us as the flight looked like it would be full.

Sure enough, the last person to board stopped at the head of the aisle and looked out over the rows of seats, then looked at Natalie, frowned, and sat in the seat next to mine. I would have felt sorry for him, except I knew Natalie was an easy-going baby and would probably be just fine. The man looked like he was only a few years older than me, so at least I'd have someone my age to talk to during the flight—assuming he wanted to chat.

"Hey," he said as he sat, glancing at Natalie again and pretty much ignoring me, then he immediately pulled out his laptop and seemed to immerse himself in reading a document. In the moment I'd looked at him, I'd noticed that he was quite attractive—strong jaw, light brown hair, blue eyes. It was obvious he didn't want to talk, and I assumed he was on his way to Seattle on business.

I turned my attention to Natalie to make sure she was happy and comfortable. As the plane took off, I put a pacifier in her mouth, and thankfully, she accepted it. The flight was just under two hours. I fed Natalie a bottle of supplemental formula partway through the flight, and before I knew it, we'd arrived. The man next to me got off as soon as the doors opened, but I waited until everyone else had deplaned. I had plenty of time before the ship left, so I was in no hurry.

When everyone else had left, I took the diaper bag out of the overhead compartment and carried Natalie to the baggage claim area. Several shuttles to the pier were waiting nearby, and the driver of one of them helped me get my bags onto the shuttle, and then Natalie and I boarded. A short time later we pulled up to the drop-off point and the ship came into view.

This is going to be so fun, I thought as I gazed at the massive ship. A worker helped me unload the bags and get them checked in, then I took Natalie to the check-in area, got our boarding cards, went through security, then headed to the boarding area. I hugged Natalie closer, excited to finally be here. I glanced around, looking for Alyssa, but didn't see her. She'd given me her room number in an email, and the plan was for me to meet up with her once I'd gotten settled in my room.

As I followed the other cruisers toward the ship entrance, I didn't see any other babies and wondered how many would be on board. Oh well, it didn't really matter. I was there to see my friend get married and to enjoy a week in Alaska. I looked up at the ship and noticed the rows and rows of balconies. I smiled, glad I had decided to splurge even more and get a balcony room. I'd figured it would be nice to be able to sit on the balcony when Natalie was napping. The room had cost more than an interior room, but since I didn't know if I'd ever go on a cruise again, I'd decided to make this trip as fun as possible.

It was our turn to enter the ship. I handed our cards to the man at the entrance and he placed them into a machine, then we walked through the metal detector. He handed the cards back to me, and I tucked them in my pocket. The first thing I wanted to do was go to our room and freshen up.

The first room we entered was decorated with bright colors, had towering ceilings, and on one side of the room I saw glass elevators.

"Look at this place," I murmured in Natalie's ear. I carried her toward the elevators and punched the button to go up. A moment later the doors opened silently and we walked in, along with some other people. I pressed the button for the eighth floor and we moved smoothly upward. A moment later the doors opened and we stepped into an area bustling with activity. Cruise ship workers were organizing stacks of luggage on multiple carts, then taking them down one of two hallways.

I walked over to the entrance of one of the hallways and looked at the range of room numbers that were down that way, then headed down the hall. I noticed that all the rooms were odd-numbered, and my room was an even number, so I went across the foyer to the other hall and walked down it, looking for my room number. A short time later I found it.

"Here's our room, sweetheart," I said to Natalie, who observed our surroundings.

I slid my key card into the slot and the door clicked. When I walked in, I immediately saw the crib that I'd ordered, as well as an umbrella stroller that I had arranged to rent while on board. I smiled, pleased that my baby's needs were being taken care of. I'd packed lots of diapers, and since I was still mostly nursing her, food wouldn't be a big issue.

I placed the diaper bag on the bed, and carrying Natalie, we checked out the room. There was plenty of closet space, and though the bathroom was small, it was sufficient. There was no tub—just a small stand-up shower. But I was certain I could manage to bathe Natalie when needed.

I paused and looked at my reflection in the large mirror. Natalie squirmed in my arms, but my eyes were drawn to my face. I'd lost all my baby weight, and my hair had grown to shoulder length since I'd chopped it off when I'd run from Trevor, and now it was back to its natural dark color. I smiled, pleased with my reflection. I didn't look so different now than when Alyssa had last seen me. My changes were all on the inside. I gazed at myself, and knew I'd changed from the innocent girl who had first met Trevor.

Holding Natalie on my hip, we left the bathroom and went onto the balcony. The Seattle skyline was right in front of us. "Look at that view," I said to her in wonder. The day was pleasantly warm—much cooler than at home—and I enjoyed the gentle breeze. After a few minutes I carried her back inside and before long her eyelids became heavy—I wasn't surprised that she was tired after our busy day. After I put her down in her crib, I picked up the phone on the desk and dialed Alyssa's room.

"Hello?" she said after only a moment.

"Hi, Alyssa!"

"Lily! You're here!"

"Yes. I'm loving it already."

"I'm so glad you made it."

"Me, too. Are you busy?"

"Not at all. Do you want me to come to your room?"

"Sure. I just put Natalie down for a nap." I gave her my room number and a few minutes later she knocked on the door. I opened it, and after she walked in, I threw my arms around her. "It's so good to see you," I said as I pulled away from the friend I hadn't seen in over a year.

She looked me up and down. "You look great. Just as beautiful as I remember."

I smiled under her compliment. "So do you. I'm so excited for your wedding."

Natalie made a noise, and I whispered, "Let's go talk on the balcony."

Alyssa nodded, then gazed down at Natalie for a moment. She looked at me and mouthed, *She's so cute.*

Thanks, I mouthed, then we walked out to the balcony. I closed the door behind me, but could see Natalie from where we sat.

"Oh my gosh, Lily. I can't believe you're here."

I grinned. "I know. I'm so glad I decided to come."

She looked at me expectantly. "Tell me everything that's happened." She paused, a look of concern and sadness on her face. "I heard Trevor died."

I told her everything that had happened since I'd last seen her—how I'd found out I was pregnant, how Trevor had become abusive, how I'd run, how he'd locked me up, how I'd gone into hiding, how I'd met Marcus, how Trevor had found me, and then, how he'd died.

She slowly shook her head. "Wow." She gazed at me for a moment. "You seem to be doing okay."

I smiled. "I really am. Marcus is my good friend now." I felt a twinge of sadness that that was all he wanted to be. "And Natalie and I have made a home for ourselves." I paused. "I'm happy."

She touched my hand. "I'm so glad."

"Now tell me about you and Ty."

Now she grinned. "I can't wait for you to meet him. He's with his parents right now, but I'll introduce you to him after Natalie wakes up from her nap."

"You said in your email that you've known him for a while, but you got together when you went home for a visit?"

"Yeah. We were friends in high school, and last summer when I went home, I ran in to him and the sparks just flew. I guess the timing was right. He's a great guy."

We chatted for a while longer, then I noticed Natalie waking up. "I need to feed her, then I'll be ready to go. Do you want to wait or do you want to meet somewhere?"

"I can wait. I'd like to see this baby of yours."

"Okay." We went back into the room and I gave Natalie some baby food, then nursed her.

"I can't believe you're a mother. You seem like you're really good at it too, but it's just weird."

I laughed. "It was weird for me at first too, but now that she's eight months old, I can hardly remember what it was like when I didn't have her." I pressed her against my shoulder and rubbed her back. "Do you want to hold her?"

Alyssa held out her hands. "Yes."

I handed her over and Alyssa cooed over her, and Natalie smiled. "I got her to smile," Alyssa said, obviously pleased.

"She's a really happy baby. I'm lucky."

Alyssa gazed at her, then looked at me. "She has Trevor's eyes."

I smiled wistfully. "I know. Even though I knew I couldn't be with him anymore, I loved him once, and I'm glad our child has beautiful blue eyes like his."

Alyssa nodded, and after a moment asked if I was ready to go.

"Yes." I put Natalie in the stroller I'd rented, placed the diaper bag over the handle, then followed Alyssa from the room.

She texted Ty to find out where he was—we were still in port so the cell signal was good. Then we took the elevator to the Lido deck, where the wedding party was gathered to eat from the buffet. I smiled as I looked at all the food laid out—I hadn't eaten in hours and was really hungry.

"There they are." Alyssa pointed to a large group sitting at several tables next to the window.

When we stopped next to the group, a man walked over to Alyssa, a smile on his face. Alyssa turned to me. "Lily, this is my fiancé, Ty."

"I'm so glad to meet you," I said.

"I'm glad you were able to come." He drew me into a brief hug, then pulled away and looked at me. "I know your being here has made Alyssa really happy."

I smiled at Alyssa, then looked at Ty. "I'm glad it worked out. I'm excited for your wedding."

Alyssa's parents, Paul and Barbara, came over to meet me. I lifted Natalie from her stroller and held her on my hip.

"What a cutie," Barbara said, touching Natalie's arm. She smiled at me. "Would you like me to hold her while you get something to eat?"

"If you wouldn't mind."

"No. I love babies." She held out her arms for Natalie and I placed her there. Natalie seemed okay with Barbara holding her, which made me feel better.

"I'll go with you," Alyssa said. "I haven't eaten yet."

Alyssa, Ty, and I walked around, seeing what food was available, then got in one of the lines.

"That was nice of your mom to take Natalie," I said to Alyssa.

Alyssa laughed. "She really does love babies. My older brother's given her two grandchildren, and I know she's hoping I'll produce some too."

I thought about Trevor's parents and their desire to spend time with Natalie, and felt guilt slice through me. They'd barely met my baby, and I'd run away from their party before they'd had a chance to get to know her. But I'd promised them I'd come for a visit in a few weeks, which helped to assuage the guilt.

We picked up our trays and selected our food, then went back to the group. I sat across from Barbara, who had given Natalie a shiny necklace to play with. As I ate, I listened to the conversation around me and looked forward to getting to know Alyssa and Ty's friends and family over the next week. I'd only met a few of them so far, and my gaze wandered among the group, trying to memorize who belonged.

As my eyes skimmed over the faces at a neighboring table, I recognized the man who had sat next to me on the flight from Sacramento. He didn't seem to notice me as he chatted with the people sitting near him. He'd hardly acknowledged me on the flight, so he probably wouldn't recognize me anyway. I watched him for a moment, taking in his perfectly straight, white teeth, and the dimple that appeared on the left side of his face when he laughed.

"Who's that?" I whispered to Alyssa.

Alyssa followed my gaze, and smiled. "That's Cameron. He's Ty's best friend."

Cameron must have felt our gaze on him, because he turned and looked our way, and when our eyes met, I felt a jolt. His eyes were the same vivid blue as Trevor's had been.

Chapter Nine

Like I expected, he didn't seem to realize I was the same woman he'd sat next to on the flight from Sacramento, as I saw no spark of recognition. He'd been completely absorbed in his laptop during the flight, so he probably hadn't even registered my presence, except to note that I had a baby with me.

Now, however, he seemed to take notice of me, which did something funny to my stomach. I wasn't sure if it was his attention, or the fact that his eyes reminded me of Trevor, but when his gaze met mine, I felt exposed somehow, vulnerable.

"He's single," Alyssa whispered in my ear.

I broke my gaze with Cameron and looked at Alyssa. "That's nice."

She tried to hide a smile. "And so are you, my dear."

I laughed. "Are you going to try to play matchmaker again?"

"Hmm. I guess that didn't work out so well the first time, did it?"

"Maybe I should have listened to you when you were pushing me toward Justin." I paused. "What's he up to, anyway?"

Alyssa smiled. "He's doing great. He and Pamela got married." She looked at me with a question. "Did you ever meet her?"

I nodded. "Yeah."

"He wanted to come on the cruise, but it just didn't work out."

"Hey, buddy," Cameron said to Ty, who was sitting next to Alyssa. "How's it going?"

I looked at him and noticed him glancing at me.

"Hey, Cam," Ty said. "Come sit with us."

I felt Alyssa nudge me in the leg, and I bit back a smile. Then I thought about Marcus and how much I cared for him—maybe even loved him. Then I thought about his new girlfriend, and how our future together was so murky. I had no obligation to Marcus. Besides, it would be fun to get to know more people on the cruise—it was just a week of fun before going back to my everyday, hum-drum life. I needed to expand my circle of acquaintances, and this would be the perfect opportunity.

"Cam," Ty said, then motioned to me. "This is Alyssa's friend, Lily."

Turning to look at him, I smiled.

"Hey," he said.

"Hi." I could see in his eyes that he found me attractive and it made me feel desirable. For the past eight months I'd been so focused on being a mother that I'd almost forgotten what it felt like to have a man show that kind of interest in me.

"Where are you from?" he asked as he slid into a seat across from Alyssa, Ty, and me.

Enjoying his attention, I smiled, and told him the name of the small town an hour south of Sacramento.

"Is that so?"

"What about you?" I asked.

"I actually don't live too far from you. I'm just up in Sacramento."

I nodded, not terribly surprised, since we'd left from the same airport. "Have you ever been to Alaska?"

"No. But I understand this is a good time of year to go. What about you?"

"No. First time in Alaska, and this is my first cruise too."

He smiled, which deepened the dimple on his cheek. "Well, maybe I can show you some of the fun things to do on the ship."

My smile grew as he made his intentions clear. "I'd like that." I paused as a thought occurred to me. Most likely he didn't know I had a baby. Would that change his mind about spending time with me? Natalie was part of me, so there wasn't much I could do about it, but I thought it would be better to make the truth known up front. "I guess you don't recognize me."

He looked puzzled. "No. Why? Have we met before?"

I laughed, secretly worried about his reaction. "Sort of. You sat next to me on your flight this morning."

"I did?" Then he looked confused. "But I sat next to a woman with a baby."

I pointed to Barbara. "Yes. Alyssa's mom is holding my daughter."

His gaze went to Natalie, who was watching the people around her, then focused back on me. He laughed, but he seemed uncomfortable. "Sorry, I guess I didn't pay attention on the flight."

"That's okay."

He didn't say anything for a moment, then he looked at Ty and asked him a question, effectively dismissing me. Though I kept a smile on my face, disappointment shot through me that his interest had shut off like a light switch the moment he'd found out I had a baby. *Oh well*, I thought. *It's probably for the best.* Then I turned to Alyssa. She frowned at me, like she understood what had happened, then we talked about her wedding plans.

As we talked, my gaze wandered to Cameron several times, and twice I noticed him looking at me. Inside I smiled, wondering if maybe there was hope there after all.

"It's time for the ship to leave," someone said.

"Let's go to the upper deck," Alyssa said to the group.

Everyone got up, including me, and I took Natalie from Barbara. "Thanks for holding her. Sometimes it's nice to eat without a baby on my lap."

She laughed. "They like to grab, don't they?"

"Yes, they do."

"I'm happy to help you out with her this week, if you'd like."

"Thank you. I really appreciate it."

She smiled warmly. "I've been on this cruise before, so if you want to do any of the excursions, I'd be happy to babysit."

I considered her offer. "Are there any excursions you recommend?"

"My favorite is the whale watching."

"That sounds like fun."

"It really is. You should consider it."

"I will. Thanks."

I put Natalie in her stroller and followed the group to the elevator, then went up one level to the sun deck. We walked to the railing and I took Natalie out of her stroller, then gazed at the view. The weather was perfect and I pressed my cheek to Natalie's as the ship slowly moved away from Seattle. Alyssa stood next to me, with Ty at her side.

"Are you going on any excursions?" I asked her.

"Well, the wedding is in our first port, but in Juneau I want to do the whale watching trip."

"Your mom was talking about that. She said it was her favorite excursion."

"Yeah, she's the one who suggested it." She smiled. "Are you going to go on it?"

"It sounds like fun. And your mom offered to watch Natalie if I went."

Alyssa's grin widened. "Do it. Come with us."

I smiled. "Okay. I will." After a while, Natalie started getting restless and I turned to Alyssa. "I'm going to take her back to my room."

"Okay."

"I'll probably just see you at dinner."

"Sounds good." She gave me a hug. "I'm so glad you came, Lily."

"Me, too." When I got back to my room, I played with Natalie until she started rubbing her eyes, which meant she was getting sleepy. I put her down, then lay on my bed, and we both napped. When we woke, we still had a while before dinner—Alyssa's party had all signed up for the later dinner time. I put Natalie in her stroller and took a walk around the ship, getting myself familiar with the layout.

When it was time for dinner, I went to the dining room and the steward showed me where my table was. I would be sitting there every night with Alyssa and Ty's group, and when I arrived, most of the group was already there. Alyssa had saved me a seat next to her—which I really appreciated since I didn't really know anyone else in the group yet.

Our waiter brought a high chair for Natalie, which I placed between Alyssa and me, and she seemed content to watch everyone. I'd fed her just before coming, so she wasn't hungry. The seat on the other side of me was empty and I wondered who would sit there, and hoped it would be someone I would enjoy talking to. It was noisy in the dining room, so talking to someone on the other side of the ten-person table would be difficult.

"Mom says the food here is really good," Alyssa said.

"Well, I'm starving, so I'm sure whatever I eat will taste good."

A moment later Cameron arrived. The only empty seat was the one next to me and he smiled at me as he sat. I wondered what, if anything, he knew about me. Surely Alyssa had filled Ty in on what had happened to me with Trevor, but I wondered if anyone else knew.

The waiters handed out the menus and I read over the choices.

There were several appetizers to choose from, as well as entrees, and everything sounded delicious. "I can't decide between these two," I said, showing Alyssa the appetizers I wanted.

"Get them both," she said.

"What?"

"Yeah. You can, you know."

"Oh."

"I know I'm getting these two," Cameron said, showing me his menu.

"I don't know if I can eat that much." I smiled at him, glad his initial friendliness seemed to be returning. "I'd better just choose one appetizer."

He grinned. "Just make sure to save room for dessert. I hear the melting cake is really good."

"If chocolate's involved, then I'm sure I'll love it."

"Oh," he said. "You're a chocoholic." He leaned toward me and whispered, "Me, too."

I smiled, enjoying his attention.

I chatted with Alyssa during the meal, but didn't want to monopolize her attention—she was the star of this cruise, after all. I turned to Cameron, who seemed to be focused on eating his entree. "So on the flight today," I began.

He looked at me and his face reddened. "Yeah, sorry that I totally ignored you."

I laughed. "It's okay. I was just wondering what you were working on. You seemed really focused on your laptop."

"I was trying to get a slide show finished for work before we set sail."

"Oh. What do you do?"

"I'm in marketing. I work for a software company and we're getting ready to launch a new product."

"Software, huh?" I paused. "I'm working on a degree in Information

Technology."

His interest seemed piqued at this. "Oh, yeah? When do you finish?"

I laughed softly. "Not for a while. I got a little sidetracked with having Natalie, so my degree's on hold for a little bit. But in the meantime, I'm building webpages for some small businesses in my community."

"Really? That's cool."

"Yeah. I like it a lot. And I love that I can work when it's convenient for me." Natalie started fussing, so I took her out of the high chair and held her on my lap.

Cameron looked at her. "How old is she?"

"Eight months."

His lips quirked into a smile. "I don't know much about babies."

"Well, I'm lucky that Natalie is a particularly easy baby."

A look of guilt washed over his face. "I have to admit, when I got on the plane and saw that the only empty seat was next to a baby, I was kind of worried." He frowned. "No, I was really worried. I've been on flights before where babies scream the whole time, so I wasn't very happy that I had to sit next to you."

I frowned. "I know."

Alarm spread across his face. "Don't misunderstand me. It turned out okay. I was wrong about your baby. She hardly made any noise at all and I was able to get my work done."

I laughed at his obvious concern that he had offended me. "Don't worry about it. I know how it is. I'd feel the same way, but I already knew—at least I'd hoped—that Natalie would be fine. It was actually kind of entertaining to watch everyone get on board, take one look at me and Natalie, and then move on. I have to admit, I kind of felt sorry for you when you got on and no seats were left." I pursed my lips at him. "I guess if you'd gotten there earlier, it wouldn't have been an issue." I paused. "Like tonight. You got stuck sitting next to me again."

He grinned. "Turns out it was okay, just like on the flight." A look of chagrin filled his face. "I have to apologize, Lily."

Confused, I asked, "What for?"

"For kind of blowing you off earlier."

I recalled the way I had felt a little hurt when Cameron had seemed to lose interest in me the moment he'd discovered I had a child. I shook my head. "It's okay."

He shook his head too. "No, it's not." He sighed. "Ty told me a little about what you've been through and I feel like a jerk for blowing you off just because you have a baby."

Now I felt awkward. "You don't have to pay attention to me out of pity, Cameron." I paused. "I'm a big girl. I can take care of myself."

He looked sort of stunned. "There's no pity involved, Lily. Just an initial moment of panic when I found out you had a baby." He gazed at me a moment and his blue eyes seemed to darken. "I *want* to get to know you better. Not only are you a beautiful woman, but your story kind of intrigues me." His face reddened a little, and his dimple showed as he smiled. "That is, if you want to get to know me."

I gazed at the sincerity in his face, and remembered Alyssa's comment that he was a nice guy, and thought about how I'd failed to listen to her before regarding both Trevor and Justin. Maybe I should listen to her this time, I thought. A smile slowly lifted the corners of my mouth. "I'd like that."

He grinned. "Now, are you ready to try some of the melting cake I was telling you about?"

My smile widened. "Absolutely."

A short time later the waiters brought out the desserts we'd ordered. Balancing Natalie on my lap, I scooped out a small spoonful of the melting cake and added a bit of ice cream to the spoon, then put it in my mouth.

"Well?" Cameron asked, watching me. "What do you think? Does it satisfy your chocolate cravings?"

"Wow. You were right. It's delicious. So rich. I'm glad they only give you a small serving of it."

"I wouldn't mind a larger serving," he said, smiling. "But I have to watch my figure."

I laughed. From what I could see, he was in fantastic shape. "Have you signed up for any excursions?" I asked.

"A couple. How about you?"

"Not yet. But it sounds like the whale watching in Juneau is a must, so I was going to do that one."

"I haven't signed up for that one. I hear it's cheaper to do some of the excursions if you wait until we dock and then sign up with people on shore."

"Really? How does that work?"

"When you get off the ship, there are booths where you can sign up to do excursions with local companies. I've been on one other cruise and it was definitely cheaper to use the local companies."

"Oh. I didn't know about that."

"Stick with me, Lily. I'll show you how it works."

I smiled at the implied invitation. "With the baby, I won't be able to do very many excursions. But Alyssa's mom offered to watch her while I do the whale watching, so I do want to do that one at least."

"There's some stuff you can do with her. Like the train ride in Skagway."

"That would be nice." I tilted my head to one side. "How do you know so much?"

He grinned. "I just did a little research."

"That was smart. I guess I just assumed I wouldn't be able to do much since I had Natalie with me. Which is fine—I'm here for Alyssa's wedding, after all. But I don't know if I'll ever get back to Alaska, so it would be nice to do a few things."

"Hey," Cameron said. "I just thought of something. Maybe Ty's younger sister can babysit for you if you want to do something on the ship. You know, there's lots to do at night."

I glanced at Ty's sister, who was sitting on the other side of the table. She looked like she was about fourteen, which seemed old enough to babysit, but I'd never left Natalie with a sitter. "I'm not sure." I glanced at Natalie, then back at Cameron. "I've never left her with a sitter before."

His eyebrows went up. "You've never been away from her?"

I thought about the hours she'd been away from me when Trevor had kidnapped her with the plan of keeping her, and felt my heart pound. "Just once, but it wasn't my choice."

He looked confused, and I wondered how much detail he really knew about me.

"It's a long story," I said.

"Well, it's up to you, obviously. But if you change your mind…"

"Thanks for the suggestion. I'll think about it."

Chapter Ten

When Natalie and I got back to our room, I was pleasantly surprised by the cute towel animal our room steward had placed on the bed. It looked like a walrus.

"Look at that, Natalie," I said as I placed her next to it. She reached out and touched it, then giggled. I picked up the schedule for the next day, which the steward had set beside the towel animal, and looked over the activities that would be available on the ship the next day—we would be at sea all day as we traveled north toward Alaska. I set the schedule on the desk, and got Natalie ready for bed.

After I tucked her in, I thought about Cameron. He really was a nice guy, just like Alyssa had said, and I wouldn't mind getting to know him better, but I knew my time with him would be minimal. I was sure he wouldn't want to be stuck with me as I was limited in what I could do. Then I thought about Marcus and how much he enjoyed Natalie, and wished that he wanted our relationship to move beyond friendship.

He'd been such a good friend to me—he'd even been there when Natalie had been born. But he was stuck in the friendship mode. Then I thought of his new girlfriend, Chelsea. He certainly wasn't stuck in the friendship mode with her.

Jealousy that she had something that I didn't bloomed inside me, but I tamped it down, not liking the way it made me feel. I had no claim over Marcus—he could do what he wanted. I'd told him how I felt about him and he'd turned me down. Clearly, he wasn't interested in anything beyond friendship.

The night I'd told him I really liked him, he'd told me he didn't think I was ready for anything more than friendship either. He'd said he thought it was too soon after all that had happened. Maybe he was right. Maybe I wasn't ready for more than friendship. Even so, I would enjoy my time with Cameron. At least he didn't have any pre-conceived ideas about what I was or wasn't ready for. He was just interested in getting to know me better. He'd even come right out and said that. I smiled in remembrance at the man who had already been vetted by Alyssa and Ty. He was Ty's best friend, after all. I felt safe spending time with him. I knew Alyssa would never lead me astray.

As I got ready for bed and climbed between the covers, I pushed all thoughts of Marcus out of my mind, and instead focused on Cameron—the man who actually had an interest in me. I smiled as I drifted off, excited for what the next day might bring.

The next morning when I was about to go to the dining room and have breakfast, Alyssa called my room phone.

"Are you up yet?" she asked.

I laughed. "I've been up for a while. That's what babies do to you—they make you get up early."

"That's kind of what I figured. Some of us are going to breakfast now and I wanted to know if you wanted to meet us in the dining room."

"Sure, that would be great."

"I want to hear about the conversation you had with Cameron at dinner." She laughed. "I couldn't hear what you were saying, but you seemed like you got along."

"Won't he be at breakfast? I don't want to talk about him if he's right there."

"No. Ty called his room, but he wasn't ready to get up yet. He'll meet up with us later."

"Okay. I'll see you in the dining room in a few minutes."

We hung up and I carried Natalie out of our room and to the dining room. Alyssa, Ty, and a few other people I hadn't talked to yet were just arriving. Someone led us to a table and brought a high chair for Natalie.

"So?" Alyssa said as she sat next to me.

I smiled, remembering how much I enjoyed talking to Cameron. "Well, I have to admit, you were right. He's a nice guy."

Alyssa grinned. "I told you." With mock-sternness, she said, "When it comes to men, you should always listen to me, Lily."

I nodded. "I know that *now.*"

"Good. Better late than never." She paused. "I was a little worried though, with the way he reacted yesterday when you pointed out Natalie."

I nodded. "My guess is that he's not comfortable around babies, and seeing her scared him."

"Yeah, that makes sense. I guess he got over it though. You guys seemed to talk a lot at dinner. Did you guys make any plans to do stuff together?"

"Not exactly. But he did suggest that Ty's sister could watch Natalie so I could do something with him on the ship."

"And?"

I bit my lip. "I've never left her with anybody before, so I'm a little nervous about it."

"Haley's great with kids. I'd highly recommend her."

"But doesn't she want to do stuff at night herself? They have a place for kids her age to hang out, right?"

"That's true. I guess the only way to find out is to ask her. I think she's coming for breakfast in a little bit."

"I'll think about it." We ordered our food and my stomach rumbled in anticipation. "How are you feeling, Alyssa? Your wedding's in two days. Are you ready?"

"Yes, I'm so ready. And it's nice that the staff here are taking care of everything so I can just enjoy myself." She paused. "I would have liked to have you as one of my bridesmaids, but we hadn't really spoken much recently."

"That's totally fine. I'm just glad I can be here."

A few minutes later Ty's sister, Haley, joined us.

"Come sit by Lily," Alyssa said, and Haley sat in the empty chair on the other side of me, which was next to Natalie's high chair.

"You're the one with the cute baby," she said as she touched Natalie's hand. "Hi, baby," she murmured to Natalie.

"Her name's Natalie," I said, pleased to see her interest.

"Hi, Natalie."

Natalie smiled at her, then banged on the tray of her high chair.

"I think she wants me to hold her," Haley said, smiling.

"I think that's a great idea." I glanced at Alyssa, a smile on my face, then took Natalie out of her high chair and gave her to Haley, who seemed very comfortable with her. Seeing them together, I warmed to the idea of asking her to babysit once or twice. It would be nice for me to be able to hang out with the grown-ups.

Our breakfast came a few minutes later, and Haley ordered her breakfast. When Haley's food arrived, I took Natalie back. "Haley, would you be willing to babysit Natalie for me once or twice at night while we're on the cruise?"

Her face lit up. "Really?"

I smiled at her enthusiasm. "Yes."

"I'd love to."

"I don't want to keep you from doing any activities that you want to do, though."

"Oh, don't worry about that. It would be fun to babysit."

"If it's at night, she might be sleeping most of the time you're babysitting."

Her smile dimmed. "Oh." She paused. "But that's okay. I still want to."

"Okay. I'll let you know when I need you." Happy that I'd been able to make arrangements for Natalie that I felt good about, I enjoyed the rest of my breakfast. "What are you going to do today," I asked Alyssa.

"I'm not sure. I think Ty wants to hit the slot machines for a little while, but that's not really my thing." She paused. "What about a massage in the spa?"

"I can babysit," Haley quickly said.

I smiled at her, thinking this would be a good chance for me to see how she did when Natalie was awake. "Okay."

"Great," Alyssa said. "I'll see when they have openings today and I'll let you know."

Later that morning Alyssa brought Haley to my room so she could babysit while we went to the spa.

"I just fed her," I told Haley, "so she should be fine as far as that goes. There are toys in the diaper bag." I looked around the room, wondering what else I needed to tell her. "You can call the number for the spa if you need me." I was glad that I knew exactly where I'd be, as otherwise it could be hard for her to track me down.

Haley held out her arms for Natalie. "We'll have fun together."

I handed her over, suddenly nervous about leaving my baby, but knew it would be fine. "We'll be an hour or so."

"Thanks, Haley," Alyssa said, hooking her arm through mine and tugging me toward the door.

"Yes, thanks," I added.

A short time later we were getting massages, and I felt myself finally beginning to relax. "This was a great idea," I murmured.

"I know," Alyssa said.

After the massage, I went to my room to see how Natalie and Haley were doing, and Alyssa went to check on Ty at the slot machines. When I opened the door to my room, I was relieved to see the two of them getting along fine.

"How did it go?" I asked, eager for a report.

"Great. She's such a sweet baby."

I smiled. "I know. She really is." I picked her up and held her in front of me. "How's my good baby girl?"

She smiled at me, clearly happy to be with Mommy again.

I turned to Haley. "We never discussed how much I would pay you."

"Oh, you don't have to pay me. It was fun."

"Are you sure?"

"Yeah. I love to babysit."

"You must be saving for something though, right?"

She looked thoughtful. "Yeah. But that's okay."

"It would make me feel better if I paid you, okay?"

She finally agreed and I gave her some cash. "Thank you, Haley."

She walked toward the door.

"Wait."

She stopped and looked at me.

"Do you know your way back to your room?"

She bit her lip. "I think so."

"Natalie's probably ready for a walk, so why don't you let us walk with you back to your room?"

Her face brightened. "Okay."

I put Natalie in her stroller and followed Haley out the door. We took the elevator to her floor and I walked with her to the room she shared with her parents. After dropping her off, I went to the Lido deck to get a soft serve ice cream cone. I filled a cone and wheeled Natalie to a table next to a window, then sat down.

Halfway through my cone, I heard a voice behind me.

"Hey, Lily," Cameron said as he stopped next to the table.

"Hi."

"Do you mind if I join the two of you?"

"Not at all."

He slid into the seat across from me and grinned, his dimple deepening. "I see you found the chocolate ice cream."

My face reddened, embarrassed that my sweet tooth was so obvious. "Yes, you caught me."

He laughed. "I'd get one too, but I had one earlier."

I smiled. "Ahh. So you're just as bad as me."

"Maybe so." He paused. "How's your day going?"

"Good. Alyssa and I went to the spa earlier to have a massage."

His eyebrows went up. "What'd you do with your baby?"

"I listened to your suggestion and asked Haley to babysit. It looks like she did a good job, too."

"Did she now?" He smiled slowly. "Does that mean you'd let her babysit in the evening so you can come out and play with the grown-ups?"

"Maybe."

"I hear the comedy shows are really fun."

"I saw those listed on the schedule."

"Do you want to go?"

"Tonight?"

"Sure."

I felt bold. "Is this a date?"

His blue eyes sparkled. "Do you want it to be?"

I didn't like the way he turned the tables on me—I didn't want to be the one to say this was a date. I tilted my head to the side. "I asked you first."

He laughed. "So you did." He stood.

I raised my eyebrows, enjoying our flirtation. "No answer, huh?"

He gazed at me for a moment. "Time will tell." Then he grinned, and walked away.

I watched him go, delighted by our budding friendship. It had been so long since I'd felt carefree—it felt wonderful. Natalie began getting restless and I knew it was past her nap time, so I strolled her back to our room, fed her, then put her down for a nap.

Forty minutes later, as I was beginning to doze while reading a book, I heard a knock on my door.

"Hi, Alyssa," I said, when I saw her standing in the hall.

"I thought you might be in here."

I held the door open in invitation. "It's Natalie's nap time."

Alyssa came in and pointed to the balcony. I nodded and followed her out, then we sat on the deck chairs and gazed out at the ocean. The clear blue of the sky, and the wide, wide ocean relaxed me. I felt far removed from my everyday life, loving the feeling of freedom that gave me.

"Cameron invited me to go with him to a comedy show tonight," I said.

Alyssa's eyebrows shot up. "When did this happen?"

I laughed at the look of surprise on her face. "A little while ago. He ran in to me on the Lido deck." I thought about our conversation. "It's unclear if it's a date though."

"Why do you say that?"

I replayed what Cameron had said, and she laughed. "He's such a flirt."

While it was fun to flirt with him, I hoped I was more than just mere entertainment to him. My sudden hesitation must have shown.

"What's wrong?" Alyssa asked.

"I just don't want him to play games with me." I'd had enough of that with Trevor, and lately it seemed, with Marcus. I needed a man who would be honest and up-front.

She reached out and touched my arm. "The last thing I want is for you to get jerked around—you've been through way too much to have to deal with that. But give Cameron a chance. He's a good guy. You'll probably only see him while you're on the cruise anyway. You might as well have some fun."

That was true. My life was normally pretty quiet and I knew I could use some excitement. Plus, the loneliness I'd been feeling since Marcus had rejected my suggestion to move our relationship beyond friendship was really getting to me. I wanted *more.* Though I'd discovered my inner strength over the last year, and knew I was capable and could take care of myself, I also longed for the love and attention of a man. Like any girl my age—I was only twenty-one after all—I wasn't ashamed to admit how much I enjoyed flirting and feeling attractive and *wanted.*

I looked at Alyssa and nodded. "You're right. I shouldn't be so serious about this. It's not like I'm going to jump in bed with him. We're just going to hang out and have fun. Nothing permanent." Something permanent is what I wanted with Marcus, but that seemed less and less likely. I needed to put aside that desire for now and just enjoy myself. No reason to think beyond that. In that direction lay heartache and disappointment.

"Right." She gently squeezed my arm. "I have some wedding stuff I need to take care of, but I'll see you later?"

"Yeah. I think I'll order something from room service for lunch since Natalie's still napping."

"Okay. I'll see you later then."

I walked her to the door, then called room service and ordered some food. I was starving—that ice cream hadn't filled me up—and it was a long time until dinner.

Chapter Eleven

That night at dinner Cameron got to the dining room before I did, and saved me a seat. I had to admit, I was a little surprised. Did he really find me that interesting? I decided to just go with it, and sat next to him. I put Natalie's high chair on the other side of me, between me and Alyssa's dad.

Between eating the appetizer and the entree, Cameron leaned toward me and said, "I asked Haley if she'd babysit for you tonight—if that's okay with you, of course."

I stared at him a moment, surprised by his boldness in arranging a babysitter for my child, but I let it slide, deciding he was just being thoughtful. And he had made it clear that it was up to me. "I suppose I should thank you." I smirked, just a little. "You must want to take me on this date really bad."

He grinned, and his dimple deepened. "Maybe I do."

The waiter set my entree in front of me—salmon and rice—and I picked up my fork, then looked at him. "What time does this date begin?"

"As soon as you say it does."

I looked at my plate, hiding my smile, excited to have some time to spend with grown-ups, then looked back at him. "Let's say, nine thirty?" That would give me time to get Natalie settled before I left for the evening.

"Sounds good."

I gave him my room number. "Do you want to confirm with Haley, or shall I?"

"I will," he said. "Since I'm the one who suggested it."

"Okay." I ate my salmon, which was delicious, and asked Cameron about his family.

"I have a younger brother, and no sisters. What about you?"

"I don't have any siblings." I sipped my water. "Are you close to your brother?"

"Not really. He's a senior in high school, so he was pretty young when I moved out."

"How old are you, anyway?"

"Twenty-six."

I nodded. "How long have you known Ty?"

"Just a few years. We were roommates our freshman year of college and got along really well. After I moved to Sacramento, we stayed in touch."

We finished our dinners and the waiter brought out the dessert menu. I read it over and decided to go with the melting cake again.

"You really are a chocoholic, aren't you?" Cameron asked.

I smiled. "Guilty as charged. Plus, those things are so good."

"I know. I told you."

A few minutes later our desserts arrived. By then I had Natalie on my lap as she'd gotten tired of sitting in the high chair. "Where are you from originally?" I asked Cameron.

"My family lives in Texas."

"I've never been there."

"I like it. We have some land there, even a few horses."

My eyebrows went up. "Oh, so you're a cowboy."

He laughed. "I've ridden a horse or two in my time."

"But did you wear a cowboy hat?"

"Of course."

I liked the imagery that came to mind—his tan showing off the blue of his eyes, his cowboy hat placed confidently on his head, his strong arms holding the reins of his horse as he galloped across an open field. I felt a little thrill as I imagined those strong arms around me. *Don't get ahead of yourself, Lily.* "What brought you to Sacramento?"

"A job offer. But I like it there. I've lived there just over a year now, and it feels like home."

Natalie started getting fussy. I tried to soothe her, but it didn't help. "It's getting past her bedtime. I'd better go put her down."

"Okay. I'll bring Haley with me when I come to pick you up." He paused, a twinkle in his eyes. "For our date."

I smiled. "Okay, see you in a while."

After I put Natalie down for the night, I went into my bathroom and added more mascara, then curled my eyelashes. Pleased with the way my eyes seemed to stand out, I smiled at my reflection, remembering what it was like to anticipate going on a date. As I gazed at myself, I felt my confidence growing. *I look good.* I could see why a handsome man like Cameron would be interested in me.

When I heard a knock at my door, I opened it to find Haley and Cameron standing in the hall. I glanced at Cameron, excitement washing over me, then focused on Haley. "She should sleep the whole time you're here," I whispered to her.

She nodded and held up a book. "I'm in the middle of a good book, so I'll be fine." She hesitated. "Is it okay if I sleep if it's getting late?"

"Of course." Then I glanced at Cameron. "I don't think I'll be out that late though." As much as I was looking forward to our evening, I didn't want to leave Natalie for too long.

He shrugged. "It's up to you."

"Okay." I smiled at Haley. "Thank you for coming over to stay with her."

"It's fine. I think she's adorable."

A moment later Cameron and I left. It felt strange to be on a date. It had been a long time since I'd been on one—since before Natalie was born. And when Marcus had taken me out back then, I'd been living a lie, pretending to be a widow named Kate. Now, I had nothing to hide. I felt liberated—I could be myself with this man and he could take it or leave it. But the more time I spent with him, the more I hoped he'd like me.

"So, where are you taking me?" I asked as he pressed the button for the elevator.

"There's a comedy show at ten, so I thought we'd head over there."

The place was filling quickly, but we found good seats. Waiters circulated among the guests, taking drink orders.

"Do you want anything?" Cameron asked.

I picked up the menu, which was on the small circular table in front of us, and read it over. "Sure."

He motioned for the waiter, who came right over to us. I ordered an alcohol-free fruity drink. Cameron glanced at me, then ordered the same thing.

A few minutes later the waiter brought our drinks, then the show began. The comedian was funny, but I noticed he picked on the people sitting in the front row. I leaned toward Cameron. "I'm glad we didn't sit up there."

"Yeah. Talk about embarrassing."

At the end of the show, Cameron turned to me. "Do you like to dance?"

"I'm not that good at it, but yeah, I like to."

He grinned. "Great. We can suck together. But at least we can have fun."

I liked his attitude, and when he stood and held out his hand, I took it. He didn't let go as we walked out of the comedy club. The warmth of his hand warmed my heart, making me feel cared about. I'd just met this man the day before, but I was really enjoying his company, and he seemed to be enjoying mine.

Marcus's face flashed into my mind, and I thought about our self-defense refresher course not long before, and how much I'd enjoyed sparring with him. For a moment I'd thought he'd felt toward me the same as I felt toward him—wanting to take our relationship to the next level. But he'd clearly stated that he didn't want that.

Now, as I walked with Cameron, our fingers intertwined, I felt the promise of a budding relationship, a relationship that had the potential of more than friendship, which, I admitted, was what I wanted. At heart, I was a traditional girl, and now that I had Natalie, I wanted to complete the picture with a husband who could also be a father. I'd had high hopes that Marcus would be that man—after all, he really cared about my sweet Natalie. But since he didn't see me as anything more than a friend, I had to move on.

I glanced at Cameron, and when he looked at me, I smiled. His blue eyes sparkled and I felt excited at my attraction to him. I *wanted* to feel attracted to him. After my experience with Trevor and Justin, I wanted to be drawn to a good man who was also drawn to me. I wanted to choose the right man.

I'd chosen poorly when I'd chosen Trevor—I'd ignored all the warning signs, as well as Alyssa's guidance. If I'd listened to her and chosen Justin, I wondered where I'd be now. Of course I wouldn't have Natalie, and I could never regret having her, but would I be happily married if I'd chosen Justin? I would never know.

Loud music with a strong beat filled the air as we approached the dance club.

"Are you ready?" Cameron asked, grinning.

"I guess so."

Still holding my hand, he led me inside the room where couples were swaying and dancing to the music. Colorful lights illuminated the room, flashing in time to the beat of the music. The energy in the room was palpable, and Cameron pulled me right onto the dance floor. At first I felt self-conscious as I danced—I hadn't been dancing in a long time—but after a little while I felt more comfortable and began to have a good time.

After a few fast songs, a slow song started. Cameron reached toward me and put his hands on my waist. Heart pounding, I put my arms around his neck. His hands slid from my sides, to around my back and he pulled me closer. I hadn't been held like that since happier times with Trevor, and I felt a mix of emotions—sadness that things had turned sour so quickly with Trevor, and euphoria that I had a chance to start fresh with someone new. I'd been through so much, I would move forward cautiously with anyone I dated, but the possibility of better things to come gave me a feeling of elation.

Cameron kept one arm securely around my waist, and with his other hand, he gently guided my head to his shoulder. I relished our closeness and willingly rested my head on his shoulder. We slowly swayed to the music and I let myself enjoy the moment, pushing thoughts of everything else out of my mind. When the song ended, Cameron released me and I took a step back. We both smiled.

"Are you thirsty?" he asked.

I nodded, and he took my hand and led me to the bar where I asked for a soda. He ordered the same, then we carried them to an empty table. The high volume of the music made it a little difficult to have a conversation, but Cameron moved his chair so our legs were touching and we could hear each other over the music.

"I don't know about you, but I'm having a good time," he said.

"I am too. I'm glad you invited me."

He smiled, and we drank our sodas. "How old are you, Lily?"

I smiled, having an idea where his question was going. "Twenty-one."

He nodded. "Okay. Just curious, but do you not like to drink? I mean, it seems like that's a favorite pastime of most of the people on the ship."

I laughed. "I've noticed. But no, I don't like to drink." I paused. "What about you?"

"I like to have a drink now and then, but it's not a big deal." He seemed to hesitate. "Do you mind my asking why you don't drink?"

"When I was little, my mom was killed by a drunk driver. When I was old enough to understand what that meant, I decided I would stay away from alcohol completely."

"I'm sorry about your mom. That's awful."

"Thanks. I don't really remember her. I was really young when it happened."

After a few minutes he held out his hand. "Ready for more?"

I nodded and took his hand and let him lead me to the dance floor. For the next hour we danced to a mix of slow and fast songs. I liked the slow songs the best, and each time one began, I eagerly went into his arms.

As midnight approached, I took his hand and pulled him off of the dance floor. "I should probably call it a night. I want to make sure everything is okay with Natalie."

"Okay."

Holding hands, we headed to my room, and a moment later we were inside. Natalie was sound asleep in her crib, and Haley had fallen asleep on my bed. I gently woke her. "I'm back," I whispered.

She opened her eyes and sat up.

"How did everything go?" I asked.

"Fine," she said as she pushed herself off of the bed. "She never woke up."

"Good." I handed her some money. "Thank you for giving up your night for me."

She smiled. "It's okay."

I glanced at Cameron and caught him looking at me, and I held back a smile. I wondered if he wanted to kiss me good-night. I knew I wouldn't be upset if he tried, but it would be awkward for him to with Haley there. I wasn't about to send her on her own back to her room—it was midnight, after all—and I hoped he wouldn't ask her to leave either.

"I can walk you to your room," he said to Haley, then he looked at me.

"That's a good idea," I said, relieved he felt as I did about her safety. "It's pretty late." I paused. "I had fun, Cameron."

"See you tomorrow?" he asked, his blue eyes bright.

I nodded, then I looked at Haley. "Thanks, Haley."

She smiled, then followed Cameron out of the room.

After they left, I made sure Natalie was comfortable, then I got ready for bed. As I tried to fall asleep, I thought about my evening with Cameron. He seemed to like me as much as I was growing to like him, and a smile grew on my face as I fantasized about him pulling me close and then kissing me. My fingers brushed across my lips, imagining what a kiss from him would feel like, and I eagerly anticipated the next day and what it might bring.

Chapter Twelve

The next morning I felt lazy—I wasn't used to getting to bed so late—and after I took care of Natalie's needs, I brought her to bed with me so I could doze a little longer. When I finally got up and got ready, it was too late to eat breakfast in the dining room, so I put Natalie in the stroller and we went to the Lido deck to get breakfast from the buffet. I found that many of the same foods were offered at the buffet as were offered in the dining room, and I had a filling breakfast.

Just as I finished eating, Alyssa and Ty came by.

"Late night?" Alyssa said, her eyebrow raised as she and Ty slid into the seats across from me.

I laughed. "How did you know?"

"Ty's mom told me Haley got back to the room after midnight."

"Oh."

Alyssa smiled. "No hope of secrets there." She paused. "Can I hold Natalie?"

"Sure." I took her out of her stroller and handed her across the table to Alyssa.

"Now, don't go getting any ideas," Ty said, eyeing Natalie warily.

Alyssa laughed.

Ty looked at me. "What do you think of my buddy, Cameron?"

I couldn't hold back a smile. "He's okay."

Ty looked surprised. "Just okay?"

I laughed. "What do you want me to say? I just met him two days ago."

"What'd you guys end up doing last night?" Alyssa asked.

"We went to a comedy show, then we went dancing."

"That sounds like fun," she said.

"It was. We had a good time." I paused. "What do you guys have planned today?"

"Not a whole lot," Alyssa said. "The ship's going to cruise up a fjord today and we'll be able to see a glacier, so that will be cool."

"I've never seen a glacier before," I said.

"We haven't either."

"Do you know what Cameron will be doing?" I asked, knowing there was no way to be subtle about the question.

Ty laughed. "No idea."

"Why don't you ask him?" Alyssa said, ever the helpful friend.

I smirked. "If I see him, I will, but I don't want to be a stalker."

We chatted for a while longer, then Ty stood. "I'm going to check out the casino."

Alyssa smiled up at him. "Okay." Then he leaned down and kissed her. She watched him walk away, then turned back to me. "I'm a lucky girl, Lily."

"I like him," I said. "I'm really happy for you."

Her face lit up. "I can't believe I'm getting married tomorrow."

"I know. It's super exciting."

"I just hope the wedding's not too early for everyone. We wanted to make sure people still had time to get off the ship and do some exploring before we set sail in the afternoon."

"I'm sure it will be fine. After all, the only reason we're all here is for the wedding."

"True."

Natalie started fussing, so I took her back. Even though I'd been lazy that morning, she'd been awake for several hours. "I think she's about ready for a nap."

"I need to go spend some time with some of my other guests anyway."

I frowned, worried. "I hope I'm not monopolizing your time, Alyssa."

"Oh no," she hurried to assure me. "I haven't seen you in ages, and I'm so thrilled you're here, I want to spend as much time with you as I can."

The warmth of her friendship made me feel loved. "I've really missed you, Alyssa."

She reached across the table and I put my hand in hers. "I've missed you too. It makes me happy to see *you* happy."

"It's been a crazy year and a half, but I've really gotten to know myself, and I've discovered I'm stronger than I thought I was."

Natalie started fussing more loudly.

"There's my hint to get going," I laughed.

"Okay. I'll see you later then."

I put Natalie in her stroller and headed back to our room. After putting her down for a nap, I pulled out a book I'd been reading, and settled in for some quiet time. Half an hour later there was a knock on my door. I set my book down and went to the door, expecting it to be Alyssa, but when I saw Cameron, I was pleasantly surprised.

"Hey, Lily." His dimple deepened as he smiled.

"Hi."

"Are you busy?"

"No. Natalie's asleep so I was just reading."

"Do you want some company?"

"Sure." I held the door open and he walked in.

He stopped next to Natalie's crib and looked down at her, and I wondered what he was thinking. When he looked at me, I motioned to the balcony. I grabbed a light jacket and then the two of us went out the balcony door.

"Wow," he said. "Having a balcony is nice."

"You don't have one?" I'd assumed everyone had gotten balcony rooms.

"No. I was trying to save money, so one of my buddies and I got an interior room."

"I considered doing that too, but I figured I might never go on another cruise, so I decided to splurge." I leaned against the railing and looked at the mountains that lined the fjord, clouds covering the tops. "I'm glad I did. Especially since I've ended up spending so much time in my room while Natalie sleeps."

"Yeah, that does make a difference."

In the background, I heard the naturalist talking over the ship-wide speakers, sharing information about the fjord. I heard her say something about whales. "What did she say about whales?"

"I think she said she'd tell us if she saw any." He gazed out over the water. "Did you bring any binoculars?"

"Yes. Alyssa suggested it."

"Maybe you should bring them out here, in case there are any whales in the area."

Excitement laced my voice. "Ooooh. That would be so cool."

He smiled, obviously amused by my enthusiasm.

"Don't *you* think that would be cool?" I asked.

"Yes, I do." His smile grew. "That's why I want you to get the binoculars."

I laughed. "Okay. I'll be right back." I went into the room and dug out the binoculars, thrilled that Cameron had come to see me. I carried them back out to the balcony and set them on the tiny table between the chairs. He was still leaning against the balcony, and I joined him. "I'm glad it's not too cold."

"Hopefully we'll have good weather in the ports we're visiting," he said. "Of course, in Alaska, the term 'good weather' might have a different meaning than what we're used to."

"That's for sure," I said. "But this time of year it should be pretty nice."

"Oh, look at that," Cameron said, pointing to a chunk of ice floating by.

"It's so pretty, but I wonder why it's blue."

"It must have broken off of the glacier. Glacial ice is really dense and compacted, and blue is the only color that's not absorbed."

Impressed with his knowledge, I said, "Now how did you know that?"

He smiled, obviously pleased that I was impressed. "I read up on glaciers a little before the cruise."

"Are you always so inquisitive?"

He thought for a second, then nodded. "Yeah."

"Well, I have a question for you."

He smiled with confidence. "Shoot."

Smiling shyly, I asked, "Why did you come to see me? Don't you want to spend time with your friends?"

He tilted his head to one side. "Do you wish I hadn't come?"

I could tell by his expression that he was teasing. "I'm happy for the company."

He straightened. "Oh, so anyone would do? As long as they keep you company?"

I paused, like I was considering it. "Mmmm, maybe." Then I

laughed. "No, I'm really glad it was you."

"Woo. You had me worried for a minute there."

"Wait a minute. You didn't answer my question."

"Oh, I'd hoped you wouldn't notice that."

I raised one eyebrow. "Well, I did. So tell me."

"Okay." He paused. "I can spend time with my friends anytime, but I just met you, and like I told you on the first night, I want to get to know you better."

"One other question." He looked at me expectantly, but I hesitated, worried to bring up the obvious. Finally, I gathered my courage. "Does it bother you that I have a child?"

Now he hesitated, which worried me. Finally he said, "That's a fair question, and since we're being honest, I will admit that I've never dated a woman with a child before. Not that I haven't had the opportunity, but it's typically something I avoid."

I slowly nodded, trying to digest his confession, and wondering what it really meant. "I don't understand then. Why do you want to get to know me better? Natalie is my world, and if you usually avoid getting involved with women who have children, why are you here?"

This seemed to stump him. He stared out over the water for a moment, then looked at me. "To be perfectly honest, I don't know. There's just something about you that draws me in. Maybe I sense a vulnerability that makes my protective instinct take over, or maybe I just really enjoy your company. I don't know."

I nodded. "Fair enough." I paused. "It's just that my heart's been through a lot of ups and downs lately and I just want to be careful."

He ran his fingers through his hair, like he was feeling uncomfortable.

"I'm sorry, Cameron. We just barely met, and here I am acting like . . . I don't know." I paused. "I'm sorry, that's all." I faced the water, my face heating with embarrassment. "If you want to leave now, it won't hurt my feelings." I waited for him to say good-bye, but instead, I felt his hand on my back. I turned to face him, wondering what he was thinking.

His eyes seemed to have softened. "It's okay. You haven't scared me off yet."

I laughed quietly. "Well, that's good."

Just then, the naturalist announced that a humpback whale was on our side of the ship. I grabbed the binoculars from the table and pressed them to my face.

"Over there, Lily," Cameron said, pointing to a spot not too far away. "I just saw the spout."

I pulled the binoculars away to see where he was pointing, then looked through them again. "Oh! I see it!" I watched for a few moments, then handed the binoculars to Cameron.

"Oh, yeah," he said as he looked through the binoculars. "That's so cool."

"I'm really excited for the whale watching trip in Juneau," I said. He handed the binoculars back to me and I looked again.

"I am too. I'll bet we'll be able to get even closer to the whales."

The whale faded in the distance as we sailed forward, and I set the binoculars on the table. "That was awesome."

His grin matched mine, and the mood from our heavy conversation vanished. I looked through the glass wall into my room and saw that Natalie was starting to wake up. "Do you want to come inside with me?"

He nodded. "Sure."

I took his hand and led him into my room. Natalie was sitting up in the crib and held out her arms to me as I approached. "Hey, baby girl," I murmured as I lifted her. I held her on my hip and turned to Cameron to see what he would do.

His eyes on her, he tentatively reached out and touched her hand. She looked at him with uncertainty, but didn't cry, which was good. He smiled at her, and after a moment, she smiled back.

"Look, she smiled at me," he said, clearly pleased.

His pleasure at my child made me happy, and I smiled.

Apparently feeling more comfortable, he tickled her neck with his fingers. She scrunched her shoulder, then giggled. I watched Cameron's reaction, and I could tell he was charmed by Natalie. I kissed the other side of her neck and she went into peals of laughter, which made Cameron laugh.

His gaze met mine. "She is really cute, Lily."

My smile widened. "Thanks. She's a really good baby."

A look of uncertainty came over him. "Do you think she'd let me hold her?"

Surprised, but thrilled with his request, I nodded. "I think so."

He held out his hands and took her from me. He held her out in front of him and gazed into her face. She stared back, her expression serious, then her eyes squeezed closed and she let out a wail. Cameron hurriedly handed her back to me. With a look of distress, he said, "I don't think she likes me."

I held back a laugh, and instead just smiled. "No, no. That's not it at all. She's just at an age where she can sometimes be scared of people she doesn't know. Especially men." She settled down after a moment.

He laughed, his mortification seeming to lessen. "I see. She's sexist."

"Maybe a little. But that's not uncommon with babies." I paused. "Plus, she just woke up and is probably hungry."

He seemed to relax. "Okay."

"I need to feed her. You can stay if you want, but I don't want you to feel uncomfortable when I nurse her."

He looked confused for a moment, then his face reddened as he must have understood what I meant. "Oh, you mean . . ."

"Yes." I smiled. "I still breastfeed her several times a day. She'll take formula, but I try to minimize that."

"Maybe I'll just leave you alone to . . . uh . . . feed her."

I laughed. "Okay."

"Do you want to meet me somewhere when you're done?"

Pleased that he wanted to be with me, and warmed by his sweetness, I nodded. "Give me forty-five minutes or so."

"Okay. Let's meet on the Lido deck, where I ran into you yesterday." He grinned. "You know, where you were when you were eating the ice cream."

"Yes, I remember."

"Bring your binoculars and I'll bring mine."

My face lit up. "Maybe we'll see more whales."

"That's what I'm hoping." He walked toward the door. "I'll see you in a while, Lily."

"Bye." After he left, I changed and fed Natalie, snuggling her close while she nursed. I gazed at her sweet face, my heart filling with love for her. I thought about Cameron and how he'd interacted with her. He'd probably had very little experience with babies, so I was delighted with his willingness to try to get to know Natalie.

Forty-five minutes later I pushed the stroller out of our room and to the glass elevator. We rode up to the Lido deck and I headed toward the meeting place. I wasn't sure I remembered exactly where Cameron was talking about, but I went to the general area and smiled when I saw Cameron sitting next to the window, looking out over the water through his binoculars.

I slid into the seat across from him. "Hey," I said, and he turned to me with a smile. "See any whales?"

"Not yet. But I've seen a few chunks of ice float by."

We watched out the window, with Natalie on my lap, and enjoyed the gorgeous view. "Look at the waterfall," I said, pointing to the stream of water rushing down the side of the mountain.

"Oh yeah. All that snow higher on the mountain is melting."

"I'm starting to get hungry," I said after a while. "What about you?"

"Yeah." He looked nervously at Natalie. "Do you want me to hold her while you get something to eat?"

I smiled. "Are you sure you want to?"

He smiled and shook his head, but said, "Yeah."

I laughed at the contradiction. "It will just take a few minutes to get some food." I placed her on his lap so that she was facing away from him. "Just let her face all the activity in the room and I'm sure she'll be fine."

"Okay."

I walked toward the buffet lines, smiling to myself, and picked up a tray. After I got my food, I went to the dessert buffet and grabbed a slice of chocolate cake, then filled a plastic cup with lemonade. As I walked back to the table, I hoped Natalie wasn't giving Cameron a hard time. As I approached the table where we'd been sitting, I felt a moment of confusion.

Is this the right table? I didn't see Cameron or Natalie anywhere. Or the stroller or binoculars, for that matter. Feeling certain that I was in the right place, alarm began growing inside me. *Where are they?* Trying to quell the alarm that crawled up my throat, I set my tray on the table and slowly turned in circles, my gaze darting from one table to the next.

Chapter Thirteen

They couldn't have gone far, I reminded myself. We *are* on a ship, after all. "Natalie," I called out, ignoring the diners who looked at me with curiosity. A feeling of deja vu crept up my spine, making the hairs on the back of my neck stand on end. *This is not like Trevor, this is not like Trevor, this is not like Trevor.* Though I chanted the words to myself, they didn't do much to calm me.

"Natalie!" I called out again as tears filled my eyes.

"Over here, Lily," I heard Cameron call out a moment later.

My head jerked in the direction of his voice, but I couldn't see him through the curtain of tears. Blinking rapidly, I wiped my eyes, and once my vision cleared, I saw him sitting at a table with Alyssa's parents, Natalie happily playing with a necklace as she sat on Barbara's lap. A mix of anger and embarrassment rushed through me. I'd been panicked for no reason, except that I had a very good reason—my baby wasn't where I'd left her.

I turned away, took a few deep breaths, picked up my tray, and calmly walked to the table. I set the tray on the table and sat in the empty seat next to Cameron. "I didn't know where you'd gone." My voice shook as I spoke, betraying the feelings I was trying to hide.

"Sorry. I saw Paul and Barbara and thought it would be fun to join them." He looked at me more closely. "Are you okay?"

Feeling a little foolish for my momentary alarm, I smiled and nodded. "I'm fine."

"I was telling them how we saw that whale earlier," he said.

Trying to push my worry aside, I focused on Alyssa's parents. "It was really exciting."

"I'll bet," Barbara said. "Hopefully there are more out there for us to see."

"I'm going to grab some food," Cameron announced, then he stood and walked away.

"Do you want me to take Natalie so you can get some food?" I asked Barbara.

"Sure."

She handed her back and I held my baby close, relishing the warmth of her small body in my arms. I felt tears threatening, but blinked slowly a few times to keep them at bay.

"We'll be back in a few minutes," she said, then she and Paul left.

"I'm so glad you're okay," I murmured in Natalie's ear. She giggled as my breath tickled her ear, then she reached out and grabbed my nose. I smiled at her, then kissed her soft cheek.

A few moments later Cameron set his tray on the table and sat down. I glanced at him, and decided to let him know how I felt—not to scold him, but because I was sure he had no clue the terror his actions had given me. "Cameron, I need to talk to you."

He turned to me, a questioning look on his face. "What's up?"

"Earlier, when I got back to the table and you and Natalie weren't there, I was . . . well, I was scared."

His brow creased. "I don't understand."

I bit the inside of my lip, wondering how much to tell him. "I'm not sure how much Ty told you about what happened to me, but there was an . . . incident . . . where Natalie . . . well, she was taken from me."

His eyes widened. "I didn't know about that." He glanced at my baby, who sat contentedly on my lap, then looked at me. "I'm sorry I moved to another table without telling you."

I just nodded, not sure what to say.

We ate our meal with Paul and Barbara, then moved to the window so we could see the beauty of the fjord as the ship cruised toward the glacier. After a while, Paul and Barbara left. "I'm fine on my own, Cameron, if you want to spend some time with your friends."

He was quiet for a moment. "Okay. Maybe I'll go see what they're doing." He paused. "Do you want to come?"

I didn't know if he meant it or if he was just being nice. "No, I'm fine here with Natalie."

"Are you sure?"

I smiled. "I'm not a big social person, so I'm perfectly happy on my own."

"Okay."

"Natalie takes an afternoon nap, so if you want to stop by my room later, we can sit on the balcony again."

He smiled. "I'd really like that."

"Great. I'll see you later then."

I watched him walk away, then I turned back to the window.

That afternoon after I put Natalie down for her afternoon nap, I settled in to read, not certain if Cameron would actually come, but half an hour later he did.

He held up two small bowls, each filled with chocolate soft-serve ice cream. "I thought you might like this."

I took one of them and smiled. "Chocolate's always a sure bet with me."

He laughed quietly. "That's what I thought."

We went out to the balcony and sat in the chairs. He took his binoculars from around his neck and set them on the small table next to mine. We ate our ice cream in silence as we watched the scenery pass by.

"Did you notice how the color of the water changed?" he said.

I went to the railing and looked at the water. "Oh yeah, you're right. Before it was kind of a murky gray, and now it's a beautiful emerald color." I turned to him and smiled. "I suppose you know why."

"Actually no, I don't."

My eyebrows shot up. "Really? I'm surprised."

He laughed. "I don't know everything."

"Evidently not."

His face turned serious. "For example, apparently I don't know that much about what happened to you."

I gazed at him a moment. "Are you sure you want to know?"

He looked thoughtful. "If I'd known, I never would have taken Natalie somewhere without asking you first."

I nodded. "That's probably true."

"You don't have to tell me if you don't want to."

I thought about it for a minute. Did I want to share my sad tale with him? So far, we seemed to be hitting it off. Would my story scare him away or make him pity me? I didn't want either of those outcomes, but if I wanted to prevent another incident like today's, it would be helpful if he knew what had happened to me in the past. I decided to give him the condensed version of events. "No, it's okay."

I sat in the chair next to his. "The short version is, I married Natalie's father and he turned out to be different than I'd thought. I left him, basically going into hiding, but he tracked me down while I was still pregnant. After Natalie was born, I let him spend some time with her, but after I'd made it clear I wasn't interested in getting back together, he took her away from me."

"Oh wow. That's awful."

The events of that day ran vividly through my mind, and for a moment the emotions I'd felt when I'd woken after Trevor had knocked me out, and then discovered that he'd taken Natalie, came rushing back. I closed my eyes. "It *was* awful." I opened them to see Cameron watching me. "That was the worst day of my life."

"How did you get her back?"

"I had something he wanted. Some money. I met him at a park to make a trade—Natalie for the money. But when I got there and he'd made sure I'd brought the money, he told me he had no intention of giving her back to me." As I thought about that confrontation, I felt adrenaline pulse through me. "When he tried to attack me, I fought back and I was able to get Natalie."

His eyes were wide as he listened, but he didn't speak.

"I went back to my house to get my purse, thinking he wouldn't be able to follow me—I'd taken his car with Natalie in the back seat. But I'd forgotten that I'd left my keys in the trunk of my car, so he showed up at my house right after I did." I paused. "At the end, he tried to strangle me, but my dog was able to get out of the backyard and she took him down. She saved me."

"So where is he now? Is he in jail?"

I smiled sadly. "No. He's dead. My dog crushed his windpipe."

Cameron gasped.

"If it wasn't for her, *I'd* be dead. Trevor was on top of me and I was blacking out."

"I am so, so sorry, Lily. Not only for what you went through, but for the scare I gave you today. Now I can see why you were upset. I would have been too."

I shook my head. "You didn't know."

He stared at me for a moment. "You are a strong woman."

I smiled, thrilled he hadn't run, or shown pity. "Thanks."

The naturalist's voice came over the ship-wide speakers, announcing that a sea lion was lounging on an iceberg floating by. Cameron and I went to the railing to see if we could see it.

"There it is." I pointed to the dark creature lying in the sun on top of the iceberg. He was nearly too big for it, but he didn't seem to mind.

Cameron grabbed our binoculars and handed mine to me, then we gazed at the sea lion as we passed.

"There's a lot of ice floating by," I said.

"We must be getting close to the glacier," Cameron said.

"Look at that waterfall." I pointed it out, but he didn't say anything, and I turned to him. He was staring at me. "What?"

He slowly shook his head. "I'm just digesting what you told me." He gazed at me a moment. "You're an incredible woman."

I held his gaze and felt electricity flow between us. Only a few inches of space separated us, and as we focused on each other, he leaned toward me. Excitement coursed through me and I lifted my chin to show that I wanted this too. He reached out and placed his hand on the back of my neck, pulling me closer. The air around us became charged with energy as his lips descended toward mine.

I closed my eyes in sweet anticipation, and a moment later his warm mouth pressed against mine, and I felt an explosion of feeling race through me. His other arm slid around my waist, and my arms wrapped around his neck. I relished the strength and warmth that his body exuded and I melted into him, the loneliness I'd been feeling making my kiss more passionate than I would have expected.

After a moment, he released my mouth and we were both breathless. He gazed at me, his blue eyes sparkling. A slow smile spread across my face, and his expression matched mine. His arm was still around my waist, and his other arm moved from my neck to my waist, so that his arms encircled me. My arms were still around his neck, but after a moment we disentangled ourselves, and smiling, turned back to the railing to look out over the water.

My thoughts were in a whirl, and I wondered if his were too. The kiss we'd shared had been amazing, and I'd thoroughly enjoyed it. Unbidden, Marcus's face flashed into my mind, and for a moment I wished it had been him kissing me like that, not Cameron. But as fast as that thought came to mind, I pushed it down, knowing that wasn't going to happen. Marcus had made his feelings clear—friends only—so I had to put up a mental *no crossing* sign in the middle of the road that led to a future with him.

On the other hand, the possibilities with Cameron were wide open, as if that road had been freshly paved, ready for traffic. I smiled at the image, then felt Cameron's arm snake around my waist. He gently pulled me closer, so we were standing hip to hip at the railing, then he leaned down and murmured in my ear, "I like you, Lily."

A smile blossomed on my lips and I turned my face so that we were only inches apart. "I like you, too."

His dimple deepened as his smile grew, then his lips pressed against my cheek.

Badly wanting to turn my head so that our lips would meet, I let him lead the way, then rested my head on his shoulder, loving the physical contact I'd been so desperately missing. His arm tightened around my waist, making me feel warm, safe, and cared about.

The ship started to turn, and the edge of the glacier came into view. As the ship continued turning, the view of the glacier widened and we were able to see the whole thing.

"Oh wow. Look at that," he said.

I gazed at the massive sheet of ice that looked like it was flowing into the water, and shook my head in wonder. "Don't you think it's fascinating to think that so much of the earth was covered with these glaciers at one time?"

He glanced at me and nodded. "Yeah. And it's cool to see how vast this one glacier is."

We stayed on the balcony, watching the view of the glacier until the ship turned in the other direction, allowing people on the other side to view it. Finally, the ship had turned completely around and we began heading back down the fjord, back the way we had come.

"I'm getting cold," I said. "Let's go back inside."

"Yeah, it is a little chilly."

A few minutes after we came inside, Alyssa stopped by. When she came in the room I could tell she was a little surprised to see Cameron there.

"Hi, Cameron."

"Hey, Alyssa." He looked at me. "I'm going to go see what Ty's up to."

I nodded, disappointed he was leaving, but happy to be able to spend some time with Alyssa. After he left, Alyssa plopped down on the bed, a grin on her face. "What's going on here?"

I laughed. "Not much. What's up with you?"

She wagged her finger at me. "Uh uh. Tell me about you and Cameron."

Now I grinned. "He kissed me."

Her eyes widened. "Ooooh. Do tell."

"There's not a lot to tell, except that he told me he likes me."

"Really?"

"Uh huh."

"And?"

Natalie began stirring in her crib.

Alyssa frowned. "Did I wake her up?"

"It's okay. She's been asleep long enough." I picked her up and held her close, letting her wake up more completely.

"So? About you and Cameron?"

I smiled. "I told him I like him too."

"Wow. I'd hoped you guys would hit it off."

I narrowed my eyes in mock indignation. "Oh. So this was in your plans all along?"

"Of course. You know how I like to play matchmaker."

"Yes. I do."

She laughed. "And it seems to be working."

"We'll see. I only met the guy two days ago."

"Haven't you ever heard of love at first sight?"

I tilted my head to one side. "Of course, but that doesn't mean I believe it. Anyway, after the bad choices I've made in the past, believe me when I say I'm not going to rush into something with someone I've just met."

"That's good, Lily." She paused. "The reason I came by was to let you know that a bunch of us are going to try doing some karaoke. Do you want to come make a fool of yourself with the rest of us?"

"Sure. That sounds like fun. I'll meet you there in a little while."

"Awesome. See you in a bit."

Chapter Fourteen

When Natalie and I arrived in the karaoke lounge, Ty was standing in front of the microphone, singing his heart out. My gaze quickly swept the room and I saw Cameron sitting with his friends. He didn't see me, so I slipped in the back and found an empty seat not far from Alyssa, parked the stroller, and held Natalie on my lap. She bounced to the beat of the music, which made me smile—she was having as much fun as I was.

Everyone clapped and shouted when Ty finished. Ty walked over to Cameron and slapped him on the back. "Your turn, buddy."

Cameron laughed. "I'll pass."

"You have to," someone said. "You're the best man."

"Yeah, come on," a few other people said.

He seemed reluctant, but Cameron got up and told the cruise ship worker what song he wanted to sing, then he stood in front of the microphone. The music started, and though he seemed hesitant at first, after a few lyrics, he seemed to get more comfortable.

I watched him from my seat in the back, enjoying the show, Natalie bouncing on my lap, and then his gaze wandered the room and landed on me. He blushed and he missed a few words, before getting back on track. I smiled, somehow pleased that my presence had that affect on him. Alyssa turned around and raised her eyebrows. I just smiled at her.

When Cameron finished, he glanced at me, then sat by his friends. I was a little disappointed that he didn't sit by me, but I had to give the man a break. He'd only known me for a couple of days, I couldn't expect him to spend every minute with me.

I watched the karaoke for another half an hour, but I left before anyone else as Natalie was getting restless. I strolled around the shops, then went to the Lido deck, before heading back to our room. As I sat Natalie on my bed, I decided that cruises weren't really meant for babies. "But I'm still glad we came," I said to her.

That evening at dinner I got to the dining room before Cameron, but didn't save him a seat or do anything else to make him feel like he needed to sit next to me. Haley arrived before he did and she sat in the empty seat next to me, with Natalie between us. I smiled at her, figuring she might even help with Natalie during dinner. Ty's mother arrived a moment later and asked if the seat on the other side of me was taken.

"No, please sit," I said.

"You're Lily, right?" she asked.

"Yes."

"I'm Ty's mom, Katherine."

We chatted for a few minutes, then I noticed Cameron approaching the table. He glanced at me and frowned, then sat in an empty seat on the other side of the table. I held back a smile, happy that he seemed disappointed that he couldn't sit by me. We didn't talk at all through dinner as the room was so noisy that it was difficult to talk across our large table. Several times though, I felt Cameron's gaze on me, and when I looked up, he smiled at me, warming my heart.

As I'd hoped, when Natalie got fussy, Haley volunteered to hold her. "She really likes you," I said.

"You think so?"

I nodded.

"I'm glad, because I think she's adorable."

"Me, too. But I thought that was just because I'm her mother."

Haley laughed. "If you want me to babysit again, I will."

"Really?"

"Yeah."

I looked at Cameron, but he was talking to someone. I turned back to Haley. "I'll let you know."

She bounced Natalie on her lap. "Okay."

After dinner I took Natalie from Haley and waited a moment to see if Cameron would come over to talk to me. He seemed engrossed in his conversation, and Natalie was getting antsy, so I stood, ready to take her back to my room. He didn't seem to notice, so I walked away from the table and toward the dining room exit.

Though dismayed that he didn't come talk to me, I knew I needed to keep my expectations down. True, he'd said he liked me, but that didn't mean he wanted to spend every moment with me. At the elevator, I pressed the button to call the car.

"Lily, wait."

I turned to see Cameron striding toward me, and a feeling of joy bloomed inside me. "Hi." The door to the elevator slid open, but I let it close without getting on.

"I wanted to talk to you," he said, stopping next to me. "I was hoping I'd be able to sit by you at dinner."

Inside, I beamed, but I kept my expression under control. "I would have liked that."

He smiled. "I guess I need to get there a little earlier next time."

I liked that idea better than me saving him a seat—how obvious would that be to everyone? Plus, what if he changed his mind? I would look foolish if I saved him a seat and he didn't use it. No, he needed to be the one to make the effort, not me. "That would help." I paused. "Was there anything else on your mind?"

"I was wondering if you'd like to go dancing with me tonight."

A thrill ran through me at the thought of being held in his arms while we moved around the dance floor. "As a matter of fact, Haley offered to babysit."

"She did? That's great."

"She's a sweet girl and she really enjoys Natalie."

"Can she do it tonight?" Cameron asked.

"I can ask her." I looked at Natalie, then back at him. "Can you hold her while I go ask?"

He hesitated. "Sure."

I handed her to him. "Don't go anywhere."

He shook his head. "No."

I smiled. "I'll be right back." I headed toward the dining room and looked over my shoulder at Cameron. He was gazing at Natalie, and she was staring at him. She looked uncertain, so I hurried to the table where Haley had moved to sit next to her mother, and slid into the seat where Haley had sat during dinner. Katherine and Haley looked at me expectantly. "Haley, at dinner you offered to babysit Natalie." My gaze went between Haley and her mother. "Are you available to do it tonight?"

Haley looked at her mother, who looked at me and said, "I'm fine with it."

"I don't want to take her away from any family activities you might have planned." I felt a little guilty for taking Haley's time when she was on the cruise.

"But I want to," Haley said to her mother.

Katherine laughed. "I said it was fine." Then she looked at me. "We don't have anything planned tonight."

"Thank you. I'll have Cameron come pick you up from your room at nine thirty."

"Okay."

Katherine turned to Haley. "Let me talk to Lily for a minute, hon."

I watched Haley walk around the table and sit by her dad.

With a twinkle in her eye, Katherine said, "I've known Cameron for a few years, and I have to say, I'm glad the two of you are getting along."

I smiled. "Me, too." I paused. "I feel kind of bad taking Haley away from other fun things she might want to do on the ship."

"To tell you the truth, Lily, though I don't mind her meeting new kids in that teen club area, sometimes it's nice to not have to worry about what she's up to. And I know she really does love babies."

"I can tell. She's really good with Natalie."

A few minutes later I walked back to the elevator and found Cameron gently bouncing a crying Natalie. He looked more distressed than she did. I held back a laugh as I took Natalie from him, and after a moment she settled down. "Thanks for holding her," I said. "You did great."

He eyed her tear-streaked face. "She didn't seem too happy about it."

"She's just a momma's girl."

"What did Haley say?" he asked.

"It's all set. I told her you'd pick her up at nine thirty."

"As long as you don't leave me alone with your baby again, I'll be fine."

He smiled when he said it, but I knew he was serious. I laughed. "Okay." I wondered if he'd feel more comfortable with Natalie if he spent more time with her, but I knew I was getting ahead of myself. We parted and I took Natalie back to our room and got her ready for bed. By the time Cameron arrived with Haley, Natalie had fallen asleep in her crib, and I'd changed into one of the dressier outfits I'd brought for the elegant dining nights—a fitted turquoise sleeveless dress.

When I opened the door and watched Cameron's reaction to my clothes, I could tell he liked the way I'd put myself together.

"You look beautiful."

His words made me glow. "Thank you." He'd changed into a pair of slacks and a button-up shirt, which he left unbuttoned at the neck. "You don't look so bad yourself." I held out my room card. "Can you keep this in your pocket? I don't have anywhere to put it."

He took it from me and a moment later we left Haley with Natalie. As soon as the door closed behind us, Cameron took my hand. The touch of his hand enfolding mine brought back the memory of his kiss that afternoon, and I smiled in anticipation of spending the evening with him.

"There's a different comedy show tonight," he said. "Do you want to go see it before we go dancing?"

"Sure. I enjoyed the one last night."

"Me, too."

When we arrived at the comedy club, we saw Ty and Alyssa sitting on one of the couches, and we walked over to them.

"Hey," Alyssa said. "Sit with us." She patted the seat next to her.

I sat next to her with Cameron on the other side of me.

"You look gorgeous, Lily," Alyssa said, then leaned toward Cameron. "Doesn't she, Cameron?"

I laughed. "Stop."

Cameron squeezed my hand. "Yes, she does."

My heart swelled. I hadn't felt this beautiful and appreciated in a long time. Though Marcus was always sweet to me, he'd firmly kept the friendship barrier up, never stepping over it to say things like that. And of course it had been a long time since Trevor and I had been in that stage of our relationship. Thinking of how Trevor had been before I'd committed to marrying him—generally treating me well— made me pause, wondering if Cameron was acting like he was for show, or if he really meant it.

I bit back a frown, upset at Trevor for making me doubt every man's motive. Would there always be a layer of suspicion between me and any man I dated? Though unhappy that the answer was yes, I thought maybe it was better that way, at least until I learned to trust my instincts.

The comedy show started, and Cameron only released my hand when he put his arm around my shoulders instead. At the end of the show, Alyssa asked if we were going dancing.

"Yes, do you want to come?" I asked, hoping Cameron wouldn't mind.

Alyssa looked at Ty, and he nodded. The four of us walked to the dance club, and I was excited to be able to spend time with Cameron, but with Alyssa and Ty too. Their wedding was the next day and I didn't know how much time they planned on spending with the rest of us afterwards, so I wanted to spend time with Alyssa while I could.

When we walked in to the dance club, a slow song was just starting, and Cameron took my hand and led me out to the floor. I felt more comfortable in his arms than I had just the night before, and relished the naturalness of our closeness.

"I hope you don't mind that I invited Alyssa and Ty to come with us," I said, leaning away from Cameron to look at his face.

He smiled down at me. "Not at all."

"Good."

He held my gaze for a moment, then guided my head to his shoulder. I didn't resist, enjoying the warmth of his strong body pressed against mine. We swayed to the music until the last note sounded. After dancing to several fast songs, he took my hand and led me to a table.

"Would you like something cold to drink?" he asked.

"Sure. A diet soda with extra ice would be great."

Alyssa joined me at the table a moment later as Ty went to get her something to drink. "Looks like you're having fun," she said.

"Yes, I am. What about you, lady-who-is-getting-married-tomorrow?"

Her face lit up. "I know. I'm so excited."

"You'd better not get to bed too late. You don't want to be tired on your big day."

"Yeah, that wouldn't be good."

The men came back with the drinks and sat next to us.

When it was time to call it a night, Cameron walked me to my room. He stopped outside my door, and when I held out my hand for the room key, he grinned. "Not yet."

A slow smile spread across my face. "Why not?"

He leaned toward me so that his mouth was next to my ear, sending a thrill of pleasure through me. "It would be a little awkward to kiss you in front of Haley," he whispered.

My heart hammered in anticipation and I smiled, then whispered. "Who said I want to kiss you?"

He pulled back with a look of surprise, but when he saw from my expression that I was joking, he smiled. "You had me going for a minute."

"I don't want you to think I hand out kisses casually."

He stared at me for a moment, his face suddenly serious. "No, Lily. I would never think that." He reached out and stroked my cheek. "After what you've been through, I imagine you're very careful about who you trust."

My heart contracted with overwhelming attraction toward him. *He really gets me. But does he deserve my trust?* I gazed at him and silently nodded.

With his thumb touching my face, his hand curved around my neck and he gently tilted my face upward. My eyes locked on his, and as his mouth descended toward mine, my eyes closed and my lips parted, and a moment later his lips touched mine. His other arm slid around my waist, pulling me against him, and my arms went around his neck. He pushed his tongue into my mouth and I eagerly tasted him, our breath mingling.

My heart pounded as my desire skyrocketed, but I wasn't ready for my feelings to become so powerful. I unwound my arms from his neck and placed them on his shoulder, then gently pushed back, forcing us apart. His pupils were dilated and I could tell he wasn't ready to stop kissing, but I was. As much as I enjoyed kissing him, I felt unexpected panic at the strength of my yearning, and I feared things getting out of control—and out of control meant the possibility of having my heart broken. He leaned toward me again, clearly wanting another kiss, but I moved back a step. "I need to check on Natalie."

He stared at me, obviously not understanding, but after a moment he took the key card out of his pocket and handed it to me. Without looking at him—I felt a mixture of embarrassment at my reaction, along with a need to control my desire—I slid the key card into the slot, then pushed the door open.

Haley had fallen asleep on the bed again, and I gently woke her. She sat up and rubbed her eyes, then groggily walked toward the door. I took my purse out of the room safe and pulled out some cash, then handed it to her and thanked her.

"Ready, Haley?" Cameron said, not looking at me.

I stared at him, waiting for him to tell me good-night, but he ignored me. Hurt by his reaction, I didn't know what to do. He opened the door and I called out, "See you tomorrow, Cameron."

He glanced at me and nodded, unsmiling, then shut the door.

I stared at the door, confused about what had just happened.

Chapter Fifteen

When I woke the next morning, I smiled, remembering that Ty and Alyssa would be married that day. Then I thought about the way Cameron had left the night before and my smile turned into a frown. Was he upset with me because I'd backed away from his kiss? Had I hurt his feelings? Did he think I didn't like him enough to kiss him?

I sighed, not sure what to do. I didn't know him well enough to guess his thought process, and I didn't think guessing was the right way to go anyway. I decided I would find some time to talk to him about it and explain why I'd pushed him away.

Natalie was still asleep, so I took a quick shower and got dressed. After she woke, I fed her, then took her out on the balcony. We'd arrived in Skagway, Alaska and I wanted to get a look. A wooden train filled with passengers sat on tracks on the other side of the pier. I looked down at the people walking along the pier between the ship and the train, and was excited to go down there and explore after the wedding.

My gaze was drawn to the mountain on the other side of the train. Trees grew between large boulders, and I noticed that most of the boulders had writing on them. It almost seemed like graffiti, except they were more like rock paintings. The sky was overcast and the air chilly and I snuggled Natalie closer, then took her inside.

I put her in her stroller and headed to the Lido deck for a light breakfast at the buffet. The wedding was scheduled for ten o'clock, which gave me plenty of time to eat and then come back to my room and get ready. As I entered the Lido deck area, I scanned the crowd to see if anyone in our party was there, but I didn't see anyone I recognized.

After I gathered my food, I held the tray with one hand and pushed the stroller with the other, then made my way to an empty table. Natalie wanted out of the stroller, so I held her on my lap while I ate, and kept my eye out for someone I knew. No one appeared, and I assumed everyone was getting ready for the wedding.

Thoughts of Cameron filled my mind as I ate, and I tried to frame my explanation for what had happened the night before. I didn't look forward to telling him that his kiss had sent powerful waves of desire through me, and I'd panicked. Why *had* I panicked, anyway? I took a bite of pastry as I examined my feelings. What was I afraid of? I could think of a couple of things—fear of getting into a relationship that would end up like the one with Trevor, or like the one with Marcus. Neither had brought me happiness. Maybe that was it. I was afraid of getting hurt.

More confident about my reasons, I finished eating and took Natalie back to our room. I changed into the dress I'd bought for the wedding, did my hair, and put on my make-up, then dressed Natalie in a cute outfit I'd gotten for her—a frilly dress, complete with a bow for her hair. At a quarter to ten, I headed to the chapel where the wedding would be held.

As I walked in, a mix of feelings rushed through me—good memories of my own wedding, sadness that my marriage had failed so quickly, and excitement for Ty and Alyssa. Not surprisingly, I didn't see Alyssa, but I saw Ty chatting with his family, and standing nearby was Cameron. My heart fluttered as I observed him in his suit. He looked so handsome and confident. The memory of his kiss went through my mind and fresh desire flooded my body, making my face flush.

He hadn't seen me come in, giving me time to observe him. He was talking to Ty's mother, his face relaxed and smiling. After a moment, Katherine's gaze went to me and she smiled. Cameron turned to see who she was looking at, and when he saw me, his relaxed manner changed to something I couldn't read. Ty tapped him on the shoulder and he turned away from me, leaving me feeling oddly bereft.

I moved to one of the benches and held Natalie on my lap, and a short time later the wedding began. First, Alyssa's older brother escorted Barbara to her seat, then Cameron escorted Katherine to hers. As he passed me, my eyes followed him, appreciating his clean good looks. Once Katherine was seated, he walked to the front and took his place next to Ty. Next, a teenage boy I hadn't talked to, escorted Haley to the front, where she stood waiting for Alyssa.

Then the wedding march began and we all stood and turned to see Alyssa on her father's arm. She looked stunning in her wedding gown and I felt tears spring into my eyes, my happiness for her overwhelming me. Her father escorted her down the aisle and she glanced at me and smiled as she passed. I hugged Natalie closer, so grateful I had decided to come on the cruise, and watched as Alyssa's father placed Alyssa's hand in Ty's.

A moment later, the officiator began speaking. I half-listened, my mind going to the memories of my wedding to Trevor, and when I was able to push that out of my mind, I gazed at Cameron, who stood next to Ty, and thought about new beginnings, and how thankful I was that I could have a second chance.

I focused on Ty and Alyssa exchanging their vows, then exchanging rings, and finally being pronounced husband and wife. I smiled through a veil of tears as Ty pulled Alyssa into his arms and kissed her with obvious passion. Everyone laughed, then clapped, then Ty and Alyssa walked back down the aisle as husband and wife.

All of those attending followed them to a nearby room where we congratulated them and had a light meal.

"You look gorgeous, Alyssa," I said, giving her a hug. "And so happy."

"Thank you." She paused, beaming. "I am happy."

"Congratulations, Ty," I said, hugging him as well.

"Thanks, Lily."

I chatted with them for a few minutes, then brought Natalie with me to the food table and picked up a glass of ice water. Trying not to be obvious, I looked around the room to see what Cameron was doing and saw him talking to his friends. He glanced my way and our eyes met, but I looked away, my feelings in such turmoil after vividly recalling my own wedding less than two years before.

I carried Natalie to a chair, and sat, observing the happy conversations in the room. A short time later Ty and Alyssa cut their cake and we all had a slice. Then Ty called for everyone's attention.

"I just wanted to thank all of you for being here," he said. "I know it was a sacrifice for a lot of you, and I want you to know how much it means to both Alyssa and me that you were able to come." He paused. "Today is our first day in port and I hope you all have a great time exploring Alaska. It's true that this is our honeymoon." He gazed at Alyssa, then looked back at the group. "But we hope to spend time with all of you over the next few days too." He held up the glass in his hand. "To family and good friends."

Half an hour later I noticed people starting to leave and decided it was a good time for me to take Natalie and explore Skagway. The ship wasn't leaving the port until nine o'clock that evening, so I had plenty of time. As I pushed Natalie's stroller toward the door, I felt a little sorry for myself. Everyone else had others they had made plans with, and excursions they'd signed up for, whereas I hadn't planned anything and was just going to explore the town.

Loneliness washed over me as I walked toward the exit. I glanced back at Ty and Alyssa, and smiled at their happiness, then saw Cameron watching me, that same unreadable expression on his face. My lips turned up in a small smile as our eyes met, and he smiled back, but made no move to come talk to me. I turned away, my brows creased, and left the room. We'd talked about going whale watching together, but that wasn't until we got to Juneau, which would happen the next day. I hoped I would have a chance to talk to him in private before then.

In the meantime, I had to go on with my life. I'd spent a lot of money to go on this cruise, and I'd never planned on having Cameron keep me company—I hadn't known he existed until a few days ago. So I would put the needs of Natalie and myself first, and enjoy the beauty of Alaska. Before getting off the ship, I took Natalie to our room and we both changed into more comfortable clothes, then I made sure I had everything I'd need to take care of her for the day, hooked the diaper bag over the stroller, and headed to the place where we would disembark.

A short time later we were walking along the pier. When I reached the end of it, I took a picture of the ship from that angle, marveling at the immensity of it. A cruise ship from another cruise line was also docked at the pier, and I watched the people coming and going. Natalie and I strolled into town, which wasn't very big, and went inside several stores.

After a while, Natalie started getting fussy and I knew it was time for a nap. She didn't seem to want to fall asleep in the stroller, so I would have to take her back to our room. As we walked to the ship, I noticed the train tracks and decided I would see about going on the train later that afternoon.

We went up the gangway and showed our cards to the security people, passed through the metal detector, then took the elevator to our room. I got her settled and then lay on my bed to read my book. When I heard a knock at my door, I went to answer it, hoping against hope that it was Cameron. When I saw him standing on the threshold, I smiled, and invited him in. Without speaking, we walked past Natalie's crib and went straight out to the balcony.

Looking out over the railing, neither one of us spoke. After a moment the silence was too much for me, and I went first. "The wedding was really nice."

Cameron turned to face me. "Yeah. Alyssa looked beautiful in her wedding dress."

I nodded.

His face softened. "You looked beautiful too."

I smiled. "Thanks." I paused. "What brings you to my room?"

"I figured this was probably Natalie's nap time and I wanted to talk to you."

Glad that he'd made the first move, I asked, "So what's going on? You hardly acknowledged me this morning."

His eyebrows pulled together. "To be honest, I wasn't sure if you wanted me to."

I tilted my head to one side. "Why would you think that?"

He chewed the inside of his mouth and looked toward the mountains, then looked back at me. "I just felt like you were giving me mixed signals last night."

Nodding, I tried to think of the words I'd planned to use to explain myself. "I'm sorry." I sighed. "When you kissed me . . ." I felt my face redden as my explanation came to mind. "Well, I just felt such a powerful . . . attraction . . . to you. And it scared me."

He grinned, his dimple deepening and his blue eyes sparkling. "Oh."

Despite my embarrassment, I smiled back.

"I don't understand what you're scared of," he said.

"Just getting hurt, I guess."

He nodded. "I suppose I can understand that. After all you've been through."

"Exactly. I guess I'm worried about investing myself emotionally into you and then you turning out like . . . others have. Others who have disappointed me."

He gazed at me a moment. "I don't know what you mean, exactly, and to be honest, I can't promise anything."

My embarrassment returned, but for a different reason. "I know. We just barely met and I'm not asking you to commit to anything, but you have to understand that I'm a little gun-shy to put . . . well, to put my heart out there." He looked uncomfortable, so I hurriedly went on. "I'm not saying I expect you to commit to any kind of relationship, but you just need to understand that I have to protect myself. Protect my heart." I stared at him a moment. "I've had very few relationships, and it seems thc ones I've had have always ended up making me unhappy. So I'm just wary." *But I'm also lonely*, I thought.

He reached out and took my hand and rubbed his thumb against my palm, sending a shiver through me. "Tell you what," he said. "Let's just take it slow. Just get to know each other." He laughed. "I mean, once this cruise is over, we may be glad to be rid of each other. But for now, we can have fun together."

I hoped he wouldn't want to be rid of me—I was really starting to like him—but I nodded. "Okay."

"What do you have planned for the rest of our time in Skagway?"

"Earlier Natalie and I walked around town, and I thought after her nap it would be fun to do one of those train trips."

"Would you mind if I came along?"

I smiled, my earlier feeling of self-pity at being alone vanishing. "I'd love to have you along."

"Great."

We talked out on the balcony until Natalie woke up, then after I gave her some baby food, the three of us went to the Lido deck and had lunch from the buffet.

"Ready to go on a train ride?" I asked Natalie as Cameron and I finished eating. I looked at him. "I hope she does okay on it. I think it's three hours long."

A look of worry crossed his face. "Do you think that's too long for her?"

Touched by his concern, I smiled. "I think she'll be okay. If anything she'll probably fall asleep by the end of it."

We left the ship, bought our tickets, and boarded the train. The views as the train took us up the mountain were spectacular, but more than that, I relished Cameron's closeness as he pressed against me in the seat. I sat next to the window, and he leaned close to me to look out.

"Look at the snow," he said, his arm around the back of my seat as he leaned toward the window.

I turned slightly, so that our faces were only inches apart, and smiled. He gazed at me a moment and I felt my heart pound as I anticipated a kiss, but he just smiled back, leaving me wanting more. Natalie was content to sit on my lap for much of the trip, and only got fussy when she got hungry, at which time I gave her formula. Eventually she fell asleep and I held her against my shoulder.

"Do you need anything?" Cameron asked. "Maybe some water?"

"Sure."

He went to the front and brought back two bottles of water, handing one to me.

When we got back to the pier, Cameron carried the diaper bag for me, which I thought was very thoughtful and sweet.

"Do you want to take her back to your room?" he asked.

"Yeah, that's probably a good idea."

We climbed the gangway back onto the ship and a few minutes later we were back in my room and Natalie was in her crib.

"I'm going to take off for a while," Cameron said.

I nodded. "I had fun with you on the train."

He smiled. "Me, too." I walked him to the door and he stopped with his hand on the door knob. "I'll try to get to the dining room on time tonight, but if you get there before me, will you save me a seat?"

"Sure."

He gazed at me a moment and I wondered if he was contemplating kissing me, but finally he smiled, opened the door, and left.

After he left, I thought about his new reluctance to kiss me and wondered if it was because of our conversation earlier. Maybe he wanted to let me make the choice, let me set the pace. I thought about that and wondered if I would have the courage to move our relationship in that direction. Or would I be like Marcus and keep Cameron at arm's length—in the friend zone.

I gasped as the realization hit me that maybe that was what was going on with Marcus. Maybe he was afraid just like I was. Maybe that was why he was keeping me in the friend zone—to keep *himself* from getting hurt. But if that was true, why would he be dating Chelsea?

I sighed, confused about what was true and what was all in my imagination.

Chapter Sixteen

That night at dinner, Cameron got to the dining room before me and saved a seat for me, which made me happy. He even had the staff put Natalie's high chair next to my seat. "Thanks, Cameron. That was very thoughtful," I said as I slid into my seat.

He smiled. "You're welcome." He held up the menu. "Have you ever tried escargot?"

I shook my head, grimacing slightly.

"Well, tonight's your chance."

"I think I'll stick with the salad."

"Well, I'm getting the escargot." He grinned. "And I'll even let you try it."

I bit my lip. "Okay. Maybe I will." When the appetizers were set on the table, Cameron looked at his escargot, then looked at me with raised eyebrows.

Laughing, I said, "It actually looks good, the way they serve it."

He popped one in his mouth.

"How is it?" I asked, my mouth stretched out in a half smile/half frown.

He nodded. "Delicious." He motioned toward his plate. "Have one."

Tentatively, I poked my fork into one, and brought it to my lips. I looked at Cameron, who watched me expectantly, then I put it in my mouth.

"Well?" he said.

"I like it."

He smiled in approval. "Have another."

I shook my head. "I don't want to eat all of your food."

He laughed. "Oh, believe me, I'll get plenty of food."

"Yeah, there's no shortage of food on this cruise." I took another and put it in my mouth.

"Not bad for a snail, huh?"

I stopped chewing for a second, then swallowed. "Yeah, until you reminded me that I was eating a snail."

He laughed, and ate the remaining three pieces. "Do you think we can get Haley to babysit again tonight?"

"I don't know," I said. "She babysat the last two nights, and Barbara is going to babysit tomorrow so I can go whale watching." I paused. "Did you still want to do that?"

"Yeah. After seeing those whales yesterday, I'm stoked to see some close up."

I smiled. "Good."

"But about tonight?" he asked.

"Yeah. I think I'd better stay in tonight. I feel guilty asking Haley again. I want her to have fun on the cruise too."

"Okay. That's cool."

I didn't invite him to my room. It wouldn't be fun to sit on the balcony at night—too cold—and I didn't want to wake Natalie by talking to him in the room. After dinner I talked to Alyssa's mom, Barbara, to make sure she was still planning on babysitting the next day.

"Yes, but I wanted to do some shopping in town," she said. "Would it be okay if I took her out in the stroller?"

I hesitated, not loving the idea, but I couldn't expect her to stay holed up in her room all day. I looked at Barbara and nodded. She was a good mom, and she had other grandchildren. Surely she could manage my baby for a few hours. "What time did you want to go shopping tomorrow morning?"

"Oh, about nine, I'd say."

"Okay. Why don't I come to your room then, and we can get off the ship together? I still need to buy my ticket."

She smiled. "That works for me."

I told Cameron that I wanted to get going by nine o'clock the next morning, and he agreed to meet me at Barbara's room at that time. Happy to have the arrangements for the next day mapped out, I told everyone good-night, and took Natalie back to our room.

At nine o'clock the next morning I knocked on Barbara and Paul's door. Barbara let me in.

"Thank you for babysitting today," I said. "I'm really excited about this excursion."

She looked at Natalie, who sat in the stroller watching us, then looked back at me. "I'm happy to do it. I had a busy day yesterday, and today I'm ready to take it easy."

I laughed. "I don't know how easy it will be to take care of Natalie."

"Oh, I'm sure she'll be fine. From what I've seen, she's a calm baby."

"Yes, she is. I'm really lucky."

A few minutes later Cameron arrived and we all left the ship together. I pushed the stroller and Cameron walked next to me, with Barbara and Paul on my other side. Cameron and I stopped at the booths a little ways past the pier to see when the next whale watching tour departed. Our timing was good as they were going to leave in fifteen minutes. We purchased our tickets, then I turned Natalie over to Barbara.

"I just fed her, so she should be fine for a few hours. There's formula in the diaper bag, and anything else she might need." I'd given her my cell number earlier, so she could call if she needed to. I leaned down to the stroller and kissed Natalie's soft cheek. "See you in a while, sweetheart."

Natalie smiled her sweet baby smile, and I hesitated. I'd never let someone else take care of her like this, and I couldn't help but worry. Barbara must have sensed my hesitation, because she touched my shoulder. I stood and faced her.

With a look of warmth, Barbara said, "I promise to take care of her like she was my own, Lily."

I smiled, feeling better. "I know you will. I'm sorry for making you think otherwise."

She shook her head. "Alyssa told me what you've been through, so I understand." She smiled. "Now go have a fun day. We'll be fine."

My worries put to rest, I turned to Cameron. "Ready?" He nodded and held out his hand, which I took. With one more glance at Natalie, I walked with Cameron toward the meeting place, excited for our morning.

We stood with a few others, waiting for the van that would take us to the Auke Harbor. A few minutes later the van arrived and drove us to the harbor, where we got on a boat. There were ten of us in the group, which seemed to be about the right number for the size of the boat. Fisher, the naturalist who was coming on the trip, welcomed us aboard.

"Our driver," Fisher said, "is going to take us really fast out to the area where we expect to see humpback whales. Once we get there, you can go out onto the top of the boat to get a better look. You'll notice binoculars by each seat. Feel free to use those."

Oversized windows wrapped around the boat, giving us a panoramic view of the water. The boat took off, and we practically flew across the water. After a short time we arrived in an area where three other boats were waiting.

"Watch for the tell-tale spout," Fisher said.

A moment later someone called out that they saw a spout. Cameron and I hurried to the top of the boat where we had a clear view of several humpback whales coming to the surface.

"I can see its tail," I exclaimed, excitement evident in my voice.

"Oh, yeah," Cameron said.

He stood right next to me, and my excitement over our adventure, mixed with my delight in having Cameron there with me to enjoy it, made me giddy. I hadn't had this much fun in a very long time. We watched the pod of whales until they disappeared from view. The boat moved slowly forward.

"We don't know where they'll surface next," Fisher said. "Watch closely as sometimes a whale will breach, which means jump out of the water. It doesn't happen often, so if you see it, you're very lucky."

A minute later I saw a spout and called it out. Several plumes of mist blew up in the air, then the whales surfaced. Everyone oohed and aahed in excitement, including Cameron and me. After a moment the whales disappeared from view. As we waited for them to surface again, Cameron put his arm around my waist and pulled me close. He leaned toward me and whispered, "I'm glad we cleared the air yesterday."

I looked up at him and smiled. "Me, too." I gazed at him a moment, hoping he'd kiss me, but he didn't, and I wondered if I should be the one to initiate our next kiss. Maybe that's what he was waiting for. I would have to find the right time—I didn't feel comfortable kissing him in front of everyone. But I was determined to let him know that I was okay with kissing.

Our boat driver moved us to another position and we saw the whales a few more times. Then, as time was getting short, he took us to a place where sea lions were lounging on a buoy. The boat slowly circled the buoy, allowing us to get a close-up look at the sea lions. As we headed back to the harbor, I wished we could stay longer and see more whales. Fisher pointed out a glacier and we stopped and took pictures, then continued back to the harbor.

At the harbor, we climbed in the van and drove back to our starting place. As we drove, Cameron had his arm around my shoulder and I leaned my head against him. "That was so much fun," I said.

"Yeah." He looked at me. "I really enjoyed spending the morning with you."

I pulled back slightly so that I was looking in his face, which was only inches from mine. "It wouldn't have been the same without you," I said, smiling.

The van stopped and he looked out the window. "Looks like we're back."

My thoughts immediately went to Natalie and how she was doing. "I wonder if Barbara's back on the ship," I said as Cameron and I climbed out of the van.

"You can call her cell phone."

"Good idea." I pulled my phone out of my purse and punched in her number. A moment later she answered. I didn't hear Natalie crying in the background, so that was good. "Hi, Barbara. This is Lily."

"Hi there, hon."

I smiled at the friendly tone in her voice. "We just got back to the pier. How did it go?"

"Your baby is an angel."

I smiled. "That, I know."

Barbara laughed. "We finished our shopping and she's sleeping on my bed as we speak."

"Well, I'll come and get her and then you'll have a couple of hours to get off the ship before we set sail."

"Oh no. My shopping wore me out. You and Cameron enjoy your afternoon. The ship sails at three, so I'll see you when you get back on."

Happy to have a couple more hours to spend with Cameron, I

smiled. "Are you sure?"

"Yes."

"Okay. I'll see you in a while." I disconnected the call and turned to Cameron. "Natalie's asleep, and Barbara said I didn't need to come get her yet." Then I hesitated. Maybe Cameron had other things he wanted to do before we set sail. Worried now that I was imposing on him, I left my question unasked.

"Great. What would you like to do?" he asked.

I looked at the tram station nearby. "The tram might be fun." I bit my lip. "Do you want to go too?"

He laughed. "What? Are you planning on going by yourself?"

My face flushed. "I didn't want to assume you were going with me. Maybe you want to spend some time with your friends."

He took my hand and stroked the back of it with his thumb, sending a shiver of pleasure through me. "Like I told you yesterday, Lily, I think we should have fun this week, because once we get back to real life, we might decide to never see each other again."

Would I decide to never see him again? I gazed at him a moment, then thought about Marcus, but that just confused me. Before coming on this cruise I'd been sure I was falling in love with Marcus, but he'd rebuffed me, and now, after getting to know Cameron, I wasn't sure what I wanted. "You're right," I said, smiling. I pushed Marcus to the back of my mind. He wasn't on this cruise, and even if he was, he'd probably have his new girlfriend by his side, not me.

We bought the tickets for the tram, then boarded. As the tram ascended, we gazed out the window.

"Wow, this view is spectacular," I said. "And seeing the ship from this bird's eye view is really amazing."

"Yeah," Cameron said. "And look out at the water, the way the ship came in."

Once we reached the top, we looked out the windows in the tram station, then walked down the nature trail. The day was sunny and beautiful, though chilly. Nevertheless, I felt wonderful—relaxed and happy and loving life. As Cameron and I walked hand in hand down the nature trail, I stopped under a large tree, deciding this would be my chance to show him that I *liked* kissing. No one else was near, and Cameron looked at me with a question on his face.

Chapter Seventeen

I smiled, suddenly feeling shy.

"Everything okay?" he asked.

I gazed at him. "Yes." I hesitated. "When we talked yesterday, there was one thing that I think I didn't make clear."

His eyebrows rose. "Oh?"

I bit my lip. "I told you how I was afraid of getting hurt."

He nodded. "That was why you pulled away when I was kissing you the other night."

I smiled, glad we were on the same page. "Right."

"And?"

"And, well, I just want you to know that I don't have anything against kissing."

He grinned. "That *is* good to know."

I stood there, waiting for him to make a move, but he just stared at me, a tiny smile on his face. Finally I said, "Well?"

He laughed. "Well, what?"

Now I was feeling impatient. "Aren't you going to kiss me?"

He shook his head. "I don't think that's a good idea."

Shocked, I just stared, my mouth hanging open a little. "Why not?" I finally asked.

"I thought we'd agreed that we were going to take things slow. You know, get to know each other. As friends."

"As friends," I echoed, my voice soft, then I turned away. *He's just another Marcus.* He touched my shoulder and I turned to face him.

He looked confused. "I thought that's what you wanted, Lily."

What *do* I want? Angry at myself for not being sure, I frowned. I thought I wanted a long-term relationship, but did I want that with Cameron? Or was he just a stand-in for Marcus? The least I could do was be honest with him. "Truthfully, I don't know what I want."

He nodded, his expression firm. "Well, until you do, we should keep things platonic." He smirked. "No point in confusing things with kissing and all that."

Though his statement made sense on a logical level, emotionally I was eager for the feelings that kissing him evoked in me. Yes, I'd gotten scared the other night by the powerful feeling of attraction I'd had toward him, but did that mean I didn't want to kiss him at all? *You're over-thinking this*, I told myself.

"Don't you agree?" he asked.

I opened my mouth to speak, but no words came to mind. Finally I shrugged. He put both hands on my shoulders, his face only inches away—close enough to kiss. My gaze flicked between his mouth and his eyes.

"Lily," he said, drawing my attention to his eyes. "You don't have to decide right now."

I nodded, a sense of relief replacing my confusion. Then a new question came to mind. "What do *you* want?" I asked.

He let go of my shoulders and looked thoughtful. "You're a special woman, and I don't want you to rush into anything that you'll later regret." He laughed. "I barely know you, but already I know I don't want to be one of the people that end up disappointing you."

"But what do you *want*?"

He stared just past me, then his gaze met mine. "Do you really want to know?"

I nodded, suddenly uncertain.

He gazed at me, and his expression became fierce. "I want to hold you and kiss you until all your doubts flee."

I gasped as a thrill of desire raced through me.

He laughed and ran his hand through his hair, then spoke quietly, almost like he was talking to himself. "I don't know what I'm saying. I just met you."

I stared at him in silence, my eyes wide.

He met my gaze and smiled. "Pretend I didn't say that."

My lips curved into a smile. "Which part?"

His face reddened. "All of it."

"I'm not sure I can forget that." My voice softened. "It was kind of poetic."

He grinned. "No one's ever accused me of being a poet before."

A group of people passed us, bringing me back to reality. "What time is it?"

He looked at his watch. "Two o'clock."

"We have to be back on the ship by two thirty."

He nodded. "Okay."

We walked back to the tram station and boarded the next tram. We were silent as we rode to the bottom. I didn't know what he was thinking, but my mind was in a whirl. Cameron had made it clear that he wanted more than mere friendship from me. The thought made me mentally hug myself. Even as he wanted me to take my time to decide what *I* wanted, there was no doubt what *he* wanted, even if he'd told me to forget what he'd said.

When we got off of the tram, he held out his hand, a questioning look on his face. I smiled and intertwined my fingers with his, then we walked toward the line of people waiting to get back on the ship.

"It's been quite a day," he said, smiling at me.

"Yes. Much better than I'd hoped."

"Which part was your favorite?"

"The whale watching. Definitely the whale watching." I paused. "What about you?"

His eyes sparkled and his dimple deepened. "I kind of liked that nature walk."

I felt my face blush. Even though we hadn't kissed, we'd opened our hearts to each other. "Yeah, that was fun too."

He let go of my hand and put his arm around me, pulling me against his side. I relished the warmth of his body against mine, and smiled as I remembered what he said he wanted to do.

Once we were back on the ship, we walked to the elevator and Cameron pressed the up button. I didn't want him to feel obligated to spend time with me, plus I hadn't seen Natalie all day, so I wanted to spend time with her. "I'm going to get Natalie and take her back to my room." The elevator arrived and we stepped on. I pressed the button for Barbara's floor. "What do you have planned?" I asked him.

"Uh, I guess I'll see what everyone's up to." He smiled. "Do you want to get together later?"

"Sure." The elevator moved upward.

"I'm not sure where I'll be," he said.

"I'll stroll Natalie around, so I'll probably run into you. If not, I'll see you at dinner."

He nodded. "Sounds good."

A moment later I got off on Barbara's floor and Cameron continued on to his. When I got to Barbara's room, Natalie and Barbara were playing with some of the toys I'd sent in the diaper bag. When Natalie saw me, she smiled, which made me feel good. "Thank you so much for watching her," I said as I picked her up.

"It was fun," Barbara said. "But I admit, I might want to take a nap after you leave." She paused. "How was your day?"

I beamed. "It was wonderful."

"I'm so glad. Did you see very many whales?"

"Yes, and it was really cool to see them."

She smiled. "I knew you'd enjoy it."

"We went on the tram."

"Oh, the view up there is beautiful."

"Yeah, it was really fun. We went on the nature walk too." I smiled, remembering the conversation I'd had with Cameron among the trees.

Back in my room, I made sure Natalie was fed and changed, then I put her in the stroller and we walked around the ship, stopping to join a trivia game in one of the lounges. I didn't see Cameron until dinner, but we sat next to each other.

"What do you have planned for tomorrow, in Ketchikan?" he asked.

"Well, we only have a few hours to be there, so I was just going to do some shopping. What about you?"

"I hear there's a rodeo there, so I was going to check it out with some of the others."

"That sounds like fun."

"Do you want to come?"

I laughed. "No. I don't think Natalie would enjoy it, but thanks."

"What about going dancing? Would you like to go tonight?"

"As much fun as that would be, why don't we put it off until tomorrow night? I don't want to keep imposing on people to babysit."

He nodded. "I understand."

The next morning Natalie and I strolled around Ketchikan, going into a number of stores. As I browsed the shelves of items, I decided to buy a little totem pole for Marcus. Even if we were just friends, I wanted to get him something so that he would know I had thought about him on the trip.

When I was done shopping, I got back onto the ship for the last time. The next day we'd stop in Victoria, British Columbia, but we wouldn't arrive until seven thirty that evening, so I didn't plan on disembarking. And then we'd arrive back in Seattle the day after that.

As I settled Natalie in for a nap, I thought over the last few days. It had been wonderful to see Ty and Alyssa get married, and now that I knew Cameron, it was hard to imagine never having met him. I smiled as I thought about going dancing with him that night—I'd already arranged to have Haley babysit—and wondered how it would go. I still didn't know what I wanted with Cameron—did I see myself getting into a long-term relationship with him, or never seeing him again once we got back to real life? Shrugging off my ambivalence, I decided I would just enjoy myself that night and not worry about the future.

That night's dinner was the second elegant night, and I wore a silky black dress with lacy sleeves. When I walked into the dining room, I couldn't help but notice Cameron's appreciative gaze. He helped me put Natalie in her high chair, then he held out my chair for me. He looked handsome in his suit, and his dimple deepened as he smiled at me.

"You look lovely," he said.

"Thank you." I scanned my menu, then turned to Cameron. "I see frog legs are on the menu tonight. Are you going to try them?"

He laughed. "I don't think I'm quite that adventurous."

"That's too bad, because I was going to ask for a bite."

His eyebrows went up. "Is that right? Well, you can always order it."

I laughed. "No way."

"So you're just trying to trick *me* into ordering it," he said.

"That's right."

"Well, your tricks won't work."

I shrugged. "It was worth a try."

He laughed.

When it was time for our date, he brought Haley to my room to babysit, then the two of us left, still wearing our elegant dining clothes.

"You really look fantastic," he murmured in my ear as he leaned toward me.

His warm breath sent a thrill of pleasure through me and I was eager to dance within his embrace—especially since that was the only time he seemed willing to get that close to me. We went straight to the dance club and onto the dance floor. The music was loud, but we had a great time.

A slow song came on and when Cameron pulled me close, I slid my arms around his neck and relished the feel of his strong body so close to mine.

"I can't believe tomorrow night's the last night," he said.

"Oh, don't remind me," I said. "I've had so much fun, it's going to be hard to leave."

He pulled back slightly and gazed at me. "The question is, is this it for us?"

I gazed back, studying his face, then whispered, "It doesn't have to be."

He smiled, then pulled me close again.

As we swayed to the music, I considered what would happen if I kept seeing him once we left the ship. Would we become serious, or would he eventually break my heart? What about Natalie? What if she got used to having him around and then he lost interest in me? The thought scared me. I didn't want to do anything that would upset my child. But Natalie and I were a package deal—if he was going to spend time with me, he would need to spend time with her. I didn't want to get involved with someone who wasn't interested in helping me raise her.

Marcus's face filled my mind's eye. He'd been there when Natalie was born, and he'd been there for me ever since. It's true that he'd seemed to put up a barrier recently, but as far as I could tell, that was because I'd scared him off by saying how much I liked him.

When I pictured Marcus dancing close with the woman his mother told me he was dating, the woman I'd never met, jealously pierced me. I squeezed my eyes closed against Cameron's shoulder, reminding myself that Marcus had been clear when he'd told me we were only friends. I had to get over any feelings of jealousy I had, and instead, be happy for him if he found someone to love.

As the thought came to mind, my forehead creased. I didn't want to think about him being happy with someone else. *But he doesn't want you*, I reminded myself. *Not like that*. Why am I even thinking about him now? I thought as I moved around the dance floor in Cameron's arms. Then I realized that it was because the cruise had been a way to step away from my everyday life—a way to not think about Marcus. But now that the cruise was almost over, reality was settling back into my mind.

"Are you okay?" Cameron asked.

The song had ended and I hadn't noticed. "Oh." I smiled at him, feeling guilty that I'd been thinking about another man while dancing with him. "Yeah. Just preoccupied, I guess."

His lips turned up into a sexy smile. "Preoccupied with what?"

I gazed into his blue eyes, and I pushed thoughts of Marcus away, instead focusing on the man in front of me. The man I'd spent many hours with over the previous few days. The man who'd said in no uncertain terms that he wanted to hold me and kiss me until all doubts about him fled. There was no question that he wanted to be more than friends. Perhaps my future did lie with Cameron. At least with him there was a chance for a future together, whereas with Marcus, that road was barred and closed. "Just thinking about how much fun I've had this week." I smiled. "Mostly because of you."

A fast song started, but he took my hand and led me to the bar, where he got both of us ice-filled sodas. He held my hand and brought me to a table where we sat close to each other so that we could talk over the loud music.

"I had a really great time too," he said. "And that was because of *you.*"

We sipped our drinks and watched the other dancers. "Are you going on any excursions tomorrow in Victoria?" I asked.

"I think a few of us are going to the Butchart Gardens. What about you?"

"No. We get in to the port so late, it would be past Natalie's bedtime by the time I got off the ship. We're just going to stay on board."

"That makes sense," he said, then he finished off his drink. "Ready for more dancing?"

I nodded, and he pulled me out to the dance floor. Knowing it was our last night together on the ship, we stayed out later than we had before. As we danced, I pushed thoughts of Marcus further and further out of my mind, and stayed focused on Cameron. Finally it was time to call it a night, and we headed back to my room to say good-night.

Chapter Eighteen

We stopped outside my door and I gazed at Cameron, waiting to see what he would do.

"Since I'll be off the ship tomorrow night, I guess this is the last time I'll say good-night to you on the ship," he said.

I nodded. "Guess so."

His lips curved into a smile. "Tonight when I asked you if this would be it for us, you said it didn't have to be." He paused. "Did you mean that?"

My smile matched his, and as I gazed into his eyes, my answer was certain. "Yes." He reached out his hand and stroked my cheek with the back of his fingers, sending a shiver of heat through me. *He's going to kiss me.*

His face became serious for a moment, then his smile returned as his hand moved to my neck. It didn't take any urging from him for me to move closer, and his other arm slipped around my waist. Our eyes locked on one another and I lifted my arms and slid them around his neck. His face was only inches from mine, and sweet anticipation flooded me.

Then I heard the door to my room open.

"Oh," Haley said as she stood on the threshold with her hand on the knob.

I jumped back from Cameron, then turned toward Haley. "Is everything okay?"

"I just thought I heard a noise out here." She smiled, obviously embarrassed. "I guess it was you guys. Sorry."

I felt myself blush. She stood there, clearly not knowing what to do. Feeling sorry for her—and a little sorry for myself for having my almost-kiss interrupted—I smiled. "That's okay." I stepped toward the door, and she held it open. I walked in the room and Cameron followed.

"I can take myself back to my room," she offered.

"No," I said, my voice soft so as not to wake Natalie. "I don't think that's a good idea. It's pretty late."

Cameron took the hint. "I'll walk you back, Haley." He looked at me. "I guess I'll see you tomorrow?"

I nodded. "Sure." I gave Haley some money. "Thanks again, Haley. I really appreciate you babysitting so much."

She took the money. "No problem. It was fun for me."

They were gone a moment later, and I was left feeling deprived. Cameron had been about to kiss me after refusing to for two days, and I'd been ready for it. But now the chance had passed. I shook my head, consoling myself with the thought that surely another opportunity would present itself before we docked back in Seattle.

The next morning Natalie and I went to the Lido deck and I got in line at the buffet. A few minutes later I took my tray to a table and held

Natalie on my lap while I ate. Though cruises really weren't meant for babies, she couldn't have been any better, and I had no regrets about coming.

"Mind if I join you?" Cameron asked as he stood next to my table.

My face lit up as I looked at him. "Not at all."

He set his tray on the table across from me, then sat down. He looked at me a moment, then started laughing.

"What?" I said, wiping my face with a napkin. "Did I get food on my face?"

He shook his head. "No, I'm just thinking about how you jumped back so fast last night when Haley opened the door."

I smiled, and I could feel the blood rushing to my face. "She surprised me, that's all."

His laughter stopped as he tilted his head to one side. "It was like you were embarrassed for her to know what we were doing."

Now my face felt even hotter. "Maybe I was."

His expression showed mock-offense. "Are you embarrassed for people to know we might like each other?"

I smirked. "I think people have pretty much figured it out. I mean, we've been sitting next to each other at dinner practically every night, and we've spent a lot of time together."

"True." He paused. "Okay. I guess I can forgive you."

My mouth fell open. "Forgive *me*? For what?"

"For not kissing me." He took a bite of his omelet.

I decided to keep playing his game. "What about you?"

He swallowed. "What about me?"

"You gave up pretty easily."

He shook his head. "I was just reading your body language."

"My body language? What was it saying?"

"The way you jumped away from me when Haley opened the door," he grinned, and shook his head. "You made it pretty clear that you didn't want to be close to me when she was watching."

"Well, I guess you'll never know." I forked a piece of pastry and put it in my mouth, watching his face.

"Never know, huh?"

I nodded.

He raised his eyebrows. "We do still have today."

"Oh, really? And what exactly are you going to be doing today?"

"I'm not sure yet. There's not a lot that I want to do today. Just hang out, I guess."

"Yeah. I looked at the schedule of stuff to do and things seem to be winding down."

"We can always watch for whales."

"That would be fun."

Once we finished eating, we went up on deck and looked out over the ocean. The day was beautiful—sunny and clear—and we enjoyed the warmth of the sunshine. After a while, I could tell Natalie was ready for her morning nap. "I'm going to put Natalie down for a nap. Do you want to come to my room? We could sit on the balcony."

"Sure. I'll give you a little time to get her settled, then I'll come."

I took Natalie back to our room and put her down for a nap, and after she fell asleep, I pulled out a novel to read until Cameron came. An hour later he still hadn't come, and a feeling of disappointment washed over me. Had he forgotten about me? I shook my head, knowing that it was silly to think I'd be the only thing on his mind. Putting aside my self-pity, I focused on the book I was reading.

When Natalie woke up, I couldn't help but feel neglected—Cameron had made it clear that he wanted to spend time with me. I put her in the stroller and went up to the Lido deck to have a soft serve ice cream. Natalie and I sat next to the window to watch the passing sea as I licked my cone. The next day at that time, we'd be flying home, and as I thought about home, I was suddenly eager to get back to my little house. Greta would be so happy to see us, I thought, smiling.

After I ate my snack, Natalie and I strolled around the ship, stopping to join in a trivia game, then moving on. Without Cameron by my side, loneliness was starting to creep back into my life. I'd had so much fun with him this past week, and I really didn't think I would have had as much fun on the cruise without him.

By the time I put Natalie down for her afternoon nap, I still hadn't seen or heard from Cameron, and was starting to think it was a mistake to tell him that we could still see each other after the cruise. Partway through her nap there was a knock at my door. Wondering if it could be Cameron, and what his excuse would be, I went to the door and opened it.

"Hey, Lily."

"Hey." I didn't invite him in.

"I'm really sorry about not coming by earlier."

"Okay." I couldn't help it, I was annoyed. I'd been looking forward to spending time with him and he'd let me down.

"After you left, I ran into Ty and found out that his dad had slipped and fallen and was getting medical attention. He was on his way to see how he was doing."

All annoyance fled and I felt bad for doubting him. "Is he okay?"

"Yeah, he'll be fine. He just got a nasty bruise, but I went with Ty to stay with him, and by the time I came to your room, you'd left."

"I'm glad he's okay."

"Can I come in?"

I opened the door wider. "Of course." I felt like a jerk. Not only had I doubted Cameron's word, but it turned out he was doing a good deed. We went out to the balcony and stood at the railing. After a moment I turned to him. "I'm sorry."

He looked at me, puzzled. "For what?"

I bit my lip. "For being kind of mad at you when you didn't show up."

He smiled. "It's okay. You didn't know what had happened."

"Still, I feel like a jerk now."

Smiling, he reached out and traced my jaw with his fingers, sending a shiver through me.

A feeling of anticipation began growing inside me—no one would interrupt our kiss this time. My gaze locked on his as his hand slid to the back of my neck. We stood close, and as I tilted my head slightly, his face descended toward mine, his mouth moving closer, closer. I closed my eyes as his lips met mine, pressing softly against my mouth. His other arm went around my waist, and my arms wound around his neck, holding him tight.

His kiss deepened, and a powerful feeling of desire grew inside me. Even as I enjoyed the feelings he stirred within me, I tried to control them, but found it nearly impossible to do so. After another moment I unwound my arms from his neck, placed my hands on his shoulders, and gently pushed him away, breaking our contact.

He looked at me, confusion clear on his face. "Is something wrong?"

I could still feel the pressure of his mouth on mine, and I pressed my lips together, trying to gather myself. Finally I shook my head.

"Then why did you push me away?"

Though I thought I knew why, I hesitated to tell him, but finally said, "I'm just not ready, I guess." What I meant was, the feelings of desire and longing he evoked in me made me uncomfortable. I didn't want to feel that way right now. Even though I liked the feelings, they reminded me of Marcus, which made me think I would end up being rejected if I let my feelings grow. It made no sense, but that was how I felt.

His face grim, he said, "This is why I told you we should take things slow." He turned away from me and looked out over the ocean. "This is why we should keep our relationship platonic."

A feeling of panic grew within me. *Just friends, just friends, just friends. All my relationships are doomed to be just friends.* But I knew it was my own doing. I had pushed *him* away, not the other way around.

He turned back to me, his face serious. "I'm not going to kiss you again. It's on you, Lily. If we're going to keep seeing each other after this cruise is over, it's up to you to let me know when you're ready to move forward." He stared at me a moment. "Agreed?"

I wasn't sure I liked having it all put on me, but I understood where he was coming from. "But what about what *you* want?" A small smile crept over my face as I thought about his comment the other day about holding me and kissing me until all my doubts fled.

He sighed. "If you aren't ready to move forward, it really doesn't matter what I want, does it?"

Fresh worry surged through me. *Am I blowing my chances with him? Will he lose interest before I get myself together?* It didn't matter. I couldn't change the way I felt. Not by force of will. Only time would get me past this barrier. As the image of a barrier floated into my mind, I thought of Marcus. Was that why he was keeping me at arm's length? Because he knew I wasn't ready for more than friendship? Or was I holding back from Cameron because of the tender state of my heart *due* to Marcus? I was so confused.

"Lily? What are you thinking?"

I gazed at Cameron. He was so honest with me and so careful about my feelings, dcspite what he may want. "You're a good man," I said without thinking.

He smiled. "I try to be." He paused. "So are we agreed?"

Reluctantly, I nodded. I didn't know what else to do.

We were quiet as we stared out over the ocean, our faces buffeted by the salty breeze.

"What time is your flight tomorrow?" Cameron asked, turning to me.

I told him.

He smiled. "I think we're on the same flight."

My face brightened. "That's great." I laughed. "Will you sit by me without fear this time?"

"Yes. I think Natalie will do fine. I can even help you with her."

My eyebrows shot up. "Really?"

"Well, I can at least help you with your luggage."

I laughed. "That would be nice."

The earlier tension gone, we chatted on the balcony until Natalie woke up, then we brought her with us as we went to have a snack.

"I'm going to miss this all-you-can-eat set up," Cameron said, then he took a bite of his sandwich.

"I know. But my waistline might be glad when it's over."

He looked at me appreciatively. "I think your waistline looks fine."

Blushing, I said, "Thanks, but I can tell I've put on a couple of pounds. It's hard not to when I have that delicious chocolate melting cake every night."

He laughed. "Yeah, that would do it." He paused. "Hey, I'm going to see if I can get into the early dining in a couple of hours since I'll be off the ship at our normal time. Do you want to eat with me then?"

"Sure."

A short time later we went to Ty and Alyssa's room to ask how Ty's dad was doing.

"He's doing fine," Ty said. "Thanks for staying with him earlier."

"No problem," Cameron said.

"Marriage seems to agree with you," I said to Alyssa as she held Natalie.

She beamed at Ty, then looked at me. "Thanks."

"Are you going into Victoria tonight?" I asked.

"Yes. What about you?"

I explained how it would be too late for Natalie.

"Ah yes. I guess I'm not used to thinking about what a baby needs." She put her finger in Natalie's hand.

"Let's keep it that way for a while," Ty said.

I laughed. "She's wonderful, but a lot of work too."

A while later I excused myself to take Natalie back to our room to feed her before our dinner.

"I'll come pick you up before dinner," Cameron said.

"Sounds good." I turned to Alyssa. "Am I going to see you before we get off the ship?"

"How about if Ty and I eat dinner with you guys?"

"That's a great idea."

At dinner, the four of us, plus Natalie, enjoyed one another's company as we ate together for the last time on the ship.

"Take lots of pictures of Butchart Gardens," I said to them.

"We will," Alyssa promised.

At the end of the meal I said my good-byes to Ty and Alyssa, promising her that we'd keep in touch after we got home, then Cameron and I finished our dessert and made arrangements to meet in the morning to disembark. A short time later he left to go on his excursion and I took Natalie back to our room.

As I carried her onto the elevator, I had to admit that it wasn't necessarily a bad thing to not have any pressure to kiss Cameron good-night, although a little kiss wouldn't have been bad. I smiled to myself and shook my head. I hated being so indecisive.

Maybe once I'm home and on familiar territory I'll be able to figure this out, I thought, feeling hopeful.

Chapter Nineteen

"See, I told you it would be painless to sit by us on the flight." I smiled at Cameron as he buckled his seatbelt in preparation for take-off.

"I know. And we got to get on first, which was cool."

I laughed. "Having a baby does have *some* advantages."

He nodded.

"I don't know about you," I said, "but I'm looking forward to getting home. The cruise was wonderful, but I'm ready to be home."

"Yeah, I suppose you're right."

We chatted throughout the short flight, and once we reached Sacramento, he walked me to my car. I put Natalie in her car seat and got the air conditioning going, then stood next to the car and faced Cameron. "I guess this is it," I said.

He smiled. "What do you mean?"

Smirking a little, I said, "I mean, will I ever see you again?"

He reached out and stroked my arm, which made me get goose bumps. His voice became soft and deep. "That's completely up to you."

I gazed at him a moment. "I gave you my cell number, and I hope you use it."

His smile grew, deepening his dimple. "I will."

He leaned toward me, and I unconsciously held my breath, but his lips brushed against my cheek. When he smiled, his eyes sparkled, and I knew he must know I would have liked more, but I didn't give any hint of my feelings, deciding to play his game.

"I'd better get going," I said.

He nodded. "Take care, Lily."

"You too."

He stood next to my car as I climbed behind the wheel and backed out of the parking space. Waving as I drove away, I smiled to myself, hopeful that he would call soon. Of course I could call him, but I wanted him to call me. Just over an hour later I pulled into my driveway, and when my house came into view, my smile grew. It felt so good to be home.

"We're here," I said to Natalie as I lifted her from her car seat and carried her into the house. Greta met us at the door and I squatted next to her and let Natalie grab her fur. Her tail wagged hard, showing how happy she was to see us. "Were you a good girl for Trish?" I asked as I scratched her head.

She panted in reply, her doggie smile wide.

I put Natalie in her swing and set it gently swaying, then went out to the car and brought in all our things. By the time I'd carried the luggage upstairs, Natalie had fallen asleep in the swing. I put her in her crib and unpacked our things, enjoying the feeling of getting everything organized and back into place.

After Natalie awoke from her nap, I put her in her stroller and walked next door to Trish's house.

"You're back," she said, a warm smile on her face.

"Yes. And thank you so much for taking care of Greta. It was so nice knowing she was in good hands."

"Oh, we're old friends now."

I smiled. "Good."

"Do you want to come in for a visit? I want to hear all about your trip."

"Sure."

We settled in the living room and she fixed us each a glass of cold lemonade.

"It's kind of strange to be back in hot weather," I said. "After being where it was cooler."

"I'll bet it was beautiful there."

"It was gorgeous. So green. I guess that's one advantage of the cooler, wetter weather."

"What was your favorite part?"

I thought of meeting Cameron and smiled, but said, "The whale watching."

"Oh, that does sound fun." She sipped her lemonade. "How was the wedding?"

"Alyssa looked stunning and it was so fun to see her getting married. I really like her new husband."

"Did you already know Alyssa's family?"

"No. The only person I knew ahead of time was Alyssa, but her family and Ty's family were really nice. Ty's younger sister even babysat for me several times."

"That must have been nice. What did you do on the ship?"

I pictured Cameron again and vividly recalled dancing with him, his arms wrapped around me, and smiled. Though I was in Marcus's childhood home, my memory of Cameron was fresh as I'd only left him a few hours earlier. "There were some fun comedy shows, and we also went dancing."

She must have seen something in my face, because she asked in a tone like she could already tell what my answer would be, "Did you meet anyone special?"

Heat rushed to my face. "Well, I did spend some time with Ty's best man."

Her eyebrows rose. "Oh? And what is his name?"

My smile grew. "Cameron."

"Where does he live?"

"Just in Sacramento."

"How nice." She seemed genuinely happy for me. She hesitated. "So you hit it off?"

I nodded. "Yeah, he's a great guy."

"How lucky for you that he doesn't live very far. Are you going to continue seeing him?"

"I think so."

"That's wonderful, Lily. I'm so glad you found someone."

I thought about her son. The man who had popped into my mind when I'd been dancing with Cameron. The man who, only a couple of weeks before, I'd thought I was falling in love with. The man who'd I'd thought was my 'someone'. Then I thought of him dating Chelsea and felt a stab of jealousy. Happiness at having Cameron in my life was marred by my feelings for Marcus. I pushed a smile on my face and nodded. "Yeah. So am I."

We talked about the rest of my trip, then I headed home, stopping by my mailbox to pick up the bundle of mail I'd had the post office hold for me. I carried the bundle into the house and set it on the coffee table, then put Natalie on a blanket on the floor. She was beginning to push herself onto her hands and knees, getting ready to crawl, and I smiled as I watched her.

I sorted through the mail, putting bills in one pile and junk mail in another, then stopped when I found a letter from Trevor's mom. Before the cruise I'd sent her a letter telling her we'd come for a visit soon, and now I would need to think about exactly when. I opened the envelope and pulled out the letter.

Dear Lily,

I'm so glad you've decided to come for a visit. Please let me know when you would like to come. I know I'm old-fashioned with sending letters in the mail, and I actually do have an email address, so if you'd prefer to email me, that would be fine.

Take care,

Marcy

She'd given me her email address, so I opened my laptop and went online, then started an email.

Marcy -

I decided to send you an email as it's so much faster—and no stamps involved :)

Natalie and I can come for a visit in a week. Would that work for you?

Lily

I sent the email, then spent some time catching up on my other online activities, including taking care of some tasks for the websites I had created for Billi and the other small business owners who'd hired me. When I received a response from Marcy before I'd signed off, I was surprised—I didn't know she spent much time online. She confirmed the date I'd set, so I called Trish to see if she could take care of Greta again. I felt guilty asking, but I didn't know what else to do.

"I wouldn't mind at all," Trish said. "But I'll be out of town then."

"Oh. Okay. Well, thanks anyway."

After we hung up, I considered what to do. Taking Greta with me was a non-starter, not after the comment Marcy had made about her family being upset that she had killed Trevor. I completely understood their reticence toward Greta, even though she'd only been protecting me. I got that they would never want to face her, but I didn't want to change the date as Marcy had already confirmed it.

I sighed, knowing the only other option was to ask Marcus to take care of her. With some reluctance, I called his cell phone.

"Hey, Lily. You're back," he answered.

For a moment I was caught off-guard, until I realized he would know it was me since my number was probably programmed into his phone. Then I focused on the sound of his voice and felt a strong tremor of longing flow through me, making me wistful that he was dating Chelsea and not me. "Hi, Marcus."

"It's good to hear your voice."

"Your's too." I silently added, *I thought about you when I was in another man's arms.*

"Did you have a good time? How did it go with Natalie? How did she do on the ship?"

I smiled. Of course he would ask about Natalie. "She did great."

"Hey, we should have lunch. Would you be able to stop by my office tomorrow?"

The thought of seeing him made my heart pound in anticipation, but would it just feel like torture to see him and know we could only ever be friends? "Sure," I said, responding before I had a chance to think it through.

"Great! I should be available by twelve-thirty."

We hung up a moment later and I leaned back against the couch and looked at Natalie, who was playing with one of her toys. "We're going to see Marcus tomorrow, baby girl," I said, and realized I was beaming.

The next afternoon Natalie and I pulled into a parking spot, and I took her out of her car seat and carried her inside.

"May I help you?" a girl a little older than me asked from behind the reception desk.

"Yes. I'm here to see Marcus Oliver."

"Please have a seat. I'll let him know you're here."

I sat in a nearby chair and held Natalie on my lap. As I waited, several groups of people came and went, which wasn't surprising as it was lunch time. Without being too obvious, I took special notice of the women, wondering if any of them could be Chelsea. What would she think of her boyfriend going to lunch with me? What would Cameron think?

"Lily," Marcus said as he entered the reception area.

My gaze went to him and I felt myself drawn to him, and all thoughts of Cameron fled. He was dressed in business casual and it suited him. As he walked toward me with a warm smile, I gazed at his incredible green eyes and knew it was hopeless—*he* was the one I wanted. *He* was the one who should be my someone.

I stood, and with Natalie in my arms, I smiled at him, but tried to keep my feelings under control, tried to keep my emotions on a friends-only level. "Hey, it's great to see you," I said.

Marcus stopped next to us and held out his arms to Natalie, who eagerly went into them. As I watched the two of them interact, I felt my heart breaking. *This* was what I wanted for myself and Natalie. A man who loved her. But he would also have to love me, and that's where the problem lay. Loving me as a friend was not enough to build a relationship on, not the kind of long-term relationship I was looking for. And I didn't think Marcus would be willing to make that kind of commitment to me anyway. Not with Chelsea in the picture. And if I was honest with myself, even if she wasn't in the picture, Marcus had made it all too clear that we were destined to be friends only.

"I'm glad she didn't forget me," he said.

As if, I thought. "It's only been a few weeks since we saw you."

"I know. But you never know with babies, right?"

I laughed, pushing aside my sorrow. "She's known you her whole life. I don't think she'll forget you that easily."

He held her in front of him, gazing into her face. "That's good." Then he nuzzled her neck, making her giggle. He smiled at me. "I love that sound."

I smiled back. "Me, too."

He held her securely against his side. "Ready to get something to eat?"

I watched the natural way he held her, and could picture him being a father to her, but as quickly as the thought came to mind, my heart reminded me that that would never happen. It didn't matter how much I wanted it. It wasn't like with Cameron, where he told me he wanted more, but was willing to let me set the pace. I'd *told* Marcus that I really liked him—who was I kidding? I *loved* him—but he'd shot me down, cleanly and clearly.

I nodded in answer to Marcus's question and held the smile on my face, but inside I felt my heart crumbling. "Where do you want to go?" I asked, proud that I'd kept my voice steady.

"There's an Applebee's nearby."

"Sounds good."

We walked out of the building together and toward my car. "Do you mind if we take your car?" he asked. "With the car seat and everything…"

"No, that makes the most sense." I unlocked the door and Marcus fastened Natalie into her car seat, then he climbed into the passenger seat. I got behind the wheel, thinking how wonderful it was to have someone else to help out, but quashed the thought the moment it came to mind. *Stop it, Lily. It's not going to happen. You're just torturing yourself.*

We drove to the restaurant and sat in the waiting area for our party to be called. Marcus held Natalie on his lap, and she played with his watch.

"So," he said. "Tell me about the cruise."

Cameron's face flashed into my mind, and I thought about how integral he was to my experience, but I wasn't about to tell Marcus about him. "It was wonderful to see my friend get married. Maybe you'll meet her one day."

He smiled. "I'd like that."

"Her husband's a great guy, and we all had fun."

"What did you do while you were in Alaska?"

"A lot of walking around the towns we visited." I reached into my purse and pulled out the totem pole I'd bought for him, then held it out to him. "I got this for you."

He took it from me and examined the intricate carving. "Thank you. This is cool." He smiled at me. "You're so thoughtful, Lily."

I smiled in return, pleased. "I'm glad you like it."

Natalie tried to grab it from him, but he held it out of her reach. "This is from your Mommy. I don't want you to play with it." He glanced at me with a grin on his face.

I blushed, but not wanting to make a big deal about my gift, I said, "My favorite thing on the trip was the whale watching. It was really cool to see them as they surfaced."

"That would be awesome. Maybe I'll have to take an Alaskan cruise one day."

"I could show you around," I said without thinking, then my face flamed red. "I mean, if I happened to be on the same cruise."

He laughed. "That would be fun. Maybe we could get a group together and go one day."

A group, I thought. That made his intentions perfectly clear. "Yeah," I nodded. "I would like that." The lie tasted bitter on my tongue, but I knew going as a group was better than not going at all.

Our table was ready and we followed the server to a booth. They brought a high chair for Natalie, and Marcus placed her in the seat.

"So what's new with you?" I asked, picking up the menu.

"Not much. Just working a lot."

I thought about Chelsea, and frowned before I could stop myself.

"It's okay," he said, obviously thinking I was frowning about him working a lot. "I really like my job."

"That's great then." I wondered if working with his girlfriend played a part in that.

"How did my mom do with Greta?"

"It's funny. At first your mom was really hesitant to watch her, but now she says they're old friends."

He laughed. "I knew it would work out."

I set my menu down. "That's one reason I called you. I'm going to Las Vegas to spend some time with Trevor's parents, and your mom will be out of town. I hate to ask you because it's a bit of a drive for you, but I don't know who else to ask. Would you be able to take care of Greta for a few days?"

"Sure. You know I'm happy to do it."

"If you want to stay at the house while you're taking care of her, that's fine with me." I wondered how that would go over with Chelsea. "But whatever works for you."

"I'll think about it," he said. "When are you going?"

I told him the dates and he nodded. We ordered our meals and they arrived a short time later. We talked about this and that, and I managed to stay away from any romantic subjects. After we finished, I dropped him off at work, and he promised to stop by for my key before I left.

Chapter Twenty

The night before Natalie and I were to leave for Las Vegas, Marcus dropped by to pick up the key. We sat on the couch, and he scratched Greta behind her ears. Natalie had already gone to bed for the night.

"What did you decide about staying here?" I asked.

"I think it would be better if I just stopped by once a day to feed her, rather than stay at your house."

Chelsea didn't like the idea, huh? I wanted to say, but instead I nodded. "Okay. I'm sorry about the drive."

"It's only about ten minutes. Not a big deal."

"Well, I really appreciate it."

He smiled warmly. "You know I'm here for you, don't you, Lily?"

I felt my heart lurch. What was he saying? I nodded. "Yes, and it's comforting to know I can count on you." As much as I wanted to say more, I had to let him lead the way.

He nodded slightly. "That's what friends are for, right?"

I almost groaned. Why did he have to keep saying that? Was he trying to make a point? Could he tell how I felt and he wanted to put me in my place? "Right."

He left a short time later, and after I closed the door behind him, I felt my shoulders slump, and tears filled my eyes. My hopes of our relationship moving past friendship seemed to be dimming. I trudged up the stairs and got ready for bed, focusing on the visit I was about to embark on.

The next morning as Natalie and I drove to Las Vegas, I thought about Marcus taking care of Greta. Would he bring Chelsea along when he came? I didn't like the idea of her in my house, but there wasn't anything I could do about it.

When we arrived at John and Marcy's house that evening, Natalie was cranky from the long drive. I carried her to the front door, but Marcy opened it before I had a chance to knock.

"Lily," she said, pulling me into a hug. "It's so good to see you and Natalie."

The warmth of her embrace made me feel welcome, and I was glad I came. "Hi, Marcy," I said as she released me.

She held the door wide. "Please come in."

I followed her inside.

"Can I get you something cold to drink?" she asked.

"That would be wonderful. It's so hot here in Vegas."

"Yes, I suppose it is, but I've gotten used to it."

I followed her into the kitchen and remembered the last time I'd been there. Trevor's older brother Chris had made it clear that he didn't want me around, and I'd left early, mortified.

Marcy handed me an ice-filled glass of raspberry lemonade. "May I hold Natalie?" she asked.

I smiled. "She's a little grumpy from our drive, but you can give it a try."

Marcy took her from me and Natalie didn't object. "Hi there, sweetheart," Marcy murmured to her.

It warmed me to see my daughter with her only living grandmother, and I was glad that Trevor's parents were so accepting of me after all that had happened. I knew they could have resented me and things could have been very different.

"Have you been keeping busy this summer?" Marcy asked as we sat on a pair of comfortable chairs.

"Yes, actually. A good friend of mine just got married, so Natalie and I went to her wedding."

"Oh, that's nice. Where did she get married?"

I smiled. "In Alaska."

Marcy's eyebrows rose. "Alaska? That's a ways to go."

"Actually, it was on a cruise ship."

She bounced Natalie on her lap, which Natalie seemed to like. "That sounds like fun. When did you go?"

"We just got back earlier this week. It was really fun."

"Was it hard with Natalie?"

"Honestly, having her along did make it harder to do things, but she's such an easy-going baby that it was fine."

"You know, I'd be happy to care for her if you were to go on a trip like that."

"Well, I'm still nursing her, so I wouldn't be able to leave her."

"Oh, okay."

We visited about other things, and when John got home, we had a nice dinner together.

"Melody and Deena are going to come over the day after tomorrow with their kids," Marcy said as we cleaned up the dishes. "I hope that's okay."

I liked my sisters-in-law—were they still my sisters-in-law?—and was happy to spend time with them. "That will be fun," I said.

On the day they arrived, Natalie had just woken from her morning nap, and soon after they got there, Deena brought up the subject of me moving to Vegas.

"It would be so wonderful for Natalie to grow up surrounded by her cousins," she said.

The last time I'd come for a visit, I'd been resistant to moving to Vegas because I'd had high hopes for a relationship with Marcus. But now that all seemed in doubt. Even so, I wasn't ready to remove him from my life—what would that do to Natalie? She adored him. Not only that, but with Cameron in the picture now, I had even more reason to stay where I was. "As much as I agree," I said, "I have a life where I live now and I don't feel like the time is right to change that."

"But what about Natalie?" Marcy asked.

I looked at her, puzzled. "What do you mean?"

She hesitated, like she wasn't sure how this would go over. "I just mean, well, don't you think it would be good for her to have a father-figure in her life?" She paused and her eyes shone with unshed tears. "I mean, since her father isn't . . . here."

I felt my stomach flutter and the room became silent, the only sound Natalie's babbles, which seemed to emphasize Marcy's point. I didn't know what to say. After a moment I said, "I have a good friend." The word 'friend' nearly stuck in my throat. "And he's really sweet with Natalie."

Marcy's eyes widened briefly, like this was unexpected.

I glanced from her to Melody, then to Deena, then focused on Natalie. I could tell none of them had expected me to say I might have another man in my life. Good thing I hadn't mentioned Cameron. They would have fallen over with shock to learn I had *two* men in my life, although my relationships with both men were complicated.

"What is this person's name?" Marcy asked, her voice even.

"Uh, Marcus." I lifted my eyes to meet hers and noticed her tears had dried.

"How long have you known him, if I may ask?" she said.

My heart began to pound at this unforeseen line of questioning. "I guess about a year now." It had actually been more than a year, but I didn't think I had to be that specific.

I heard a soft gasp and glanced at Melody, who'd put her hand over her mouth. Then my gaze went to Marcy to see how she was taking the news.

Not well, that's how. She stared at her lap as if doing a difficult word problem, then she looked up at me and frowned. "So, you were 'friends' with this man while you were hiding from Trevor?" When she said the word 'friends' I could hear the air quotes in her voice.

I felt a need to defend myself, though I'd done nothing wrong. "He lived in the house next door." I could almost hear their thoughts: *How convenient.* "He's just a friend." For once I was glad of the distance he'd kept between us as I knew my protestations would be sincere.

Marcy sighed. "I don't mean to be so . . . well, so dramatic, Lily." She paused. "But you must understand how this makes me feel. I mean, my son," her voice began to waver, "has only been dead for a matter of months and already you've found a replacement." Tears overflowed her eyes and ran down her cheeks. "No, let me correct that. You found a replacement *before* he even had a chance to *live*." She stood abruptly and fled the room.

Tears of sympathy and shame filled my eyes as I watched her go, and I turned my head away from Melody and Deena, not wanting them to see how upset I felt. Thankfully, their children were playing outside, so at least I didn't have to hear any uncomfortable questions about why I'd made their grandmother cry. After a moment I placed Natalie on the floor as she'd gotten squirmy—perhaps she felt the tension in the room.

"I don't blame you," Melody said softly.

I felt a hand on my shoulder and turned to see Deena smiling through her own tears. "Neither do I," she said.

Their kindness brought on a fresh surge of tears and I wiped at my face impatiently. "Thank you."

"It's been hard for her," Deena said. "He was her baby."

I glanced at Natalie, and felt my heart clench. I had a good idea how Marcy felt—I'd felt something similar when *her* baby had taken *my* baby. The difference was, he'd *chosen* to behave in a way that had gotten him killed. Over the last few months I'd learned to forgive him for what he'd done—there was no point in holding a grudge against him. But I was sympathetic to Marcy's plight. She missed her son terribly, but she was still trying to build a relationship with me for Natalie's sake.

I turned so I was facing Deena and Melody. "I didn't want him to die." Now my voice shook. "He's Natalie's father. In the short time I saw him with her, he was good to her."

Melody shook her head. "It all seems so pointless. I mean, why did he have to die? Why couldn't you guys have worked it out?"

Deena gasped. "Melody," she said sharply.

Melody looked between us. "That's what Chris has such a hard time with. He doesn't get why it came to that." Her voice softened. "Neither do I."

"Have you read the police report?" Deena asked her.

"Of course," she said. "But that just shows one side of the story." She glanced at me, then looked at Deena. "Don't you wonder what Trevor would have said in his own defense?"

The way they were talking, like I wasn't even in the room, made me angry. *They* hadn't been there when I'd woken from my unconscious state to find myself tied up and my child missing. *They* hadn't been there when Trevor's hands had wrapped around my neck, choking the very life out of me. *Their* lives were neat and tidy, and *their* husbands had never taken their children with the idea of giving them to another woman. They had no idea what it was like to be me.

"I tried to make it work," I said evenly. "But he wanted what I couldn't give him. He wanted to get back together, but he'd killed my love for him and I just couldn't do it."

"But why couldn't you just *share*," Melody asked. "I mean, plenty of divorced people co-parent. I don't understand why you guys couldn't work it out to both be in Natalie's life."

"Is this really the time?" Deena asked, obviously uncomfortable.

"No, it's okay," I said. And it was. It was better to hash this out sooner, rather than later. Get it over with. Evidently, Melody had been harboring certain thoughts and misconceptions about what happened—her husband probably did too. It was better to clear the air.

"Well?" Melody said.

"I completely agree with you," I said.

Melody's forehead creased, like she didn't quite believe me.

"As soon as Trevor found me—and don't doubt that he spent a lot of time tracking me down—I knew I would have to work with him, and though I admit I wasn't happy about it, I came to accept it." I paused, remembering seeing him with Natalie and how it seemed to come so naturally to him. "He was good with her. But he couldn't stand the fact that she was *connected* to me. I don't mean physically—although as a newborn she completely depended on me for her sustenance—but as her mother." I gazed at her with a look that said *you must understand*. "I'd just finished carrying her in my womb for nine months and gone through a grueling labor and delivery. She was—and is—a part of my heart. That is a bond he not only couldn't understand, but that he couldn't break, as much as he wanted to."

Tears filled my eyes and I spoke with passion. "And, oh boy, he wanted to. He *told* me that he was going to . . ." I swallowed around the lump that formed in my throat, but it was still hard to speak as the tears were thick in my voice. "He was going to give *my* baby, *my* child, to a girlfriend he had on the side." My eyes narrowed in memory. "He *stole* Natalie from me. He *told* me I would *never* see her again."

I took a moment and gathered myself, then locked eyes with Melody. "Does that sound like a man who is willing to co-parent?"

Her mouth had fallen open and I wondered if she'd missed that part of the police report—or maybe I hadn't put that much detail into it.

"I didn't know," she finally muttered. She blinked a few times and said again, "I didn't know."

"There are lots of things you don't know," I said quietly but firmly.

I felt Deena's hand on my shoulder again, and I placed my hand over hers. I didn't know either of my sisters-in-law very well, but was grateful for Deena's unwavering support, as well as her husband's. Natalie began fussing and I picked her up and held her.

"I think she's getting hungry." I smiled at them to show I had no hard feelings, then took Natalie into the kitchen to give her some baby food, then put her down for a nap. When I came back into the living room, Deena and Melody were talking quietly, but abruptly stopped when I walked in the room.

Wondering if I should leave them, I stood on the threshold a moment.

"It's okay, Lily," Melody said. "You can join us."

I nodded, then sat in an empty chair.

"I'm sorry I jumped to conclusions," she said. "I should know better."

"It's okay," I said.

"No, it's not." She frowned. "I know Chris has some ideas about what happened, but from what you've told me, he's wrong, too." She paused. "I'm going to tell him what you told me. Maybe he'll soften towards you."

"Of course I'd like it if he did," I said. "But whether he does or not, I'm going to live my life the best way I can, and I'm going to care for Natalie in the way I think is best."

"I know," Melody said. "It's just that I want us to all be able to be together without the tension and anger and sadness."

"You're very wise, Melody," Marcy said from the entrance of the room.

I looked at her reddened eyes and felt my heart ache in empathy. I could only imagine how she must still be grieving for her lost child.

She sat in a chair near mine and smiled at us. "I'm sorry about my outburst. I just get so emotional sometimes."

I completely understood why she would, but was she still upset that Marcus was in my life? I couldn't tell, but it wasn't something I could change. I didn't *want* to change that. In fact, I hoped he became a more permanent, and more important part of my life. Then I wondered if she'd overheard any of my earlier conversation with Melody and Deena. I didn't think so as I hadn't seen her when I'd taken Natalie into the kitchen to feed her. Did she have feelings similar to Melody's? Feelings she was hiding from me?

Chapter Twenty-One

Emotionally wrung out, I had no intention of bringing up any more Trevor issues—or Marcus issues for that matter—and I was grateful when the conversation moved in another direction. After clearing the air with Melody, I felt lighter, although I wondered when the inevitable conversation with Marcy would happen.

The four of us chatted for a while longer, then Melody and Deena left, needing to get home.

"I hope you enjoyed visiting with them," Marcy said to me as we watched them drive away.

"I did. Thank you for inviting them over."

We walked back inside and I helped her get dinner started. We had a pleasant evening, and she didn't bring up the subject of Marcus until just before I was set to leave the next morning.

"I know you're young, Lily, and life goes on for you, but I hope you'll reconsider moving closer to family here in Vegas."

The fact that she considered me family, even though my only connection to them was Natalie, filled me with warmth, and I smiled. "I'll keep it in mind. But like I said, I have ties to where I live now and I really like it there."

"Does this Marcus person have anything to do with that?"

I bit my lip, uneasy with the idea of talking about my love life—or lack thereof—for fear of upsetting her. But then decided she deserved my honesty. It was about the only thing I had to offer. "To some extent, yes."

She sighed.

"Truly, Marcy, he is just a friend." I decided not to tell her that I desperately wanted it to be more than that.

"Family is more permanent than friends, Lily. Always remember that."

In my life that wasn't necessarily true. I had no living blood relatives, so my friends *were* my family. I was thankful for Marcy and John and everyone else in Trevor's family, but I really hadn't spent a lot of time with them and didn't know if I could really count on them in a crunch. For that matter, I wasn't one hundred percent certain I could count on Marcus in a crunch.

I frowned as a feeling of loneliness grew inside me as I was reminded that I really couldn't count on anyone besides myself. People in my life had good intentions, but when push came to shove, who would really be there for me?

"I'd better get going," I said, feeling down. "We have a long drive ahead of us."

Marcy pulled me into a hug. "I'm so glad you came." She looked at me steadily. "I want you to know that you're always welcome here."

My feelings of self-pity lifted a little at the strength of her sincerity. "Thank you. I really appreciate knowing that."

As Natalie and I drove north, I turned my thoughts away from Las Vegas and back toward home. The drive was long, but uneventful, and when I pulled into my driveway, I breathed a sigh of relief, happy to be home again, and with no plan to go anywhere.

I carried Natalie to the front door and heard Greta moving around on the other side, then unlocked the door and went in.

"Hi, my good girl," I said to Greta as I squatted next to her with Natalie in my arms. Her tail wagged and she danced around, happy to see us.

I went into the kitchen to pour myself a cold drink, but stopped in my tracks when I saw a lovely flower arrangement sitting in a vase. "Marcus is so sweet," I said out loud as I reached for the card tucked into the flowers.

I opened the envelope and slid out the card.

Lily,

Just wanted you to know that I've been thinking about you. The cruise wouldn't have been the same without you.

Cameron

I blinked twice as my mind readjusted to the fact that the flowers were not from Marcus, but were from Cameron. How did they get in the house? Had he stopped by? How did he even know where I lived? Confusion and uncertainty swept over me, and I decided I would call Marcus for an explanation.

I carried Natalie upstairs and nursed her before putting her down for a short nap, then carried our things into the house and unpacked. Once I felt settled, I sat on the couch and called Marcus's cell phone. It went to voice mail and I left a message, letting him know I was home.

A while later I heard a knock at the door. As I leaned toward the peephole I smiled, wondering if it would be Marcus—although it was a little early in the day for him to be dropping by. My smile faded when I saw Mary, my landlady, standing on the other side of the door.

"Hello, Lily," she said when I opened the door.

I hadn't spoken to her in quite a while—normally I just mailed her a rent check every month and didn't hear from her or her husband. "Hello. Please come in." I held the door open and she followed me inside. "What brings you by?"

She smiled sadly. "I'm afraid I have some bad news for you."

I tensed, wondering what she was going to say. "What is it?"

She sighed. "My son and his family have run in to some difficult financial circumstances, I'm afraid, and they need a place to live."

"Oh no." I could see where this conversation was heading, and I felt my body stiffen.

She nodded. "Yes. I've so enjoyed having you as a tenant, but after a lot of thought and discussion, Edward and I have decided we need to let our son and his family move in here."

My shoulders slumped. I was on a month-to-month rental agreement, so I had no choice in the matter. My lips compressed as my thoughts flew.

Mary put her hand on my arm. "I'm so sorry to do this to you, Lily."

I sighed, thinking about Marcy's desire for me to move to Vegas. Maybe this was a sign that I should move there. "It's okay, Mary. I understand. Family has to come first." I paused. "When do I have to be out?"

"By the end of September." Her brow furrowed. "Will you be able to find something else by then? My son and his family will need to move in by October first."

"I'm sure I can find something." I relaxed a bit, knowing I still had a sizable amount of money in the bank from the sale of Dad's house, plus his life insurance policy. Natalie and I would be okay. I would just really miss this place. We'd made it our own, and it was the only home I had.

Mary smiled, her face relieved. "Good." She turned to go. "I'll be in touch, but please let me know how your search goes."

I nodded. "Okay."

She left a moment later and I sank onto the couch, my mind in a whirl. Trying to stay focused on the issue at hand, I considered my options and knew I had to make two decisions. One, where to live—here or in Las Vegas. And two, should I continue renting, or should I buy a place? The idea of buying had great appeal. If I bought a house, what happened this afternoon wouldn't happen again—no one could suddenly tell me I had to move. Now that I was no longer hiding from Trevor, I could purchase a home for Natalie and myself, and know that I could stay there as long as I wanted.

I smiled as the idea of buying a place grew on me. If I stuck to a budget, I could use the money I'd kept in the bank and keep my mortgage extremely low. True, I would deplete my cash reserves, but buying some security for Natalie and myself would be a good investment.

The idea of buying firmly in my mind, I started to think about where to buy. I opened my laptop and went online, pulling up a website that listed homes for sale, then did a search for houses in Las Vegas. There were many that I felt I could afford, and I browsed the options until I heard Natalie waking up.

By evening, I was no closer to deciding where to live than I'd been when Mary had first stopped by that afternoon, and when someone knocked on the door, I was glad to have the interruption. I peered through the peephole and smiled when I saw Marcus standing on my porch.

"Hi," I said when I opened the door. "I'm glad you stopped by."

"Hey, Lily." He held out the key.

I took it from him. "Do you want to come in?"

He seemed uncomfortable, but finally nodded.

We sat on opposite ends of the couch, and Natalie played on a blanket on the floor.

"How was your trip?" he asked.

"It was good." I thought about the intense conversation I'd had with my sisters-in-law. "I'm glad I went."

"That's good."

He seemed quieter than usual and I wondered what was up. "I have some news," I said, thinking about my house hunt.

His eyebrows pulled together, as if he was upset. "Oh yeah?"

Did he somehow know that I was going to have to move? His mother was friends with Mary, so it was possible. But why would that be upsetting? Trish wouldn't know I was thinking about moving to Vegas. "Yeah. Mary, my landlady, stopped by earlier. Her son and his family need to move in here, so I have to be out by the end of September."

Marcus looked surprised. "Oh."

Evidently he didn't know.

"What are you going to do?" he asked.

I smiled. "I decided that I don't want to rent anymore, so I'm going to buy a place."

He seemed to relax. "That's exciting. Do you know what area you want to focus on?"

I bit my lip. "That's what I'm trying to decide." I gazed at him as I spoke, curious to see his reaction. "Trevor's family really wants me to move down to Las Vegas so that Natalie can be with family."

His brow creased for a moment, then his expression smoothed out. "What do *you* want?"

I want to stay here with you, I thought. "I don't know," I said instead.

"That's a big decision."

Disappointed he hadn't said something to encourage me to stay, I nodded. "I'm going to have to decide soon. I only have five weeks until I have to be out of here."

"If you decide to stay in the area," he said. "I know a realtor who can help you find a place."

Was that his subtle way of telling me he wanted me to stay? I desperately hoped so, and realized I'd already made my decision. I couldn't leave him, not as long as there was any hope of a future together. "Oh. Well, why don't you give me his number and I'll see what's available around here." I smiled. "Might as well start with a place I'm familiar with."

He seemed to brighten. "Great."

We were quiet for a moment and I suddenly remembered the flowers. "Hey, Marcus?"

"Yeah?"

"I was wondering about the flowers in the kitchen."

His earlier agitation returned. "They were delivered when I was here feeding Greta, so I put them in the kitchen for you. I hope that's okay."

That made sense. "Yes, that's fine. Thanks."

His brow creased again. "Well, I'd better get going. I'll get my friend's number for you." He stood and walked toward the door.

I followed him, not knowing what to do to get him to stay longer. "Thanks again for taking care of Greta." I laughed. "I don't have any plans to go anywhere now, so I shouldn't have to ask you again."

He smiled. "It's no problem." He opened the door, then turned to me. "Maybe the place you get will be close to where I live, then if you need me to watch her it will be easier."

I nodded, not sure what to make of his comment. I watched him get into his car, then drive away, and wondered what to make of the mixed messages I seemed to be getting from him.

As I fed Natalie some baby food for dinner, I glanced at the flowers Cameron had sent and thought about Marcus's strange reaction to them. He'd seemed a little unsettled when he'd told me about them being delivered, and I wondered if he'd read the card, or if his mother had told him about me meeting Cameron on the cruise. But I didn't understand why my dating someone would bother him. He'd made it clear enough that we were only friends. Not only that, *he* was dating Chelsea.

I shook my head, confused by his behavior, then finished feeding Natalie.

The next day Marcus texted me the name and phone number of the realtor he knew, and I immediately called him.

"I'd like a place with two to three bedrooms, and two bathrooms would be nice," I said.

"I'm sure I can find lots of places to show you," Russell said. "Let me look through the listings and I'll get back to you."

After I ended the call, I smiled, excited now to move forward with this new plan. Later that day, Russell called me back, and we scheduled time to look at several houses the next day, Saturday. A few minutes later my phone rang again, and I wondered if he needed to change the appointment. I looked at the caller ID and didn't recognize the number.

"Hello?"

"Hey, Lily," a male voice I didn't recognize said.

"Who is this?"

He laughed. "It's Cameron."

"Oh! Hi, Cameron." I smiled, my spirits rising. Here was a man who was really interested in me—as more than a friend.

"I can't believe you've forgotten me so quickly. And after I sent flowers too." He paused. "You did get the flowers, didn't you?"

"Yes, and they're beautiful." I paused, wondering again how he'd gotten my address, and knowing there wasn't a subtle way to ask. "How did you know where to send them?"

"I asked Alyssa." He hesitated. "I just realized that you might think I'm some sort of stalker. Honestly, I'm not."

I trusted Alyssa's judgement. "I don't think Alyssa would have given you my address if she had any worry about you being like that."

"Good. I'm glad we cleared that up."

"Well anyway," I said, "It's been a crazy few days."

"What's going on?"

I told him about having to move and that I was going to look at houses the next day.

"Do you want some company?"

"Really? You'd come all the way here to help me look?"

"Sure. Why not?"

"I'd love it," I said, the idea making me happy. "I could use a second opinion."

"Great. What time should I come?"

"We're supposed to start at ten in the morning."

He laughed. "No sleeping in for me."

I smiled into the phone. "Hey, it was your idea to come."

"Yes, and I'm willing to give up a little sleep to spend time with you."

"Good." I gave him my address and we hung up a moment later. When I went to bed that night, I was excited not only to house hunt, but to have Cameron there with me. As much as I wanted Marcus to be in my life, he just didn't seem interested, and I didn't know how to change that. In the meantime, I would spend time with Cameron. Maybe *he* was the one I should be focusing on. Ty and Alyssa thought he was a great guy, and from all accounts, they were right. I'd made the mistake of not listening to Alyssa before, and I didn't want to make the same mistake twice.

Chapter Twenty-Two

"Good morning, beautiful," Cameron said as I let him into my house.

"Good morning." My smile widened as my eyes met his, and I felt my body react to his presence, the memory of the few kisses we shared filling me with desire.

"It's great to see you," he said.

"I'm glad you suggested coming down." I wondered if he would kiss me before the day was through. "It will be fun to have you along on my house hunt. I can use a second opinion."

"I'm here to help."

I handed him a stack of papers. "Russell sent me the listings for the houses we're going to look at." I tapped the one on top. "We're supposed to meet him at this place first."

He hefted the small stack of papers. "Wow, there's a lot here."

"I don't have a lot of time to find a place, so I have to get busy."

"Hopefully they don't all start looking alike."

I frowned. "I know." I turned to Natalie, who was watching us from her swing. "Let me just grab Natalie and we'll get going."

"Okay."

A few minutes later we were driving to the first place, using the GPS on my phone to guide us. We pulled up to the house a short time later. Russell showed us around, but the place didn't feel like home to me. We went to several more places, but nothing jumped out at me. Either there wasn't enough of a yard for Greta, or the bedrooms were too small, or the location didn't feel safe.

I expressed my concerns to Russell.

"Have you considered getting a fixer?" he asked. "That way you get more for your money, the location you want, and the space you need. But you'll have to put some work into it."

I turned to Cameron.

"Don't look at me," he said, grimacing. "I'm no Mr. Fix-It."

"I can do some basic stuff, like paint," I said, turning back to Russell. "But beyond that, I don't know if I can afford to hire someone."

"Think about it," Russell said. "And if you want, I can take you to look at some places that might fit your needs better. At least they would have the potential of fitting your needs better."

"Okay."

Cameron, Natalie, and I headed back to my house, with me feeling discouraged. "I really thought I'd find something promising today," I said.

"You just barely started looking. I'm sure you'll find something."

"It's just that I don't have a lot of time. Mary's son needs to move in by October first, so I have to be moved in to a new place by then." My stomach knotted up as the stress of being homeless came to mind. "I have to find a place for Natalie's sake."

"What's the worse that can happen if you don't find a place?"

Cameron asked as we pulled into my driveway. "You have to live in a hotel for a few weeks? Put your stuff in storage?"

I felt the tension seeping away. "You're right. We'll be okay." I turned off the car and smiled at him. "Thanks for keeping a level head."

He grinned. "It's easy when I'm not the one who has to move."

We went inside, and I fed Natalie some baby food.

"She looks like she's ready for a nap," Cameron said.

I looked at him and nodded, realizing that he'd never held her the whole time we'd been house-hunting. I couldn't fault him for that—not everyone was like Marcus. I frowned at the thought, but quickly pushed a smile onto my face and laughed. "I know how she feels. This house-hunting is exhausting." I turned back to Natalie, who was rubbing her eyes, and finished feeding her the jar of baby food.

A moment later Cameron said, "I should probably head back to Sacramento."

I set the empty jar of baby food on the counter and turned to him. "Already?"

He smiled. "I've really enjoyed spending the morning with you, Lily, but I have some other commitments this afternoon."

I felt my heart sink. *He's bored with me already, or he has another date.* Both thoughts added to the discouragement I was already feeling. I nodded. "Sure. Okay."

He moved to stand close to me, then put his arms around me. "When can we get together again?" he murmured in my hair.

I smiled, thinking maybe he wasn't bored with me after all. "My schedule is wide open."

He pulled back and looked at me. "What about next Saturday?"

I nodded, feeling better about him. "Yes. Let's plan on that."

He grinned. "Great. I'll come down next Saturday morning. You know this area better than I do. Do you want to see if you can think of some things to do?"

"Besides house hunting?"

He frowned. "Yeah. There is that."

"There's a good chance I'll still be looking next Saturday. I doubt I'll be lucky enough to find something this week."

"Well, if that's what you need to do, then that's what we'll do."

"Are you sure?"

He nodded. "I admit, it's not my favorite activity, but I'm here for you, Lily."

His words echoed what Marcus had been telling me, and for a moment I paused, thinking of the man who I *really* wanted to be with. Then I focused back on the man who was standing in front of me. "I appreciate that. But I can manage to house hunt on my own. I'd rather reserve our time for something that we would both enjoy."

"Okay. We can play it by ear then. We'll see where your house hunt stands at the end of the week."

"Sounds fair."

He smiled and pulled me against him.

The heat of his body wrapped around me and I felt my heart rate escalate, and again wondered if he would kiss me before he left. But then Marcus's face filled my mind and I thought about kissing him. Was Cameron just a stand-in?

Natalie started fussing and Cameron released me. I turned back to my baby girl and wiped her face, then lifted her from her high chair.

"Well, I'll call you later in the week to see how things are going," Cameron said.

I nodded, knowing he wasn't going to make the first move to kiss me, and not certain I wanted to kiss him just then. Conflicting feelings washed over me—if it was really Marcus I wanted, it wouldn't be fair to Cameron for me to lead him on. But if Marcus had no interest in that kind of relationship with me, I didn't want to lose Cameron.

I walked him to his car and we stopped next to his door. The warm sun flowed over me and I smiled at him.

He reached out and stroked my arm, his gaze meeting mine.

"Remember, Lily. It's up to you."

I felt my heart skip a beat and knew he was referring to where our relationship was going to go. Where did I want our relationship to go? I was no closer to an answer than I'd been on the cruise. I gazed at him, my eyes drifting to his lips, which turned up into a smile.

With Natalie on my left hip, I wasn't in the best position to pull him into a kiss, but after a moment I reached my right arm toward him. He obviously understood what I was trying to do, because he leaned toward me. I'd only meant to give him a quick kiss on the lips, but as soon as our mouths touched, he pulled me close—Natalie and all—and our kiss deepened.

Desire swept over me, making me breathless, and I felt the same panic I'd felt on the cruise beginning to engulf me. Forcing it down, I allowed myself to become lost in the moment. It felt so good to be *wanted*, even if it was by the wrong man. My eyes shot open at the thought. Did I really believe Cameron was the wrong man for me? And if I did, what was I doing here, standing in my driveway, kissing him?

Pushing those thoughts to the side, I closed my eyes and focused on Cameron and the fact that he was a good man, a man recommended by Alyssa, whom I trusted completely. When I stopped analyzing everything and second guessing myself, I was able to enjoy the warmth of his embrace and the security I felt in his strong arms. It seemed obvious enough that he really liked me, and I relished the feeling.

A moment later he released me, a sparkle in his blue eyes.

I gazed at him, wanting to make this work. "Are you sure you need to leave?"

He smiled, like he knew the effect he had on me, then nodded. "I do. I promised a friend I'd help him move."

I felt my insides flutter. He was helping a *male* friend. With a grin, I said, "What is it with you and people who are moving?"

He laughed. "I know, right? I don't know how I let people drag me into their moving dramas."

I smiled back. "Well, hopefully mine won't be a drama."

He paused. "I'll see you in a week."

"I look forward to it." And despite thoughts of Marcus, I really was looking forward to spending time with Cameron. Maybe it was the kiss we'd just shared and the feelings he evoked in me, but I hoped there *could* be a future for us. I just had to open my heart to him and push all thoughts of Marcus aside.

A moment later Cameron climbed into his car and drove away.

That evening, Alyssa called.

"How are the newlyweds?" I asked, pleased to hear from her.

"We're great. But what I want to know is, what's going on with you and Cameron? Have you heard from him since you got home?"

I smiled. "Yes. In fact he came over today and went with me to look at houses."

"Really? That's fantastic." She paused. "So you like him?"

My smile dimmed slightly. "I think so."

"What do you mean, you think so? Why wouldn't you? Like I keep telling you, he's a great guy."

"I know. And I think he's great too. It's just that . . . well . . . I told you about Marcus, right?"

"Yes."

"I really like him." I stared at the wall across from me.

Alyssa sighed. "No offense, Lily, but I don't know this Marcus person, but I do know Cameron. So I'm on team Cameron."

I laughed. "So we have teams now?"

She laughed in response. "Yes, we do."

"Oh, Alyssa. I don't know what to do."

"What do you mean?"

"Marcus is so good with Natalie, and he's been there for me. And, well, I just really, really like him. But when I told him how I felt, he brushed me off. And now he's dating some woman he works with." I paused, gathering my thoughts.

"And what about Cameron?"

"That's where I'm confused. I know he likes me—he's told me as much—and he's so sweet, letting me set the pace, but I just don't feel as strongly toward him as I do toward Marcus. And, well, he doesn't seem as interested in Natalie as Marcus is."

Alyssa was silent for a moment. "Look, you can't blow him off because he's hesitant around Natalie. I don't think he has any experience with babies, so you need to cut him some slack there." She paused. "You just need to focus on who makes you happy."

I nodded. "I know." Then in a near whisper. "I know."

"And, Lily?"

"Yeah?"

"Just be careful. I don't want to see you getting hurt. You've been through enough."

I could hear the sincerity in her voice. "I will."

We said our good-byes and I set the phone down. Greta pressed her nose into my hand and I scratched her head. "What do you think, girl? Who do you like better?" I watched her face, but she had no answers for me.

I rested my head against the back of the couch and stared at the ceiling, thinking about the two men in my life. But was Marcus really "in my life"? He was a friend, there was no doubt of that, but when I'd told him how I felt, he'd shot me down. And now he was dating Chelsea.

If being more than friends with Marcus wasn't a possibility, what would I do? Trying to be honest with myself, I considered the options. I could allow the relationship with Cameron to develop and see where it led. Or, I could end it with Cameron and just allow myself to be happy with my role of friend in Marcus's life.

But would I be happy in that role? I shook my head. No, I would definitely want more. Especially if he was the only man in my life. So, I thought, my stomach churning, if he has no interest beyond friendship, maybe it's time to start backing away from him. How else can I protect myself from being hurt? The more time I spend with him, the more I love him, and the more I open my heart up to being hurt.

Yes, I thought. I need to erect barriers between Marcus and my heart.

The next evening after I put Natalie to bed, I heard a knock on my door. I looked through the peephole and saw Marcus standing on the porch. At first I smiled at the unexpected visit, but my smile quickly turned into a frown as I remembered my decision the night before. Putting a friendly smile on my face, I opened the door.

"Hey, Lily," he said, his face open and sincere. "How are you?"

"Good."

He motioned toward his parent's house next door. "I just had dinner with my parents and thought I'd stop by to see how your house hunt is going."

I felt silly just talking to him at the door. "Do you want to come in?"

"Sure."

He followed me into the living room and we sat on opposite ends of the couch.

"Is Russell showing you many houses?"

"Yes. He took me to a number of places yesterday." I left off the fact that Cameron had come along.

"Great. Did you find anything that looks promising?"

"Not yet."

"Well, I'm sure there's something out there that will be perfect for you and Natalie." He paused. "When are you going to look again?"

"Russell said he'd line some places up for tomorrow afternoon."

"Perhaps I could come along. You know, give a second opinion."

I hesitated, but felt my earlier resolve to create distance between us slipping.

Obviously noticing my hesitation, he said, "But if you'd prefer to go on your own, I understand."

Quickly shaking my head, I said, "No. I'd like it if you came along."

He tilted his head to one side. "Are you sure?"

Feeling slightly ridiculous now for even considering putting distance between us, I nodded. "Yes." Then my eyebrows drew together. "But what about work?"

"I've been putting in a lot of late nights. I'm sure I can leave a little early for a change."

Renewed excitement about my search flooded me, and I smiled. "Great."

Chapter Twenty-Three

The next afternoon Marcus arrived at my house right on time and I opened the door. "I just need to get Natalie and we can go."

"Let me help," he said.

"Thanks."

I watched as he walked into the living room, where Natalie was playing on a blanket on the floor. He scooped her up and held her in front of him, then gently rocked her in the air, sending her into a fit of giggles.

My heart swelled with love for him as I watched him interact with my daughter. *Why can't Cameron be so natural with her?* Frowning at myself for comparing the two men, I pushed thoughts of Cameron aside and decided to just enjoy being with Marcus, even though I was certain I would feel sad later.

He turned toward me. "Ready?"

"Yes."

We walked out to my car together and he fastened Natalie into her car seat.

"I hope Russell has some good places to show me today. I've only been looking for a few days and already I'm stressed."

He turned to me and smiled. "You'll find the right place for the two of you."

I gazed into his incredible green eyes and forced myself to focus on what he was saying. "I know. I'd just like it if it happened today."

He nodded. "Hey, do you want me to drive? Then you can focus on looking at the neighborhoods we drive through."

"Great idea." I handed him my keys, then began walking to the passenger door.

"Hold on a sec, Lily." He walked past me and opened the passenger door, holding it for me while I got in.

He closed it once I was in my seat, and I watched him through the windshield as he walked back to the driver's side and climbed in. *Why does he have to be so wonderful?*

He glanced at me, a smile on his face, then put the key in the ignition and started the car. I was silent as we drove to the first house, my thoughts in a jumble. One part of me thought about the house hunt and what I would see that day. Another part of me couldn't stop thinking about Marcus and how much I loved having him sitting so close to me. I allowed myself to fantasize about us being a family, going on a drive—just me, my perfect husband, and our daughter.

"We're here," Marcus said as we pulled up to a house.

I felt my face flush, as if he knew what I'd been thinking, but I looked toward the house, my face averted from him, so he couldn't see my embarrassment.

"It has good curb appeal," he said as he turned off the car.

I nodded.

"There's Russell," he said.

I saw Russell's car pull into the driveway and I reached for the door handle.

"Let me get that, Lily," Marcus said.

I turned to him, a smile on my face. "I appreciate you being such a gentleman, but we're going to be getting in and out of the car quite a bit today. Maybe you should let me do this myself?"

He grinned. "Yeah, I suppose that makes sense." He paused. "I'll get Natalie out."

"Thanks." I climbed out of the car and watched him gently extricate Natalie from the straps of her car seat, then hold her against his shoulder. For a moment I envied the closeness to Marcus that my daughter enjoyed.

"Hey there, Marcus," Russell said as he walked toward us. "What a nice surprise to see you."

They shook hands, then Russell turned to me and started giving me the stats on the house. We all walked into the house and looked through the rooms.

"What do you think, Lily?" Russell asked when we'd gone back out front.

"It's okay. It looks like it's in good shape, but it's a little small." I glanced at Marcus before looking back at Russell. "I know it's just Natalie and me, but whatever I end up buying, I plan on staying in for a long time. And I hope to expand my family one day."

"Sure," Russell said. "I understand. I have another place I want to show you that I'd like you to consider."

"Okay."

He gave us the address and we all climbed into the cars and drove to the house. As we pulled up, I immediately noticed that the front yard needed some work, but the house looked larger than the last place. We got out of the car and Russell met us on the driveway.

"Now, you need to keep an open mind," he said to me.

I didn't like the sound of that. He told me how much the seller was asking and it sounded like a good deal for the amount of square footage. "What's the catch?" I asked.

He smiled. "It needs a little work."

I groaned. "I told you I can't afford to hire anyone to fix a place up."

"Let's go inside and have a look around, okay?"

"Well, I'm here, so I might as well." I glanced at Marcus, who was holding Natalie, but he didn't say anything. A moment later we all walked into the house. A small entry opened up into a comfortable family room. Stains dotted the carpet, but I knew that could be changed out. A wood-burning fireplace was nestled in the corner, and a large sliding glass door led out to the backyard.

Russell slid open the door, and we walked out onto a large, covered concrete patio. My gaze went from side to side, taking in the large, weedy yard.

"It definitely needs some work, but it's a good size," I said. "Lots of room for Greta to run around." We went back inside and into the eat-in kitchen. "There's plenty of cupboards and counter space." I looked at the floor. "The vinyl floor looks a little beat up, so I'd want to put in tile, but it's workable." I turned to Russell, a feeling of home washing over me. "I'm glad you brought me here."

He smiled, clearly pleased with himself. "I thought you might like it." He pointed back to the entry. "There's a good-size living room off of the entry."

We walked back to the entry and into the living room. Again, the carpet needed to be replaced, but the room was spacious, with a picture window looking out over the front yard. "I like it." My gaze took in the walls. "I'd want to paint, but I can do that." I glanced at Marcus and smiled. He smiled back as if he could sense my excitement. My gaze went to Natalie, held securely in his arms, and I felt an overwhelming sense of peace. Not sure what that meant, I tucked it away for later evaluation, and followed Russell to the hallway, which led to the bedrooms.

"There are three bedrooms, including the master, but they're all a pretty good size," he said. "Plus there are two full bathrooms, and one of them is part of the master."

I looked into the two guest rooms and smiled. "Decent closet space." I peeked into the first bathroom. "Needs some updating, but it's okay." Next we went into the master, and my gaze went around the room. "There's plenty of space in here, though it needs a coat of paint, and the carpet is gross." Then I went into the master bath. "It's not too big, but it will work. And again, I'd want to update it."

I turned to face Russell and Marcus. "I like it. I'm not quite sure how I'll manage all the work that needs to be done, but it feels like home." I thought about Cameron's statement that he wasn't handy at all, and wondered who I could hire to do the work—and how much it would cost. It didn't matter, this place felt right.

"Are you ready to make an offer?" Russell asked.

Fresh excitement swept over me as I realized I was about to buy my first house. I glanced at Marcus, who had been silent the whole time. "What do you think?"

"I think you like this place," he said, smiling.

My smile widened. "Yes, I do."

"Then you should go for it."

I looked around the space and felt my smile falter a bit. "I have to admit, I'm a little worried about the work that needs to be done."

He adjusted Natalie in his arms. "What is it that's worrying you?"

I bit my lip. "I'm just a bit overwhelmed about where to find people to do the work. I've never hired anyone to do this kind of thing before." I paused. "And I'm a little worried about the cost. Buying the house will take almost all of my budget. I won't have much left over to hire someone."

He shook his head, his face relaxed. "Don't sweat it, Lily. I'll help you."

I wasn't sure what he meant, but felt confident that he would come through for me. I nodded, then turned to Russell, my earlier excitement returning. "Let's do it."

We went into the kitchen and he drew up the paperwork for the offer.

"I'll submit the offer and let you know as soon as I hear anything," he said.

Relief that I'd found a place for me and Natalie flooded me, and I grinned. "Great."

A few minutes later Marcus, Natalie, and I were back in my car.

"It's a good area," Marcus said as he drove out of the neighborhood.

"Yes, I think so too." My gaze examined the houses and yards near the house I wanted to buy, and I felt confident that this would be a safe place to live. I turned to Marcus. "Thanks for coming."

He smiled. "I don't think I did much to help."

I laughed, then said in a soft voice, "It was just nice having you there."

He looked at me and his smile faltered a bit, then he looked back at the road without speaking.

My brow creased. I was confused by his reaction. Did he regret coming? Was he afraid I might think he wanted more than friendship? Of course I did, desperately, but I knew it was out of my hands. I looked out the passenger window, my excitement about buying my house tempered by my sorrow over Marcus.

A short time later we pulled into my driveway. I climbed out of the car before Marcus had a chance to open the door for me, then walked around to Natalie's side, where Marcus was unbuckling her car seat. He kissed her cheek, then handed her to me.

My heart flip-flopped to see him treat her like he would surely treat his own daughter, and my sorrow that he would only be a friend intensified. I held her to me, and breathed in her baby scent, comforting myself that she would always be my daughter. "Thanks again, Marcus."

"No problem. Let me know when you hear back from Russell."

"I will." I hesitated. "Do you want to come in?"

He shook his head. "No, I've got some things I need to do."

I nodded. *Chelsea. Of course.* "Okay."

"See you later, Lily."

He drove off a moment later and I carried Natalie into the house.

Two days later I heard back from Russell. The seller had accepted my offer and my terms to close within two weeks. Ecstatic, I picked Natalie up from her swing and danced around the room.

"I'm buying a house," I cried out. "I'm buying a house."

Greta barked in alarm, but I just laughed. Natalie had no idea what was going on, but she must have sensed my joy because she giggled as we spun around the room. Finally I sat on the couch and held Natalie on my lap. "What color do you want your room, baby girl?" I kissed her soft cheek and held her close.

Then I thought about the projects I would need to do and mentally listed them: replace all the carpet, replace the kitchen floor with tile, update both bathrooms, paint all the rooms, fix up the front and back yards. As the list grew in my mind, I began to feel overwhelmed and my exhilaration dimmed.

"How am I going to do all this?" I said out loud. But then I remembered Marcus's statement that he would help me. I pictured the earnestness in his face and knew I could count on him. But then I thought about Cameron. How would he feel if he knew I was spending time with another man? Should I tell him? Afraid of his reaction and that he might walk away, I decided to say nothing for now. After all, there was nothing to tell regarding Marcus.

But I had promised Marcus that I'd tell him once I'd heard back from Russell. I called his cell phone and he answered right away.

"I got the house," I said in response to his greeting.

"That's great, Lily. Congratulations." He paused. "We need to celebrate. I'm taking you out to dinner tonight."

I grinned. "Okay." I had to admit, I was a little surprised he'd been so spontaneous in his offer. Wouldn't he want to check with Chelsea first? Not my concern, I reminded myself.

That evening at dinner, Marcus was as sweet as ever with Natalie, and it suddenly occurred to me that maybe it was really her that drew him to me. Did that mean if I didn't have her, he would no longer want to spend time with me? How ironic, I thought. Cameron's interest in Natalie was minimal—he just seemed to be interested in me. But Marcus seemed to be the opposite. Why couldn't I find someone who had both of those qualities rolled up into one?

Pushing aside my silly thoughts, I focused on enjoying my time with Marcus, regardless of why he chose to be with me.

"I'm glad the seller agreed to close on the sale in two weeks," I said as I sprinkled salt onto my steamed vegetables.

Marcus nodded as he swallowed his steak. "Do you want to get started on your projects as soon as you close?"

"I haven't even looked for carpet yet, but I guess I should paint the rooms before I have it installed." I took a bite of the steamed broccoli.

"What about the tile work in the kitchen and bathrooms?"

"You said you'd help me find someone to do it."

He smiled. "No. I said I'd help you *do* it."

"Wait. You mean do the work myself?" I felt panic edging in. "I don't know the first thing about that."

His smile grew. "That's why I'll be there to help."

My mind immediately went to the day he'd helped me put in Greta's dog door. He'd pretty much ended up doing the whole thing himself. But what I most vividly recalled was the way he'd knelt behind me when he was trying to show me how to use his power tools. A rush of warmth cascaded over me at the memory.

How would it be if we worked together again? I didn't know if I could handle it when I knew it wouldn't lead anywhere. But what other choice did I have? I didn't feel comfortable spending a lot of money hiring people, and Cameron had made it clear he wasn't the handy type.

I nodded, resigned to the idea. "Okay. Thanks."

"On Saturday I can go with you to look at tile," he said.

"Shouldn't we wait until I close on the house?"

"You don't have to buy the tile yet, but I think you should know what you want to get, and then once you close on the house, we'll just need to buy it. Then we can get started right away."

I smiled, starting to see the possibilities. "Maybe we can get it done before Natalie and I move in."

"Exactly."

"Thanks, Marcus. I really appreciate all you do for us." And I did. Whether he was just doing it for Natalie's sake or not, he made my life a little easier.

He gazed at me, his green eyes bright. "Like I've told you, Lily. I'd do anything for you."

As I stared back, I felt something pass between us, and for a moment hope flared in my heart, but then I thought about his statement only weeks before that we could only be friends, and my hopes plummeted back to earth.

I nodded, a tiny smile on my lips, but I couldn't speak as it seemed my throat had swollen with unshed tears.

Chapter Twenty-Four

Late the next afternoon I put Natalie in her stroller and wheeled her outside for a walk. Greta was on a leash and the three of us walked down the street past Trish and Jeff's house. As I passed, I noticed an unfamiliar car in their driveway. We walked for half an hour, in which time Natalie fell asleep, before turning around and heading toward home.

As I approached Marcus's parent's house, I saw Trish standing in the driveway talking to a woman with blonde hair.

"Lily," Trish called out, then waved me over.

Holding tightly to Greta's leash, I pushed Natalie's stroller up Trish's driveway.

Trish went to Greta and scratched her ears. "Hello, Greta," she murmured.

I smiled to see that they really had become old friends. "She really likes you, Trish."

Trish stood. "She's a good dog."

"I completely agree."

"Lily," Trish said, motioning to the woman standing next to her. "I'd like you to meet Chelsea."

I felt my eyes widen, but I quickly gathered myself and put a smile on my face. "Hello," I said, examining the woman closely. I thought she must be several years older than me, and dressed in her slacks and flattering blouse, I had to admit that she looked lovely. Her blonde hair was cut in a stylish way, and her smile was genuine—making me wonder if Marcus had told her much about me.

"We were just talking about the surprise birthday dinner party we're having for Marcus on Saturday night," Chelsea said.

"Yes," Trish added. "And I wanted to invite you and Natalie."

"Oh." Caught off guard not only by the invitation, but also by finally meeting Chelsea, I scrambled to think of a reason to refuse. As much as I liked to spend time with Marcus, the thought of seeing him with Chelsea made my stomach churn, and I knew I would only be torturing myself if I subjected myself to an evening of witnessing their love for each other. "I'm sorry, but I won't be able to make it," I finally said, still having no legitimate excuse.

"Oh," Trish said. "That's too bad."

I'd been so focused on my house hunt, that I'd forgotten Marcus's birthday was coming up. It wasn't actually until Monday, but I hadn't even thought of what to get him. Greta tugged against the leash. "I'd better get these guys home."

"It was nice meeting you," Chelsea said.

"You, too." I wheeled the stroller around and walked back toward the street and to my house. Once safely inside, I carried Natalie up the stairs and put her down in her crib, then I went into my room and collapsed on my bed.

Now that I knew what Chelsea looked like, it was impossible to keep the image of her with Marcus out of my mind. Mini-films of them huddled together at work, dancing late at night, gazing at each other and kissing, paraded through my mind. I couldn't seem to control the visuals as they stubbornly marched into my head and refused to leave.

I squeezed my eyes closed and felt tears flow down my cheeks. Angrily, I wiped at my face. Why was I even getting upset? Trish had told me weeks ago that Marcus was interested in Chelsea. Deep-down, had I doubted her? Well, there was no doubt now. I'd seen her face to face. At Trish's house, no less. Planning a surprise party for Marcus.

After a short while I was able to get my emotions under control, and just then, my phone rang. I picked it up and looked at the caller ID. Cameron. *At least I have him*, I thought, feeling sorry for myself. "Hello?"

"Hey, Lily. How's the house hunt going?"

"Cameron, it's so good to hear from you." I felt my mood lifting to know there was a man who cared about me. True, he would never be Marcus, but he was a good person. "It's going great, actually. I found a place and the seller accepted my offer."

"That's fantastic." The enthusiasm in his voice was unmistakable. "Do you know when you'll be moving in?"

I laughed. "Why? Are you available to help me move?"

"Somehow I always seem to get pulled into people's moving dramas. So, yeah. I'll make sure I'm available."

"I don't have a specific date yet, but before I move in I need to do some work on the place."

"Oh yeah? So you decided to go for a fixer?"

"The place was perfect, and it felt like home. It just needs some paint and some updating."

He was quiet for a moment. "You know I'd like to help you, but I wasn't kidding when I said I'm no handyman."

I laughed. "It's okay. I have it covered."

"Are you sure?"

"Yes." But now when I thought of spending time with Marcus, I felt sick inside. All hope seemed to be gone. Clearly, he was with Chelsea now. I couldn't blame him—he'd told me we were only going to be friends. It was only in my mind that I'd held on to a slim tether of possibility.

Now Cameron laughed. "Good. Off the hook."

With some difficulty, I focused back on Cameron. "Yes."

"Do you still want to get together on Saturday?"

Several thoughts raced through my mind. I already had plans to shop with Marcus, but could I go through with it? If I cancelled, he'd surely ask why. What could I tell him? And eventually I would need his help to shop for tile. No, I would push myself to go, as painful as it would be.

But what about Saturday night? Marcus would be at his party with Chelsea and I would be sitting home alone. Unless I invited Cameron over. I could make dinner and we could spend time with Natalie. Now that all possibility with Marcus had ended, I needed to work on my relationship with Cameron, give him some time to get to know Natalie better.

"Yes," I finally said. "I'll be busy for part of the day, but why don't you come over in the late afternoon? I can make us dinner."

"Great. I'd love that."

I smiled when I heard his eagerness, and once again I felt drawn to him, his undisguised desire to spend time with me wrapping around me like a soft blanket. It was exactly what I needed just then, and I felt my heart swelling with affection for the man I'd had so much fun with on my Alaskan cruise. "I'll see you on Saturday."

"Yes. Take care of yourself, Lily." He paused. "And that cute baby of yours, too."

Thrilled that he mentioned Natalie, my smile widened. "I will. Bye, Cameron."

I set my phone down and stared at the ceiling, amazed by how my emotions could rocket from one extreme to another in such a short period of time.

Saturday morning dawned sunny and bright. It was Labor Day weekend, and the morning was cooler than it had been lately. As I waited for Marcus to arrive, my mind bounced between thinking of him with Chelsea, and thinking about my date with Cameron that night. My emotions ran the gamut too, making me anxious. Natalie must have felt my unsettled mood, because she was fussier than usual that morning.

"It's okay, baby girl," I soothed as I held her in my arms. "Everything will be okay."

I had no idea if I was telling her the truth, but I hoped speaking the words out loud would convince myself as much as comfort her.

When Marcus knocked, Greta raced to the door, all wagging tail and lolling tongue. I laughed at her excitement, which helped to settle my mood a bit. I swung the door open and invited him in. I'd put Natalie in her swing, hoping that would calm her, and she had quieted.

"Good morning," Marcus said, a smile on his face.

"Hey."

"Are you ready for some tile shopping?" He was obviously in a great mood.

I wondered what his mood would be like that evening when Chelsea and his mom surprised him with a party. "I suppose." His positive attitude was contagious and I found my spirits lifting. "Do you have some places in mind where we can shop?"

"Of course."

"Great. Let me just get Natalie, and we can go."

A short time later we were loaded into my car. I suggested Marcus drive since he knew where we were going.

"Do you have any idea what you want?" he asked, glancing at me.

I gazed at him, and unbidden came the thought, *I want you to love me*. My face heated and I turned away, looking out the window.

"Lily?" he asked.

I took a quick breath, then turned back, a faint smile on my face. "No."

"Well, that's no problem. I'm sure you'll get a better idea once you see what they have."

I nodded, staring at his profile as he drove. I wanted to reach out and stroke his face, and imagined doing it, then him turning to me with love in his eyes, and confessing that he's loved me all along.

"What?" he asked, glancing at me with a smile, apparently feeling my eyes on him.

"Nothing." Embarrassed at being caught staring, I said, "Just wondering how much experience you really have with installing tile."

"Oh, I see," he laughed. "You're worried I'm going to mess it up."

"Exactly. I mean, you come pretty cheap. And you haven't even given me any references." He looked at me and I narrowed my eyes. "How do I know I can even trust you?"

"You caught me. Now you know I'm only in it for the money."

I laughed. "Yeah, because I pay so well."

"I've helped my dad with some tiling projects over the years, so I've done it before."

"Good, because I have no clue what to do."

"Here we are," he said as he pulled into a parking space in front of a large building. He got out of the car and opened my door for me.

I climbed out and stood next to him.

"They have so much to choose from," he said. "I know you'll find something you like."

I nodded. "Okay."

He must have sensed my uncertainty. "Don't worry, Lily. I'll be there every step of the way."

I flashed back to the day Natalie was born, and how he'd been in the delivery room. He'd truly been there for me at one of the most important events of my life. How could I give up on a future with him so easily? But then, how could I *make* him love me as more than a friend? If he didn't feel that way about me, if he didn't feel that spark, then I didn't know how I could change that.

Resigned to loving him from afar, my shoulders slumped and I sighed.

"Hey," he said, slipping one arm around my shoulder and pulling me against his side. "It really will be fine."

I melted into him, desperately wanting to throw my arms around his neck and have him hold me close, but I knew I couldn't take the rejection right now. Not when my emotions felt so fragile. He released me, leaving me feeling bereft, and walked around to Natalie's door. I followed him and waited while he took her out of her car seat, then watched as he held her in his arms.

"Do you want me to take her?" I asked.

"No. I don't get to see her very often, so I want to hold her while I can." He laughed. "Before you know it, she'll be so active that she won't want anyone to hold her. I have to take advantage of her willingness to be held while it lasts."

My love for him surged, and I couldn't imagine anyone else being a father to her. Tears filled my eyes and I blinked to clear them.

He didn't seem to notice my emotion and turned to go into the tile store. I followed him and a moment later we stood in front of a wall of tile displays. Pushing aside my thoughts of a father for Natalie, I focused on the task at hand. As I perused the choices, I felt my anticipation for the project building. *I was buying a house.* "There are so many," I said. "And I like a lot of them."

"Good. Just try to picture how they would look in your kitchen."

I turned to him and grinned. "*My* kitchen."

He returned my smile. "That's right."

We walked up and down the display aisles. "I like this glass tile." I pointed to a sheet of blue and gray squares. "Can I use them for a backsplash in the kitchen?"

"You can do whatever you want. It's *your* kitchen."

I laughed. "Maybe I should rephrase that. Will *you* put these in the kitchen as a backsplash?"

His eyebrows rose. "I'll show you how to do it."

As I gazed at the tile, I felt my confidence growing. "We don't have to use any power tools, do we?" I turned to him and smiled.

He must have remembered installing the dog door, because he smirked. "No. I won't make you use the power tools."

My smile dimmed. "So there are some involved with this project?"

"We'll need to use a tile saw sometimes."

"Oh." My confidence in truly doing this on my own plummeted.

He laughed. "Don't worry about it. I'm not going to leave you on your own."

Relief swept over me because I knew he would never do that. "You rock, Marcus. Do you know that?"

He grinned. "Yes, as a matter of fact, I do."

I gently shoved the arm that wasn't holding Natalie. "Now, don't get a big head or anything."

He laughed. "Never."

We spent the next hour picking out tile and the other supplies we would need, then we went to another store and I found carpet and paint that I liked. By the time we finished, I felt much better about the project and much less overwhelmed.

"I think Natalie's getting tired," I said as we walked out to the car. Her head rested against Marcus's shoulder and her eyelids drooped.

"What about you?"

"I have to admit, I'm kind of worn-out after all this decision making."

He nodded. "Not to scare you, but picking stuff out is the easy part."

I grimaced. "I don't think I want to know that."

He laughed. "You'd find out soon enough."

We drove to my house and he carried Natalie in, then brought her up to her room. I watched him settle her in her crib—she'd fallen asleep on the drive home—and my heart swelled with feelings of tenderness for the man standing in my daughter's room.

We tiptoed out of her room and went into the living room. I still needed to plan the meal I was making for Cameron, but I wasn't eager for Marcus to leave. In fact, I wished it was *him* who I would be cooking for that evening. As much as I liked and was attracted to Cameron, he just wasn't Marcus.

"Well, I'd better get going," he said. "I have some things to get done before tonight. My parents invited me over for dinner later, so I just have a few hours."

I noticed he said his parents had invited him for dinner and he hadn't mentioned Chelsea. In fact, when I thought about it, I'd never heard him utter her name. Was that to spare my feelings? "I hope our errands didn't keep you from getting your other things done."

"No, it's fine." His eyes softened. "I enjoyed spending time with you and Natalie today."

Me and Natalie, I thought. Not just me. "Me, too," I said, pushing down my disappointment.

"Once you close, we'll have lots of work ahead of us." He grinned. "But I promise, once we're done, you'll be really glad you did all that work."

"I hope you're right."

He reached for the door knob. "Trust me."

"I do," I said, mentally adding, *Completely*.

He smiled, then left. I stood in the doorway and watched him climb into his car, then waved as he backed out of the driveway. An image of Chelsea filled my mind, and I wondered if he would be spending the rest of the day with her. Frowning, I closed the door, then sat on the couch, trying to change my focus to Cameron and the time I would spend with him.

It's true that I didn't feel toward him like I did with Marcus, but at least Cameron had a romantic interest in me. I just had to allow myself to let my feelings for him grow, and then everything would be perfect.

Chapter Twenty-Five

Late that afternoon Cameron knocked on my door. Before answering his knock, I took a deep breath, and slowly released it. I could do this. I could push aside thoughts of Marcus and focus on my budding relationship with Cameron.

I turned the knob and pulled the door open. "Hey, there," I said, a bright smile on my face.

"Hey, gorgeous." He held a bouquet of flowers.

His thoughtfulness, added to his words, warmed my heart, and I felt drawn to him. Impulsively, I threw my arms around him. His free arm wrapped around my waist and I felt his strength as his arm tightened protectively around me.

"Thank you, Cameron," I murmured into his shoulder. "You're so sweet." Though tempted to kiss him, I restrained myself, wanting to see how things went before going there. I loosened my arms, and he released me.

"These are for you." He held out the flowers.

I took them and breathed in their scent. "Thank you. They're so pretty."

"For a pretty lady," he said, smiling.

My voice softened. "Thank you." Backing up, I said, "Come in."

He followed me into the kitchen, where I put the flowers in a vase, then filled it with water from the sink faucet. "I'm glad you came down," I said, setting the vase on the table.

"Can I just say I'm glad we don't have to look at houses?"

I laughed. "It wasn't that bad, was it?"

"It's just not my favorite thing to do."

"Oh yeah? What do you like to do?"

"Hmmm. I like to go on whale-watching expeditions with beautiful women."

I laughed. "What else?"

He walked over to me and put his hands on my shoulders, and dropped his voice. "I like when you kiss me."

A thrill raced through me, and without thinking, I slid my arms around his waist and pressed my cheek to his chest. His arms tightened around me and I reveled in his closeness. Yes, he wasn't Marcus, but the strength of his affection, and the warmth from his body drew me to him like metal to a magnet, powerfully and irresistibly.

"I like hugs too," he murmured in my hair.

I tilted my face to his, my smile wide and inviting, and he closed his eyes as his mouth descended toward mine. Our lips met and desire tore through me. His arms tightened around me, snugging me close, and our mouths pressed together hungrily.

As we kissed, an image of Marcus passionately kissing Chelsea filled my mind, and jealousy lanced through me. Distracted by thoughts of Marcus, my ardor toward Cameron cooled, and I gently pushed him away. His eyes were filled with desire, but I couldn't bring myself to kiss him when my mind stubbornly refused to dislodge Marcus from my thoughts.

"I need to check on Natalie," I said lamely as I turned and walked out of the kitchen and toward the stairs. She'd been asleep for a while, so it wasn't unreasonable for me to want to look in on her, but I knew that was just an excuse to put some space between myself and Cameron so I could think for a minute.

Shaking my head as I trudged up the stairs, I felt frustration at myself. I needed to make a choice, and soon. It wasn't fair to Cameron to encourage him when my heart was with another man—even if that man would never be mine.

I walked into Natalie's room and saw her lying on her back, her fingers curled around her toes, babbling to herself. I smiled, my heart swelling with unconditional love for my daughter, and leaned over her crib. "You're awake, baby girl."

Her eyes went to my face and she smiled, filling me with joy. I reached toward her and she held out her arms, and I scooped her up and held her close. "At least I know you'll always be my sweet Natalie," I murmured in her ear.

She giggled as my breath tickled her ear and I laughed with her. After changing her diaper, I carried her downstairs and into the kitchen, where Cameron stood next to the counter. He smiled at me, but I could tell he felt a little neglected.

"Sorry. I heard her waking up." That wasn't true, and I think he knew it, but he didn't comment. I set her in her high chair and went to the cupboard to get a jar of baby food. After opening the lid, I held it out to Cameron. "Do you want to feed her?"

His eyes widened. "Uh. I guess?"

I smiled, pleased that he was making an effort. He took the jar and spoon from me, then sat in the chair across from Natalie.

"Just put a little bit on the spoon," I said.

He glanced at me and nodded, then scooped out a small amount of pureed carrots. He moved the spoon toward her lips, and she opened her mouth and accepted the food. He looked up at me and laughed. "I guess she knows what to do."

I nodded. "Yes. She's a good eater."

He gave her another bite and quickly seemed to get the hang of it. "This is actually pretty easy."

Just then, Natalie pressed her lips together and the last mouthful oozed out onto her chin.

"You spoke too soon," I said, trying to hold back a laugh.

He stared at her, obviously not sure what to do. I took the spoon from his hand and expertly cleaned off her face, and she opened her mouth to accept the food I placed in her mouth.

"You're really good at this," he said, obviously impressed.

"I've had some practice." She spit out the next bite and I set the nearly empty jar on the counter. "I think she's had enough of the carrots." I wiped her face, then lifted her from the high chair and held her out to Cameron. "Can you hold her while I fix a bottle?"

"Uh, okay." He took her with some reluctance, and she stared at him as she sat on his lap.

I smiled to myself as I went into the kitchen to fix a bottle of formula. My breast milk hadn't been filling Natalie, so I'd resorted to giving her supplemental formula. It only took a moment to have her bottle ready, and I handed it to Cameron to see what he'd do.

He looked at me with one eyebrow raised.

I nodded. I was delighted to see how he managed to hold Natalie in the crook of one arm and put the bottle in her mouth with his free hand. Natalie wrapped her tiny hands around the bottle and happily drank her formula.

"I guess she likes this," Cameron said, obviously proud of his success.

"Yes, she does."

He held her until she'd finished the bottle, then he looked uncertain about what to do next.

"I'll take her," I offered, and he handed her over. I smiled at him, happy he'd been willing to feed her, but I wondered how he really felt about it. Had he just been trying to please me, or had he enjoyed the process? "Do you want to go outside?" I asked.

"Sure. It's nice today."

I walked toward the back door and pulled out the plastic barrier from the dog door that had kept Greta from coming in. She burst through the opening and went directly to Cameron, thoroughly sniffing him. To Cameron's credit, he scratched her head and stroked her body, winning him points with both Greta and me.

"She seems to like you," I said.

"She's a pretty dog," he said, gazing at Greta's face.

"I think so too. And she's very sweet with Natalie." I opened the door to the backyard and Cameron walked outside with me, then I closed the door. Greta came through her door a moment later.

Cameron gazed out over the yard. "It's nice out here." He looked at me. "What's the backyard like at your new place?"

I frowned. "It needs some work." I paused. "It has potential though."

"It's worth it then, don't you think?"

I nodded. "I hope so. Hey, do you want something to drink? I made lemonade earlier."

"Sure," he said.

I grinned. "Will you hold Natalie for a second?"

He took her from me and seemed like he was getting more comfortable with her.

I went into the house and fixed two glasses of lemonade, then carried them outside and set them on the small table I'd recently gotten. "Here you go."

"Thanks." He held Natalie out to me and I took her and held her on my lap.

We chatted for a while and I really enjoyed his company.

As the evening wore on, I couldn't help but think about the party that was taking place next door. Had Marcus been surprised? Had he noticed that I wasn't there? Did he care? Forcing thoughts of Marcus out of my head, I smiled at Cameron. "I think I should put dinner in the oven. You must be starved by now."

"I could eat."

"Well, lucky for you, I made the casserole earlier, so I just need to heat it up. But I also want to make a salad." I stood to go inside.

"Do you need any help?" he asked, standing as well.

"No, but you can come talk to me."

He smiled. "Sure."

I put Natalie in her swing, and after dinner was ready, we carried the food outside and set it on the table. Natalie had fallen asleep in her swing, so I left her there while we ate. Greta stretched out on the grass, soaking up the last rays of the sun.

Half an hour later Greta leapt up from the grass and ran through the doggie door and into the house.

"What in the world?" I asked, surprised.

Cameron looked at me with a question on his face.

A moment later I heard my back door opening. Startled, I jerked my head to the door, and when I saw Marcus pushing it open, with Natalie in his arms, I nearly gasped. *What is he doing here?And why is he holding Natalie?*

Marcus's gaze went directly to Cameron and I knew he must have seen him through the window before opening the door. I watched several emotions work their way across his features before his gaze settled on me.

"Hi, Marcus," I said, standing. "What's going on?"

"I stopped by and no one answered the door, but I heard Natalie crying, so I came in." His gaze flicked to Cameron before coming back to me. "I didn't mean to interrupt. I just wanted to make sure everything was okay."

I reached for Natalie. "I didn't hear her crying." He handed her to me. We stood there for a moment in uncomfortable silence, then I motioned toward Cameron. "Marcus, this is Cameron. I met him on the cruise." I didn't know why I felt the need to point that out.

Marcus stepped toward Cameron and they shook hands. "Nice to meet you," Marcus said.

Cameron nodded, but seemed unsure what to do about the man who was obviously familiar with me and my child—comfortable enough to just walk in and pick her up.

"Well, I'll get back to my parents' house," Marcus said, focusing on me.

"Okay. See you later."

Marcus smiled at me and nodded, and left through the gate without acknowledging Cameron. I looked at Cameron with uncertainty, wondering what he must be thinking. He gazed back, confusion clear on his face.

I motioned vaguely toward the gate. "His parents live next door." As if that explained everything.

"Does he just stop by like that often?"

"Um, sometimes." I sat in the chair across from Cameron. "But I've always answered before."

Cameron was quiet, like he was trying to put together the pieces of a challenging puzzle. Finally, he nodded. "Dinner was delicious, Lily."

"Thanks."

He pushed his chair back and stood. "I'd better get going."

Alarmed that I would never see him again, I blurted, "Marcus is just a friend."

His lips compressed. "Sure."

Confused about why he doubted me, I kept my mouth closed. Had my reaction to Marcus's presence given away my true feelings? I thought I'd kept my expression neutral—besides the surprise I'd had that he'd walked in, of course.

Cameron walked toward the kitchen door. "Thanks for an enjoyable evening."

"Do you really have to go?"

He clenched his jaw. "Yeah. I do."

I felt any possibility of a future with him slipping away, but felt helpless to stop it, as helpless as I felt when it came to making Marcus fall in love with me. "Well, thanks for driving down."

He nodded and walked into the house. I followed him to the front door, but stopped on the threshold. He turned to me, a sad smile on his face. He paused, like he was going to say something, then shook his head and walked to his car.

I watched him drive off, then stood on the porch, stunned by how the evening had ended so abruptly. A breeze brushed across my face, and carried with it was the sound of people singing happy birthday at the house next door. I turned my face in that direction, but couldn't see anything, although once the song ended, I heard applause echoing in the night.

I turned and went into my house and closed and locked the door behind me as tears filled my eyes and trickled down my face. Feeling very alone, I carried Natalie into the kitchen where I fed her dinner, then I carried her upstairs and put her to bed. I went into the living room and sat on the couch, turning on my eReader so I could lose myself in a world of someone else's creation.

After a while I found myself drifting off, and when I heard a knock at my door, I startled awake. I looked through the peephole and saw Marcus standing on my porch. Puzzled about why he was there after what had happened earlier, I opened the door.

"Hey, Lily."

I thought he looked tired, although it was only about ten o'clock. "Hi."

"Is it okay if I come in?"

"Sure." I opened the door wider and he walked in. We stood in the entry and I gazed at him expectantly.

"I just wanted to apologize for barging in on you like that," he said.

I smiled tentatively. "It's okay."

He shook his head. "I saw a strange car out front, and I have to admit, I was worried about you."

I nodded, acknowledging to myself that I had very few visitors. In fact, Marcus was pretty much the only person who ever came by. "Why did you stop by in the first place?"

"Remember how I told you that my parents had invited me for dinner?"

"Yeah."

"Well, they had a little surprise party for me."

"Your birthday's Monday, right?"

He nodded.

"Well, that was nice of them to throw you a party."

He had a half-smile on his face. "I guess so. But I just wanted to get away for a few minutes, so I came over here." His brow creased. "I wonder why they didn't invite you to the party. My mom knows we're friends."

"Oh, well, uh, she did, but . . . I already had plans." That was a total and complete lie, but since he'd seen Cameron at my house, he had no reason to doubt me.

He nodded and laughed. "Yeah, and again, sorry about interrupting."

"It's okay, really."

He looked at the wall behind me, as if thinking, then his gaze came back to my face. "So you met this guy on that cruise?"

"Cameron, yes."

"He must be the one who sent you those flowers."

I nodded, uncertain where he was going with his questions.

He was quiet for a minute. "Okay. Well, I guess I'll see you later." He smiled, but it had a tinge of sadness in it. "That is, unless Cameron's going to help you with your house?"

I shook my head. "No."

His eyebrows went up.

"He's not very good at that kind of thing."

Marcus clenched his jaw as he looked at me. "Good thing you have me then."

"That's what friends are for, right?"

He gazed at me a moment, then nodded. "Right." Then he turned and left, leaving me more confused than ever.

Why had he seemed upset with me?

Chapter Twenty-Six

On the day I closed on my house, my joy was edged with sadness. I hadn't heard from Cameron since the night he'd come for dinner—the night Marcus had stopped by unexpectedly. I also hadn't spoken to Marcus since then. I'd wanted to wish him a happy birthday, but every time I'd picked up my phone to call him, the thought of our awkward conversation had stopped me. But now that I'd closed on my house, I would need to call him so we could move forward on our projects.

With the key in my pocket, I drove to my new house, and as I pulled into my driveway, a feeling of euphoria swept over me. This would be my home and I could live there as long as I wanted. I'd used enough of the money from the sale of my childhood home and Dad's life insurance policy to make my mortgage payments manageable, without completing depleting my funds, and felt confident I would be able to make my payments.

I carried Natalie to the porch, then slid my key into the lock. I swung the door open and entered the house, *my* house. I grimaced as I looked at the stains on the carpet, but when I visualized the new paint on the walls and the new carpet on the floor, my grimace turned to a wide grin. It would be gorgeous.

I walked through all the rooms, letting my imagination take over, picturing freshly painted walls, with my furniture arranged just so. Stopping in the room that would be Natalie's, I swung her around, making her giggle.

"What do you think, sweet girl? Do you like your new room?"

I imagined watching her grow up there—her first day of Kindergarten, having other little girls over to play, getting ready for her first date—and knew I had made the right choice in buying this place.

Carrying Natalie, I walked into the kitchen and let my gaze wander the room. I pictured the tile I'd picked out with Marcus and visualized it laid out on the floor and knew it would improve the look of the room.

"Guess I'll call Marcus," I said out loud. I looked at the stained carpet, but not wanting to place Natalie on it, I held her on my hip while I dug my phone out of my purse. The call went to voice mail and I left a message. "Hey, Marcus. It's Lily. The house is mine now, so give me a call when you have time." I paused, wondering what else to say, and wondering if he was still even willing to help me. Finally I said, "'K. Talk to you later."

I put the phone back in my purse and stared at the wall as I spoke. "If he doesn't want to help now, I don't know what I'll do." Sighing, I carried Natalie out to the car and drove home.

Alyssa called late that afternoon.

"What's up with you and Cameron?" she asked, after some chit chat.

"What do you mean?"

"Ty was talking to him last night and when Ty asked how things were with you two, Cameron brushed him off, like he didn't want to talk about it. So what's going on?"

I told her how we'd been having dinner when Marcus showed up, and then Cameron abruptly left.

"Who does this Marcus guy think he is, Lily?" She paused. "Maybe I shouldn't say this, but his behavior reminds me of Trevor."

"No," I immediately said. "He's nothing like Trevor. Nothing."

"But you said he just walked in to your house. That kind of scares me. You know, after all that happened with Trevor."

I opened my mouth to speak, but hesitated, considering her point of view. How would Trevor have reacted if he'd walked in on me having a date? He would have made a scene, I thought. And he would have made me pay somehow. No, Marcus isn't like that at all. In fact, his reaction was the exact opposite. When he saw Cameron, he just left, and besides stopping by to apologize—something Trevor never would have done—he hadn't contacted me at all. "No," I finally said. "Believe me, I would recognize Trevor-like behavior, and Marcus is nothing like him."

"Okay. If you say so. But if Marcus is just a friend, why do you think Cameron reacted like he did?"

I shrugged and shook my head. "I was wondering the same thing."

"You must have some idea, Lily."

I bit my lip, wondering if I should confess my true feelings for Marcus. "I have no idea," I finally said, not wanting her to feel sorry for me.

"Hmm. Well I hope you guys can work it out."

"Me, too." But deep inside, I didn't think we would, and after I ended the call with Alyssa I sat glumly on the couch, feeling sorry for myself. Greta must have sensed my despondency, because she pressed her nose against my leg, drawing my attention away from myself and onto her.

"You want to play?" I asked. "Natalie should sleep for a little longer, so this is a good time to throw the ball for you."

I went out back with Greta on my heels, and I threw the ball for her until I was worn out. The physical activity felt good, and I sat on the back porch and smiled as Greta stretched out in the shade of a tree. I hoped she would like her new yard. As I gazed out over this yard, I thought about all the good memories I had. Of course there were some bad ones too, all of them involving Trevor, but I pushed those aside, knowing I couldn't change the past, and instead focused on the memories that made me happy.

I especially liked thinking about the times Marcus had worked with me on self-defense moves. Smiling, I recalled the feel of his arms around me as he acted out attacking me from behind. Then I thought about the way he had helped me put the doggie door in—he'd knelt right behind me and held my hands as he'd shown me how to use his jigsaw—and felt my body heat with longing.

"Lily, are you back there?"

I nearly gasped in surprise, then turned toward the back gate at the sound of Marcus's voice. Greta raced toward the gate to see what was going on. "Yes," I called out, my heart pounding to have him appear right when I'd been thinking about him. "Come on back."

A moment later he walked through the gate, a smile on his face. "I got your message."

I returned his smile, thrilled to see him there—maybe he'd gotten over whatever had seemed to upset him that night. I stood as he approached the porch. "I was at my new house when I called you."

He nodded. "That must feel good to say."

My smile grew. "Yes. I'm really excited to move in."

"Do you still want to do all those projects?"

"Yes. In fact when I was there, I was trying to picture how everything would look when we're done, and I think it will look great."

"I think so too." We both sat down in the chairs next to the table. "When do you want to get started?"

"As soon as possible. But I need to at least get it in shape for me and

Natalie to be able to move in."

"What do you want to get done before you can move in?"

"I think if I can get the rooms painted and the carpet put in, that should be enough to make it livable."

He nodded. "Okay. Do you want help with painting?"

"If you have time, then I wouldn't mind some help."

He glanced away, then looked at me. "Maybe your boyfriend can at least help with that part."

I felt myself blush and I stared at my lap before meeting his gaze. "He's not my boyfriend." At least I didn't think he was. We'd spent a lot of time together on the cruise, and he'd come to see me twice since then, but we'd never established our relationship as boyfriend and girlfriend.

"Well, whatever he is, I don't want to intrude on something he might want to help with."

Should I admit that Cameron hadn't called since the night Marcus had unexpectedly stopped by? Why would he even care? "I'll check with him," I said, not wanting him to know that Cameron had evidently lost interest in me already.

He nodded and stood. "Okay. Well, let me know when you're ready for my help."

I smiled up at him, wondering how Chelsea felt about him offering to help me. "I will."

He left a moment later, and I went inside to check on Natalie. She was still sound asleep, so I made a list of the things I needed to buy so that I could get started on painting.

The next day, after spending some time doing maintenance on the websites I managed, I took Natalie to the hardware superstore where Marcus and I had gone before, and I arranged to have someone come out and measure for the carpet, and then bought the paint and other supplies I needed.

We drove directly to the house and I sat Natalie on the floor long enough to spread out a large sheet over the stained carpet, then I placed her on that while I did the prep work for painting. As I put painter's tape on the door frame, I thought about Marcus's suggestion that I ask Cameron if he wanted to help with the painting, but I couldn't bring myself to call him. He'd left so abruptly that night, I was afraid that if I called him he would just confirm what I suspected—he wasn't interested in seeing me anymore. Instead, I pretended like he was just too busy to call, and I worked on the painting myself.

By the time Natalie and I left, I'd done most of the prep work. I planned on coming back the next day to finish it up and begin the actual painting. The measurement guy was scheduled to stop by the next day as well.

When I pulled into the driveway at my house that evening, I was shocked to see Cameron sitting on the steps to the front porch. I parked the car and took Natalie out of her car seat, then walked up to the porch with a tentative smile on my face. "Hi, Cameron."

"Hey." He stood as I approached.

"How long have you been here?"

"Not too long. I tried to call you, but it went to voice mail."

"I was at my new place, prepping it for painting. I didn't hear my phone ring."

He looked sad as he nodded.

"Do you want to come in?"

"Sure."

I let us in and we sat on the couch, and I held Natalie on my lap. "So what brings you here?"

He let out a short sigh. "I just felt like we needed to talk, and I decided to risk driving here without calling first." He laughed. "Luckily, you came home."

I nodded, feeling tension building between us as to why he was there. "What's going on?" I finally asked.

He sighed again, then said, "I don't think I've made it a secret that

I'm interested in you, Lily."

I gazed at him, wondering where this was going, but stayed silent.

"And you made it clear from the start that you aren't sure how you feel," he said. "I appreciate your honesty, but I think I know now that there's no future for us."

My eyes widened as I felt any chance with Cameron slipping away. "What do you mean?"

He pressed his lips together for a moment. "When your . . . neighbor . . . stopped by that night, I could see in your face how you feel about him. And, well, I can't compete with that."

Blood rushed to my face to be called out on the feelings I'd thought I'd kept private. Was it so obvious how I felt? How pathetic was I? I didn't argue with Cameron, because deep down, I knew he was exactly right. Instead I chewed on my lip and waited to see what he would say next.

"We haven't known each other long," he said. "But in that time, I've really grown to care about you, Lily." He nodded and stood. "If you ever want to talk," he paused and smiled. "You have my number."

I stood as well, feeling terrible, like I'd led him on in a way. "I'm sorry, Cameron. Truly."

He reached out and stroked my face. "It's okay, Lily. I hope you find happiness." He smiled sadly. "You deserve it."

I pressed his hand against my face and smiled. "You really are a good man, Cameron."

He smiled without speaking, then pulled his hand away and left. I closed the door behind him and carried Natalie into the kitchen, feeling numb.

Now what? I thought. Marcus is involved with Chelsea—and even if he wasn't, he told me we can only be friends. And now the only man who had a romantic interest in me has told me can't compete with my feelings for Marcus.

I put Natalie in her high chair and went to the cupboard where I kept her jars of baby food. As I took out a jar, I noticed that my hand shook. I took a deep breath and released it slowly, then focused on feeding Natalie. After she was fed and happy, I decided it might help if I called Alyssa to talk things over. I had no one else—no one—to talk to, and I desperately needed another opinion.

I put Natalie in her swing, then dialed Alyssa's number.

"Hey, Lily," she said. "How's everything?"

At the warmth in her voice, I felt a lump form in my throat and it was painful to speak. "Not so good."

"What's wrong?"

I swallowed, trying to ease the feeling in my throat. "Cameron just left." I paused, trying to gather my emotions.

"Yeah?"

"He broke it off with me." My voice cracked as I spoke, and I realized I was more devastated than I had initially admitted to myself.

"What? Why'd he do that?"

I repeated what Cameron had told me.

Alyssa was silent for a moment. "Is what he said true? How do you really feel about this Marcus person?"

I smiled at the way she spoke about Marcus, because I knew she only cared about what was best for me. Then, in a quiet voice I said, "I love him."

She sighed. "I have to tell you, Lily. This feels a little bit like Justin all over again."

I thought about Justin, the good man who had liked me—who I'd met through Alyssa—and how I'd chosen Trevor over him. I knew now that that had been a mistake, but I didn't think this was like that. Marcus was nothing like Trevor, although Alyssa made me doubt myself and my judgement. "It's not."

"I sure hope you know what you're doing."

I had no clue what I was doing, and in fact it seemed my chances of finding someone to love had diminished. "Me, too," I said.

We hung up a short time later and I didn't feel any better about things than when I'd called her. In fact, my level of self-doubt had gone up. But it wasn't like I'd broken things off with Cameron. That was a decision he'd made. I couldn't force myself to feel toward him like I did toward Marcus, as much as I wished I could.

Instead, I would just have to live with the idea that the most I could expect from Marcus was friendship. I would have to be satisfied with that, and hope that I could even keep that once he and Chelsea became more serious.

Chapter Twenty-Seven

The next day Natalie and I went to our new house so I could paint. Even though it would have been nice to have help from Marcus, I was embarrassed to tell him that Cameron wouldn't be helping me. Besides, I'd painted before and knew it was something I could do on my own. Marcus would be helping me enough with the tiling and I didn't want to take advantage of his time.

I set out several toys for Natalie and put her in the middle of the living room on the sheet I'd laid out, hoping she would be happy. She was getting good at crawling, so I put the tray of paint on the kitchen counter so I could at least keep her from getting into it.

It didn't take long to cover one wall with paint, and I stood back and admired the improved look.

"What do you think, Natalie?" I said to her as she sat on the sheet, a toy in one hand. She blinked at me, and I smiled at her sweet face.

Taking advantage of her contentedness, I continued painting and before long I'd completed the first coat.

By the end of the day I'd painted the first coat in most of the rooms —it didn't hurt that Natalie had taken a long nap—and the carpet measurement guy had come by. Exhausted but happy, I brought Natalie home.

The next day Natalie was less cooperative, and though I was able to finish the first coat on all the rooms, I hadn't been able to start on the second. The carpet installation was scheduled for three days later, so I had to finish painting before then, and when Marcus called that night to see how things were going, I hesitated, not wanting to admit I was doing it all myself. "It's going okay," I said.

"Have you scheduled the carpet installation?"

"Yes."

"And when is that?"

I nearly gulped. "Uh, in three days."

"But you and your . . . friend . . . finished painting, right?"

"Not exactly," I murmured.

"Well, what do you have left?"

"I still have to do the second coat."

"On the whole house?"

I nodded, and with meekness, said, "Yes."

He was quiet for a minute. "You're doing this all yourself, aren't you?"

I was silent, embarrassed to have been caught.

"Lily?"

"Yes, okay? I'm doing it by myself."

"Why? I thought you were going to see if your friend could help."

I shook my head, not willing to explain. What was I supposed to say? *He decided not to see me anymore because it was obvious to him that I'm in love with you.* No, that was not going to happen. "He couldn't."

He sighed. "You were supposed to tell me. It's too much for you to do on your own." He paused. "And what about Natalie? What are you doing with her while you're doing all this work?"

Why did I feel like he was scolding me? "I'm a grown woman, you know. I don't have to answer to you or anyone else."

He was quiet and I immediately regretted my harsh tone.

"Look," he finally said. "I just want to help. I hate to see you struggling on your own if you don't have to." He paused. "But if you don't want my help, I respect that."

Oh no. Now what had I done? I desperately needed his help, but I'd offended him. I pushed down my pride. "I'm sorry, Marcus. I didn't mean to get so defensive. To tell you the truth, I really could use your help."

"Good. Tomorrow's Saturday, so I'll plan on spending it with you." He paused. "If that's okay. I don't want to intrude on any plans you may have."

What about Chelsea? I wanted to ask, but didn't want to utter her name. Maybe if Marcus spent more time with me and Natalie, he would forget about Chelsea. I pictured her face and knew that wasn't likely, but a girl could dream. "No, that would be great."

"Okay. After we finish painting, we can buy the tile and other supplies we need."

I nodded, my anxiety over not getting the painting done in time lifting. "Sounds great." And I liked the way he'd said "the supplies *we* need." Like this was *our* house.

"Okay. I'll see you first thing."

Marcus arrived early the next morning. Natalie had slept later than usual and when Marcus arrived, I was just fixing her some breakfast.

"Let me help with that," he said, taking the jar of pureed bananas from my hand.

I smiled, happy to hand it over so I could finish cleaning up the kitchen. As I wiped down the counters, I watched him feeding Natalie and felt my feelings of love for him grow even more, if that was possible. Now that Cameron was no longer in the picture, I'd given up on battling my feelings for Marcus.

Even though our future seemed to only hold friendship, it was too exhausting to deny the way I felt about him. I loved him, plain and simple. Even though he didn't feel the same, I couldn't stop myself from feeling the way I did. That was like telling the sun to stop shining.

"She's a good little eater," he said, turning to look at me, a smile on his face.

"I know. I just hope she stays that way."

A short time later I drove us to my new place.

"I'm excited to see what it looks like so far," Marcus said as we walked to the front door.

I unlocked the door and we walked inside. "It's amazing what a coat of paint can do."

"Wow, Lily. It looks great."

I beamed under his praise. "Thanks."

"I'll bet we can get the second coat finished today."

"Really?"

He examined the place where the walls met. "I don't think we need to cut in again, so if we just have to use the roller, it will go fast."

"That would be great. I want to make sure it has plenty of time to dry before the carpet installers come on Monday." I sat Natalie on the floor next to several toys.

"We should be fine."

I gazed at him as he stood looking at the wall, and I wanted to wrap my arms around him and feel his strong arms around me. Just having him here with me made me feel protected and secure, like everything would be okay.

He turned and looked at me, and an emotion I couldn't read swept over his face, then was gone. "Ready to get started?" he said, his voice soft.

Had he seen the unguarded love in my eyes? My face heated with embarrassment and I walked over to the cans of paint on the kitchen counter. "Yes."

I poured some paint into the tray and a few minutes later we were applying the second coat. An hour later we'd completed two rooms.

"This goes a lot faster when two people are doing it," I said as I stood back and admired the finished kitchen.

He tilted his head to one side. "If you'd called me in the first place, I could have helped you from the start."

I turned to face him, feeling chagrined under his stare. "I guess I didn't want to take your time since I know the tile work will take longer to do."

He gazed at me. "Lily, how many times do I have to tell you that I'm here for you?"

My heart pounded at the intense look he gave me, and my attraction to him was almost overwhelming. It took all of my self-restraint not to fling myself into his arms and profess my love for him. Before I had a chance to respond, his cell phone rang.

He pulled it from his pocket, looked at the caller Id and sighed, then answered. He paused as he listened to someone speaking. Then, "No, I can't. I have plans all day today." He gave me a quick smile as he listened, then, "Yes, that's right." He frowned as he listened. "Look, this isn't a good time." "Okay, bye." He slid the phone back into his pocket, then focused back on me.

"Everything okay?"

"Yeah. Nothing you need to worry about." He smiled brightly. "Okay, what room do you want to do next?"

I kept my own frown from forming as I answered him, but inside I wondered who he'd been speaking to and what they were talking about. Was it Chelsea? If so, he sounded irritated with her. What did that mean? I tried not to think about it, and instead focused on the job at hand.

Partway through painting the bedroom we were in, Natalie became fussy.

"Go ahead and take care of her," Marcus said. "I'll keep working on this."

"Thanks." I picked Natalie up and brought her into the kitchen where I prepared a bottle and fed her, then put her down for a nap in the living room, where I'd set up a playpen. When I got back to the bedroom, Marcus was just finishing, and I smiled, pleased with the progress we were making.

By the time Natalie woke up, we'd finished the rest of the rooms.

"I can't believe we finished," I said.

"Why?" He grinned. "I told you we would."

"Yes, but maybe I didn't quite believe you."

He laughed. "You shouldn't doubt me, Lily."

I smiled in return. "Okay. I won't make that mistake again."

"Good. And now that we're done, do you want to buy the tile?"

"Sure. But I need to get some boxes so I can pack my stuff. Once the carpet's in, I'll want to get moved in."

He nodded. "Okay."

We bought the tile and brought it back to the house, then bought some boxes at the hardware superstore.

"Is your friend going to help you move?" Marcus asked as he set the broken-down boxes on the floor of my current place.

I looked at him and shook my head. "He won't be able to make it." I put Natalie in her swing and turned back to Marcus.

A look of annoyance crossed his face. "Forgive me, Lily, but he doesn't seem like much of a friend."

I pressed my lips together, wondering how I could explain Cameron's absence without revealing that he'd dumped me. I didn't know why it was important to me that Marcus believe Cameron was still in my life—maybe I didn't want him to feel sorry for me or worry about me, or maybe since he had Chelsea, I didn't want him to know I had no one. "He lives up in Sacramento and it's hard for him to get away from work sometimes." Both true as far as I knew.

Marcus nodded. "Okay. Whatever. I'll see if my Dad can help me move your stuff." He looked around my small living room. "It shouldn't take too long." He turned to me. "What day did you want to move?"

Guilt that he was doing so much for me washed over me. As much as I wanted to tell him I could do it myself, in reality, I couldn't, so I had to swallow my pride and let him help. "Uh, I guess on Tuesday? I can start moving the small stuff myself, but if you and your dad can move the big stuff, that would really help." I paused. "But if Tuesday doesn't work for you guys, we can do it whenever you can." I bit my lip. "Sorry."

His brow creased. "What are you sorry about?"

Pity for my lackluster—or nonexistent, really—love life, plus my total dependance on Marcus for so many things, not to mention my unrequited love for him, left me feeling dejected and melancholy. Tears flooded my eyes and I blinked, trying to force them back, but when I spoke, my voice shook, and the tears insisted on making their presence known. "I just feel like a burden sometimes," I choked out as a tear slid past my eyelashes and tracked down my cheek. My voice dropped to a whisper. "Sorry."

He reached out and pulled me into his arms, holding me tightly against him.

Several emotions roared through me—euphoria at being in his arms, comfort and security, and a powerful and overwhelming love toward this man I wanted to spend the rest of my life with. My trickle of tears turned into a torrent, and I sobbed against his chest, sorrow that what I wanted so much was beyond my grasp.

"It's okay, Lily," he murmured into my ear. "Everything will be okay."

We stood that way for several minutes and I wanted to stay in the safety of his arms forever, but eventually my tears stopped and my sobs slowed to an occasional sigh, and his arms loosened from around me. Though I didn't want to move away from him, I couldn't very well stand there forever, and at last I stepped back.

He put his finger under my chin, forcing my eyes to meet his, then he wiped a stray tear from my cheek. I gazed into his eyes, willing him to love me, *just love me*, but he just stared back, and I couldn't read his emotions.

"You'll never be a burden," he finally said, smiling gently. "Don't ever feel that way." His green eyes sparkled. "Not with me."

I nodded slightly, and he moved his finger away from my chin. I knew my face must be a mess, so I excused myself and went into the bathroom. Staring at myself in the mirror, I tried to figure out why he seemed to be stuck in the friend-zone, but then a thought occurred to me, and I gasped.

Maybe he felt toward me like I felt toward Cameron. Though I'd wanted to build a relationship with Cameron, I couldn't get past my feelings for Marcus. Maybe Marcus *wanted* to feel more for me than friendship, but he was in love with Chelsea. Of course maybe he was perfectly happy being just my friend, but in either case, that's where he was stubbornly staying.

My shoulders slumped as I realized that as much as I loved Marcus, and as much as I wanted him to love me back, he couldn't make himself love me like that, just like I couldn't make myself love Cameron. Fresh tears flooded my eyes, and I allowed them to fall for a minute, then I took several deep breaths until I was able to get myself under control. I splashed cool water on my face and blew my nose, took one last look in the mirror, then opened the door. When I came out of the bathroom, Marcus was holding Natalie in his arms, a bottle to her lips.

He looked at me and smiled. "She was getting hungry. I hope it's okay that I went ahead and fixed her a bottle."

It was more than okay, and I nodded. "Yes, thank you."

"Are you okay?" His face showed his sincere concern.

I gazed into his incredible green eyes. "I'll be fine." I hoped the words convinced him, because I had no idea if they were true.

He stayed long enough to put the boxes together, but then he stood to go.

"Thank you again for your help," I said.

He nodded. "I'll check with my dad about moving the big stuff on Tuesday and I'll let you know if that works for him."

I walked him to the door, and after he left I began packing, afraid that if I didn't keep busy then my thoughts would focus on my bleak future and I'd dissolve into a puddle of tears.

Later that evening Trish called and invited me over for brunch the next day.

Chapter Twenty-Eight

"Hello," Trish said, opening her door. "Please come in."

I carried Natalie into the house and she squirmed to get down. I set her on the floor as Trish and I sat in the living room, and she immediately began crawling across the carpet.

"She's going to be walking before you know it," Trish said.

"I know. Then it will be even harder to keep up with her."

"She's at a fun age, but a busy age."

"That's for sure."

Trish turned her attention from Natalie and over to me. "How is the move going? I understand Marcus is helping with some projects?"

"Yes. He's been great. We finished painting all the rooms yesterday, and tomorrow I'm having new carpet put in." I smiled. "I'm hoping to start moving my stuff in on Tuesday."

"It's very exciting to buy your first place. I remember when Jeff and I bought our first house. It needed some work too, but once we'd gotten it to where we wanted it, we really enjoyed it."

I nodded. A short time later we went into the dining room.

"Is Jeff going to join us?" I asked.

"No. He won't be home until tomorrow, so it's just us."

"Okay."

I held Natalie on my lap as we ate and chatted companionably. Toward the end of the meal, she smiled and said, "I wanted to talk to you about something, Lily. Something a little sensitive."

I set my fork down and focused on her. "Okay."

"Has Marcus ever talked to you about Chelsea?"

I shook my head as my stomach began to churn. "No."

"Hmm. Well, as I've told you, they've been dating, but lately they've been having some . . . well, some issues."

I felt really uncomfortable with her telling me this, and I had no idea why she was doing it. "I'm not sure . . ." I began.

"No, you need to know this," Trish said, cutting me off. "It concerns you."

My forehead furrowed in puzzlement. "Okay."

"One of their issues seems to be the time Marcus is spending with you, Lily. Helping you, as it were."

The way she said it made it sound like she thought there was more to our relationship than friendship. "What are you saying?"

"Well, Chelsea is beginning to think that Marcus is cheating on her. With you."

My laugh came out loudly and unexpectedly.

"You find this funny?" Trish said.

I shook my head and covered my mouth with my hand. "No. It's just that she is so far from the truth, that it's . . . well, it's laughable."

Trish seemed to relax. "Oh."

"I'm still not sure why you're telling me this. Isn't this something they should be working out between themselves?"

"Of course, but if I can be completely frank with you, I told you because I'm . . ." She looked away from me with an expression of discomfort, then met my gaze. "I suppose I'm asking you to discourage Marcus from spending so much time with you."

What? I wanted to shout. "But he's going to help me with some projects on my house."

"Isn't there someone else who could help? What about that man you told me you met on the cruise? Cameron, I believe you said."

I shook my head. *This is unbelievable.* "I'm not seeing him anymore."

Trish's eyebrows flew up. "Oh." Her expression smoothed out. "I didn't know that."

How could you? I wanted to ask.

"When did this happen, if I may ask?" she said.

"Just a few days ago."

"Does Marcus know?"

I shook my head. "No."

"Perhaps you should keep it that way."

What an odd request. "Why?"

She smiled tightly. "I just don't want to confuse matters."

I had no idea what matters she was talking about.

"Will you do that for me, Lily?"

"I can't promise that he won't find out."

"Of course not. But if you don't tell him, I don't know how he would find out."

Something about her request felt wrong, but I wasn't sure what it was. Was it because she was asking me to lie to Marcus by omission? But why would she think he'd even care? We were just friends. Why would my relationship with Cameron—or lack thereof—matter to Marcus? Did she think if Chelsea found out, that she would trust Marcus with me even less? If Chelsea knew, would she forbid Marcus from helping me? What would I do then?

"Lily?" Trish pressed.

Reluctantly, I nodded. "I suppose."

She smiled. "Thank you."

As Natalie and I walked home, I wondered how much of Trish I'd see in the future. Once I no longer lived next door, would she invite me over any more? And did I want to go over if she did? It seemed every time I went, she had some sort of bombshell to drop on me.

On Monday morning Natalie and I went to our new place to wait for the carpet installers. Once they'd arrived, I let them in, excited to see how the place would look after they'd finished. While they worked, I left Natalie in her car seat, which I'd set on the kitchen counter, and scrubbed the kitchen floor. Then I let her crawl around while I scoured out the kitchen cabinets and applied shelf paper. The seller had left the refrigerator, and of course the stove, and I cleaned those as well.

After several hours the carpet had been installed, and as I carried Natalie from room to room, looking at each space, I smiled, thrilled with how my new place was shaping up.

"I think we're ready to move in," I said as we stopped in her room. I let her crawl on the new carpet as I scrubbed the bathrooms, then I took her home.

On Tuesday I spent the morning taking loads of boxes from the old place to the new one, and putting things away as I went. I'd brought Greta over and she was loving exploring her new backyard. As she whined at the sliding glass door to be let in, I realized I'd need to put in a doggie door soon.

By that night, when Marcus and Jeff came to move the big things, I was getting tired of the whole moving experience. Marcus had borrowed a truck from a friend and it didn't take long to move everything over to the new place—one advantage of not having much stuff. At the new place, I directed them where to put each piece of furniture, and before long everything had been moved over.

"I think that's it," Marcus said.

"Yes. Thank you both so much. I couldn't have done it alone."

"I'm happy to help," Jeff said.

"We both are, Lily," Marcus said, smiling. "I'll come over tomorrow after work and we can start planning the rest of our remodel strategy."

"Sounds great." I wondered how much I would see him once we'd finished all the work we were going to do, but decided not to think about that just then.

After they left, I put sheets in Natalie's crib, as well as my bed, and then fed Natalie and put her down. I spent the rest of the evening getting things organized and by the time I fell in to bed, I felt really good about all I had gotten done.

The next day I cleaned the old place, then called Mary and let her know I was out.

"Thank you, Lily. You were a great tenant. I'm sorry I had to do this to you."

"It actually worked out fine. I bought a place of my own and I'm loving it already."

"Well, I'm glad to hear that." She paused. "You take care now."

"Thanks, Mary. I really enjoyed living here."

That evening Marcus came by and brought some fast food he'd picked up on his way over. "I hope you haven't eaten yet." He set the bags on the kitchen table, then picked Natalie up from the floor, where she'd been crawling around.

"I haven't. Thanks for bringing this." I smiled as I watched him interact with my daughter, then remembered Trish's request that I not tell him that I was no longer seeing Cameron, and my smile turned into a frown. When Marcus turned towards me, I put the smile back in place. "I'll grab some plates." I took plates out of the cupboard, then set them on the table, and Marcus joined me at the table.

"The new carpet really makes a difference," he said, balancing Natalie on his lap as he ate.

"I know. And I love the colors on the walls. It's already starting to feel like home."

"Good. Now we just need to rip up the vinyl in the kitchen and bathrooms and lay the tile."

"Yes," I said. "And put up the backsplash in the kitchen." I glanced toward the cupboards. "One day I'll update the cabinets and counter tops, but that can wait."

"So, when do you want to start on the floors?"

"I'm ready when you are."

He grinned. "Let's start tomorrow night."

My eyes widened. "Okay."

He laughed. "Are you having second thoughts?"

"No, but I'm just a little scared about what's involved. Painting the walls is one thing, but ripping out old floors and putting in new is another. It's not like carpet. Right?"

"You're right, but it won't be hard."

Greta barked at the back door to be let in. I glanced toward her, then looked at Marcus. "That reminds me, can you help me put in a dog door for Greta?"

"Sure."

I smiled, then walked to the sliding glass door and let her in. She raced over to the table, eager to be with us. Marcus scratched her head with his free hand, Natalie held securely on his lap with his other.

"Let me take her," I said, reaching toward Natalie. "I'm done eating."

He handed her over and finished his food, then helped me clear off the table. "I'll bring my tools over tomorrow," he said.

"I'll make us dinner."

"Sounds like a fair trade." He smiled. "I like your cooking."

"It's the least I can do."

He stared at me a moment. "Last night you said you couldn't have done this move alone." He smiled gently. "As long as I'm around, you should never feel alone, Lily."

My heart pounded at his words. What was he saying? What would

Chelsea think? Should I care about her? Did I have any obligation to make sure their relationship stayed intact? "I appreciate that."

He nodded. "I'll be back tomorrow."

"Okay." I walked him to the door, and after he left, I pondered what he'd said. Was he just talking to me as a friend, or was he starting to feel more? The latter idea thrilled me, but I didn't want to fool myself and read more into it than what he'd meant. I put aside my need to try to read between the lines and got Natalie ready for bed.

That night I dreamed that Marcus had declared his love for me, and when I woke the next morning the feelings of joy I'd experienced in my dream stayed with me, and I eagerly looked forward to him coming over that night.

Chapter Twenty-Nine

"I'm going to be a little late," Marcus said, when he called me that afternoon. "I have some work-related obligations I need to take care of first."

I frowned as I wondered if those obligations involved Chelsea. If they did, why didn't he just say so? As I thought about it, I realized he'd never even said her name to me. Why? Did he think I was too fragile to know that he was dating another woman? Was my love for him all too apparent and he was completely aware of how I felt, but he didn't want to hurt me? Or was he just keeping me in the wings, in case things didn't work out with Chelsea?

My earlier feelings of joy evaporated, and my tone was sharper than I'd intended. "We can do it another time, Marcus. You don't have to put your life on hold to help me with my project, you know."

He was silent and I wished I could take my words back.

"If you don't want me to help you, then I understand." He paused. "If you have . . . others . . . to help, just tell me."

Heat flooded my face. He thought Cameron was going to help. What a joke. "I'm sorry. That's not what I meant. I do need your help. I just . . . well, I guess I just don't want you to feel obligated."

"Lily, how many times do I have to go over this with you? I'm happy to help you. Really."

I sighed. "If you need to postpone, I understand. It's not a big deal."

"No. I'll be there, but I'll just be a little late." He seemed to hesitate. "You might want to have dinner without me tonight."

"Oh. Okay." So this did involve Chelsea. "I'll see you when you get here."

When he finally arrived, tools in hand, his mood seemed subdued and I wondered what had happened.

"Natalie's already gone to bed," I said as I followed him into the kitchen.

"We'll try to keep the noise down then." He set his tools on the kitchen floor and turned to me. "I'm sorry about our conversation earlier."

I shook my head. "There's nothing to be sorry about."

He clenched his jaw. "It was kind of stressful at work today."

"Don't worry about it. It's already forgotten."

He smiled, and his mood seemed to improve. "Great. Let's get started then."

We spent the rest of the evening ripping up the vinyl in the kitchen.

"I think that's enough work for one day," he said as he swept up the last of the debris. "Tomorrow we can start on the cement board."

I stared at the wood subfloor and frowned. "Now that we've started, I hope we can get it done soon. I hate to think of Natalie crawling on this."

"It shouldn't take too long."

Friday evening Marcus came over and I wondered how Chelsea felt about him spending a Friday evening with me, but shrugged it off—I had enough problems of my own without worrying about hers.

"I made us dinner," I said, setting out the casserole I'd baked.

"Smells great," he said.

Natalie sat in her high chair and worked on a baby cracker while we ate.

"How many teeth does she have now?" Marcus asked, watching her.

"Just two."

He smiled at her and she smiled back. "It sure is fun seeing her personality develop."

"I know. It's hard to remember what life was like before she was here." My brow creased. "Or to imagine what life would be like without her."

Marcus turned to me. "That won't happen again. He's gone now and no one can take her from you."

I smiled. "I know. But I can't help thinking about what happened. It was so terrifying."

He nodded. "I can't even imagine what you must have felt."

I was quiet for a minute, then I shook my head. "Enough of that. I'd rather think about the present. When Mary called me to say I had to move, I felt panic, but look where I ended up." I gestured to the space we sat in. "It all turned out great in the end." I smiled at Marcus. "And thanks to you, it will be even better soon."

"Are you ready to get started?"

"Yes."

After cleaning up, Marcus began laying the cement board. I watched as he spread thin set on the sub floor.

"Do you want me to do that? I mean, it is my house."

On his hands and knees, he looked up at me. "If you want to do it, then you can. But I'm fine with doing it."

I held Natalie on my hip and smiled down at him. "Well, if you're okay doing it, then I'm good with giving you moral support."

He laughed and turned back to the task.

I continued to watch. "You make it look easy," I finally said as he scooped out some thin set and dropped it on the floor, then began spreading it with the notched trowel.

"Thanks. It's really not that hard."

After I put Natalie to bed, I watched as he screwed the cement board to the subfloor, and I was glad he was fine with doing the hard labor.

When he finished, he turned to me with a smile. "Since tomorrow's Saturday, we'll have lots of time to put in all the tile. I'm borrowing a tile saw from a buddy, so we should be able to get the whole thing done."

I laughed. "I like how you say 'we', but really, it's 'you'."

He grinned. "It makes me happy to do this for you."

Love towards him rushed through me, and I smiled, but deep inside I felt an ache in my heart that he would never be more than a friend.

"I'll come over first thing and we'll get started on the tile," he said.

Pushing aside my melancholy, I nodded. "I'm excited to see what it looks like with the tile in."

"Once it's in, we'll let it set for a day, and then on Monday night we can grout it."

"Okay."

By the time he arrived the next morning, I'd already fed Natalie and we were ready to get started.

"I'll set the tile saw up on the back patio," he said.

Before long we were laying tile on the kitchen floor, and I was able to see it taking shape. "I really like this," I said as I handed a tile to Marcus.

"Yeah, I think you made a good choice."

We worked for several hours, then when it was time to mix up a new batch of thin set, we stopped to take a break. I'd put Natalie down for a nap, and Greta was locked outside, so it was just the two of us. I spread a blanket out on the carpet in the family room, then set out the sandwiches I'd made.

I'd been thinking about what Marcus had said about how helping me made him feel happy. It was one thing to help me out a little, but he was going above and beyond. Why? Was it possible his feelings ran deeper than friendship? The mere possibility filled me with hope and I considered asking him, but fear that he'd shoot me down again made me hesitate.

He must have sensed that I had something on my mind, because as we sat quietly together eating, he said, "What are you thinking about, Lily?"

My eyes met his, and I paused, then decided I'd had enough of guessing. "I was just thinking about what you said last night. About how helping me made you happy."

He smiled and his green eyes sparkled. "Yeah?"

Now what? I thought. "What else makes you happy?" I finally said.

He was quiet for a minute. "Really, it's spending time with those I care about."

Chelsea's face flashed into my mind, and I stared at the floor before meeting Marcus's gaze. My heart pounded as I opened my mouth, and after a moment I gathered the courage to speak. "Like Chelsea?" I watched his face, waiting for confirmation that we had no future together.

He looked confused. "What?"

Painful as it was, evidently he needed me to spell it out. "I know you've been dating a woman named Chelsea. Does she make you happy?" As I looked at his face, I realized that if I truly loved him, if she was the one who made him happy, I would need to step aside. And I would do it. For him.

His brow creased and he shook his head. "What makes you think I'm dating Chelsea?"

"Aren't you?"

He shook his head.

My eyebrows rose as the truth dawned on me. *He wasn't dating Chelsea. Trish had lied to me*. But why? Regardless, I didn't want to be responsible for putting a wedge between him and his mother. "I guess I assumed that. I know she helped your mother plan your party." That was partly true, and I hated not telling him everything, but I didn't feel comfortable calling his mother a liar.

He laughed and shook his head. "I did go on a few dates with her."

So it was true. But I'd had lunch with Trish only a few days earlier, and she'd made it sound like they were actively dating. Confused, I waited for Marcus to explain.

"And my mom did get her involved in planning my party, but I think my mom likes her a lot more than I do."

"Oh."

"So to answer your question, no, I'm not dating her."

A feeling of lightness swept over me, and I smiled.

"What about you?" he asked. "What makes you happy?"

You do, I wanted to say. "Natalie makes me happy. And this house makes me happy." My smile brightened. "And having you help me makes me happy."

His smile dimmed. "What about your friend? Cameron?"

I laughed softly, ready to tell him we'd broken up, then I remembered the promise I'd made to Trish. But now that I knew he wasn't dating Chelsea, why would it matter if he knew Cameron and I were no longer seeing each other? Then, in shattering clarity, it all came together. *Trish doesn't want her son to get involved with me*. I felt my heart drop. What did she find so abhorrent about me and Natalie that she would lie to me, and then manipulate me to mislead her son about Cameron?

I felt my face redden, and suddenly I felt inadequate, like damaged goods, even though I knew I'd done nothing wrong.

Marcus obviously saw my discomfort, although he misread the

reason behind it. "It's okay. You don't have to tell me about him."

Mixed feelings, raw and bright, pulsed through me. Shame for lying to Marcus, Trish, and Jeff when I'd first met them, setting the stage for her to distrust me. Guilt for making a bad choice in Trevor that led me to this place in my life. Joy that I had Natalie, despite all that had happened. Gratitude that Marcus was in my life, even if we were only going to ever be friends. And finally, despair that I would never find lasting happiness.

Hot tears pushed at the backs of my eyes, and I stood, not about to sob in front of Marcus again. "I need to check on Natalie," I said, using my go-to excuse.

"Okay."

I could feel his eyes on me as I went down the hall and into the master bathroom. I locked the door behind me and pressed my palms flat against the counter as I gazed at myself in the mirror. *Don't cry, don't cry, don't cry,* I chanted to myself, not wanting to end up with the tell-tale red eyes that would give away my emotion. I blinked several times and swallowed around the lump that had formed in my throat, then splashed cool water onto my warm cheeks.

I breathed in and out slowly, getting myself under control, then finally left the room, stopping to check on Natalie on my way back to the kitchen. She was still asleep. When I reached the kitchen, I saw Marcus on the patio, cutting a piece of tile, and I sighed, relieved to be able to focus on the task at hand.

He came inside, gave me a quick smile, then spread thin set on the back of the tile and put it in place, adding spacers near the corners. "Looks like we should get this done before the day's over," he said.

I nodded. "That's great."

"Can you hand me a full-size tile?"

"Sure." I picked one up and held it toward him, and as he took it from me, his hand brushed mine. A current of energy surged between us, and he paused and looked at me, an unreadable expression on his face.

"Thanks," he said, a smile lifting his lips, then he spread thin set on the tile and placed it in position.

I stared at the back of his head, an overpowering feeling of love sweeping over me. *I love you*, I thought fervently. Then in barely a whisper I said, "I love you."

His head whipped in my direction. "What? What did you say?"

My eyes wide, I shook my head. "Nothing."

He stared at me a moment, then pushed the tile into place, moving it back and forth to seat it in the thin set.

I pressed my hand to my mouth, mortified that he'd heard me, and shocked at myself that I'd uttered the phrase out loud. Then my gaze went to his face. I could only see his profile, but it looked like he was smiling.

Chapter Thirty

Natalie cried out from her bedroom, and I walked away from the kitchen and toward her room, my face crimson.

He heard you, I thought. He knows what you said.

And he seems happy about it.

Not sure what this meant, and not daring to hope, I lifted Natalie from her crib and held her warm, sleepy body against me. After changing her diaper, I carried her to the family room and put her in the high chair.

Marcus was outside cutting tile again, and I smiled as I gazed at the way his body moved as he worked—so sure of what he was doing. I opened a fresh jar of baby food, and began spooning the food into Natalie's mouth. When I heard the back door sliding open, I turned to see Marcus coming inside. He smiled at me, and I thought I saw a twinkle in his eyes.

Carrying the cut tile, he paused next to Natalie's high chair and smiled down at her. "Is that good?" he asked her. She smiled back, her mouth moving as she ate, and he laughed. He glanced at me, went into the kitchen, buttered the tile, and placed in its proper place, then placed spacers around it.

My gaze kept wandering over to him as I fed Natalie, and when she was done, I set her on the carpet to crawl around. She wanted to crawl to Marcus, so I had to keep picking her up and moving her away from him. "She really likes you, Marcus," I said as I picked her up for the fourth time.

"*She* does, huh?"

I noticed the subtle emphasis he put on the word 'she', and felt myself blush as he watched me. I nodded.

He set spacers in the corners of the tile he'd just placed, then looked at me, his expression becoming more serious. "When is Cameron going to come see your new place?"

"He's not," I said, before I had time to reconsider.

Marcus tilted his head to one side. "Oh?"

"We're not seeing each other anymore." There. I'd said it. And I only felt a little guilty for breaking my promise to Trish.

"Oh." Marcus gazed at me a moment. "Can you hand me a tile?"

That's it? Now I felt really foolish for the three words I'd uttered before Natalie woke up. I picked up a tile and held it out to him.

As he reached for it, his eyes met mine, and I felt immobilized by his magnetism. "Thank you, Lily."

I let go of the tile and he turned his attention to the bucket of thin set, scooping some out and placing it on the back of the tile, then scraping the notched trowel across it, forming deep grooves. I stood there as he placed the tile in position and moved it back and forth to create adhesion, then placed the spacers at the corners.

He looked up at me and smiled. "I think it's time for you to try this."

"What about Natalie?" I pointed to her as she picked up one of her toys.

"She seems to be occupied." He stood and motioned to the place he'd left off. "Come on, Lily. I'll help you."

I remembered the last time he'd helped me with a project—putting in the dog door at my last place—and felt my body burn with desire. "Okay," I said, kneeling in the place where he'd been.

He knelt nearby and handed me a tile and the trowel. "You've been watching me all morning, so I think you know what to do."

I nodded. "Okay." I scooped out some thin set and dropped it onto the back of the tile, which I balanced on the palm of my left hand. It was heavy and I found it awkward to hold it steady with only one hand as I attempted to butter the back. "This is harder than it looks."

He laughed. "You'll get the hang of it."

The grooves on the back of the tile looked nothing like the neat, even lines he always created. "Uh, I don't think this is quite right."

"Well, let me help you with that. If it's too thick, the tile won't be level with the ones next to it."

"Oh. That would be bad."

"Yes." He knelt behind me and put his arms around me, helping me hold the tile in my left hand with his left hand, and then he placed his right hand over mine on the trowel.

My heart rate skyrocketed and I closed my eyes, relishing his warm, muscular body pressed against mine.

"Are you paying attention, Lily?" he murmured in my ear.

My entire body was at attention, only not to what he was trying to teach me. "Yes." My voice came out in a whisper and I opened my eyes as I tried to focus on his lesson.

"You need to use the trowel like this." His voice was deep and soft next to my ear, and his breath was warm and smelled of mint. His hand guided mine until the grooves were right.

I turned my head toward his until our lips were nearly touching, but I could only see him with my peripheral vision. "Thank you," I murmured. I saw his lips turn up into a smile and I longed for him to kiss me.

He pulled back slightly. "Now place the tile in the next open space."

Trying to be a good student, I did as instructed, and wiggled the tile back and forth like I'd seen him do. "How's that?" I asked, looking for praise.

"You did a good job."

I smiled, proud of myself, but also wishing I needed his direct assistance again.

"Now, place the spacers around the edges, and make sure the tile is pressed up tight to the one next to it."

I want to be pressed up tight to you. I felt myself heat at the thought, and was glad he couldn't see my face. When I was done, I turned slightly to see his reaction.

He examined my work, then looked directly at me and smiled. "Good job. Now let's see you do one all by yourself."

Feeling more confident, I picked up a tile, then saw Natalie crawling toward us. "Uh oh. The little helper's coming." I looked at Marcus and he looked at his hands, which had thin set in places.

He laughed. "I'll lure her away from you."

"Okay." I watched as he walked across the sheet we'd laid out earlier to keep thin set from getting on the new carpet, and knelt on the floor.

"Come here, Natalie."

She gazed at him, then looked at me, then at him. Finally she turned in his direction and started crawling.

I don't blame you, I thought, smiling.

Marcus stood and disappeared down the hall, and Natalie crawled after him. A few minutes later he reappeared, his hands clean, and Natalie held against his chest. "How'd you do?" he asked as he walked over to where I knelt.

"Better this time." I held up the tile for his approval. "Is that right?"

He nodded. "Looks good to me. Place it, and then use the level to make sure the tiles are even."

"Okay." As I set the tile in place, I fervently wished he was kneeling behind me. I'd enjoyed his closeness tremendously. I put the level across the two tiles and smiled at him. "I think it's level."

"Awesome."

I grinned. "I can finish this row, if you want."

"It's your house, Lily. You should do it."

My smile grew. He was right. This was my house. He kept Natalie entertained while I finished that row. I stopped when I got to a place that needed a cut tile. Standing, I brushed off my knees and admired what I'd completed. A sense of accomplishment flooded me.

We continued working, and between the two of us we kept Natalie occupied until it was time for her afternoon nap. After I put her down, I came back into the kitchen to see the progress Marcus was making. Though I enjoyed doing some of the tile work myself, I was happy to let him help, as after a while my back and knees became sore.

"Wow. Just a few left," I said.

"Yep. And we're almost out of thin set, but I think we'll have just enough."

A short time later he held the final tile in his hands. He looked at me. "Do you want to do the honors?"

"Sure." He stood and handed the buttered tile to me. I took it from him and carefully placed it in the only space left, seated it, then turned to him with a smile.

"Perfect, Lily." His eyes gleamed with an unspoken message, and I felt a warm glow building inside me. "Just wait until we add the grout," he added. "Then it will look finished." He held his hands up. "I'm going to get cleaned up."

"Okay." I watched him carry the bucket to the backyard, then begin washing it, along with the trowel. His movements were graceful and sure, and when I recalled the feel of his body next to mine, his hands helping mine to butter the tile, I wondered when I would feel that closeness with him again.

I couldn't be sure if he'd heard me say *I love you.* If he had, why hadn't he said anything in response? Unless he was trying to think of a way to let me down gently. Then I thought about my feeling just a moment before, when he'd said *Perfect, Lily.* Was I imagining the feeling I thought I'd gotten from him? Did I so desperately want him to love me that I was conjuring up what wasn't really there? A small frown played at the corners of my mouth, but I battled it back, and forced it into a smile as he came back into the house.

"You'll want to stay off of the tile at least until morning," he said. "To make sure they're cemented into place."

"Okay."

He grinned. "That means you can't use your kitchen, which means I'll need to take you and Natalie to dinner tonight."

I shook my head, worried about having to face him across a table after embarrassing myself with those three little words. "You've done so much for us already."

One side of his mouth quirked up. "Are you turning me down?"

"Well, no. I guess not. I just don't want to take advantage of your generosity." *Or have to listen to you tell me how it will never work between us—how we're meant to only ever be friends.*

He laughed. "If I didn't want to take you to dinner, Lily, I wouldn't have offered."

Obviously I would have to face my future, whether I was ready to or not. "Okay."

"Good. I'm going to go home and get cleaned up, and I'll come back in a couple of hours to pick you guys up, okay?"

I nodded. "Okay."

He left a few minutes later, and I headed to my bathroom to get ready. Even if he was going to break my heart one more time, I wanted to look my best. By the time he came back, I'd put on a dress that made me feel pretty and confident, although in reality my confidence was flagging.

"You look beautiful, Lily," he said, his green eyes sparkling with obvious appreciation.

His sincere compliment helped my confidence grow, and I smiled. "Thank you."

"Let's take your car," he said. "If that's okay."

"Sure."

He picked Natalie up from where she was crawling on the floor, and carried her out to my car, securing her in her car seat, then he opened the passenger door for me and helped me in. He drove to the restaurant, and after a short wait we were seated in a booth, with Natalie in a high chair.

"Today was very productive," I said, after ordering my food, trying to keep the conversation away from our relationship, not yet ready to hear the dreaded word—*friend.*

"Yeah. It was hard work, but it turned out great."

After our food came, I gave Natalie a piece of my roll and she kept herself busy chewing on that.

"How's your food?" Marcus asked.

"Delicious. Thanks for taking me here."

We chatted about what was left to do on my house, and talked about when we would work on each step, then Marcus looked at me, his expression unreadable. My stomach began to churn and I knew the moment I'd been dreading had arrived.

He rested his forearms on the table and leaned forward, gazing at me a moment. "I heard what you said today."

There was no question what he was talking about, and my mouth fell open to have my admission pointed out so boldly. Then I pressed my lips together, and my face went crimson.

His smile grew. "You don't need to feel embarrassed, Lily."

I stared at him in silence, mortified that he had, in fact, heard me. He'd known how I felt for all these hours, but hadn't said anything until now. And now he was going to tell me that he was sorry, but if I wanted to remain friends, I would need to scale back my feelings. What if I couldn't do that? Would he want to cut back on the time he spent with me so as not to encourage me? I felt a flutter of panic at the idea. I *needed* him in my life. I gazed at him, not knowing what to say, my stomach in knots.

He reached across the table and took my hand. Energy charged through me at his touch, and my gaze went to our intertwined fingers, then to his face. His incredible green eyes sparkled, and an unexpected surge of hope pulsed through me.

"Lily, over these last few months, as much as I've fought it, I've finally learned to accept the way I feel about you."

I blinked a few times, my mind racing. Where was he going with this? Did I dare hope? Just then, Natalie began banging on her tray and babbling loudly, evidently not liking us ignoring her. I tried to pull my hand from Marcus's, but he held it firm.

"She's fine," he murmured, then he reached out with his free hand and stroked her face, shushing her, and she settled down.

My love for him blossomed even more as I watched the way he was so gentle with my child, and when his focus shifted back to me, I found my gaze riveted to his, wary and hopeful at the same time.

He smiled. "As I was starting to say before the little princess interrupted . . ." His face became serious, and his gaze turned intense as his grip on my hand tightened slightly. "I love you, Lily. You and Natalie."

My lips parted in stunned surprise, and a small gasp flew from my mouth. My heart soared as my mind fought to take it in. *Did I hear him right? He loves me?* "You do?" I finally managed to whisper.

He nodded.

"But you said we could only be friends." As I gazed at him, I feared

I was only dreaming, but the sounds in the restaurant, and the smell of the food on my plate were too real to only be in my mind.

"I was wrong. Like I said, I've been fighting my feelings, but deep-down, I've known all along that I was in love with you."

His words slowly sunk in, but after wanting this for so long, I was afraid to let myself accept them. What if he didn't mean it? "I don't understand," I finally said. "Why were you fighting your feelings?"

His hand gripped mine as he gazed at me. "I was afraid of getting hurt, of putting my heart out there to be trampled." He paused, looking thoughtful. "The moment I witnessed you giving birth to that little girl . . ." He looked at Natalie, then back at me. "That was it for me. But then your . . . husband . . . showed up, and, well, I felt like you'd betrayed me."

"I'm so sorry I lied to you." The old shame flared bright inside me, and I tried to pull my hand away again.

He held on. "I'm over that, Lily. Totally and completely."

I forced myself to relax and *believe*, trying to focus on the here and now. "Thank you."

"But after he died," he continued, "And you were all alone, I felt a need to protect you. Both of you. And that protection extended to protecting your heart. You'd just been through a traumatic, life-altering experience. I didn't want to take advantage of that by trying to win your heart, so I decided I needed to just be your friend, and I pulled back." He sighed. "When you told me you really liked me, I was elated, but I was afraid. Afraid that I was just the first man you'd spent time with, and that what you felt for me wasn't real. I didn't want to take the chance that either one of us would get hurt."

His brow creased. "So I pushed you away. I thought I was doing what was best for both of us—giving us time. But then you went on that cruise and met . . . Cameron. When I was staying at your house taking care of Greta, and those flowers arrived for you, I felt panicked, like I'd messed up, let you get away." Anguish filled his face. "And when

I stopped by and Cameron was at your *house*, eating dinner with you, I was crushed."

He paused, clenching his jaw. "I decided that if I really loved you, I would stay in the background and just be your friend." He laughed, but it sounded grim. "That was the hardest thing I've ever had to do." Then his face lit up, and the sparkle came back into his eyes. "But today, when you whispered that you love me, I couldn't believe it. I wasn't even sure I'd heard you right, but the look on your face when I asked you what you said?" He laughed, and the sound was pure joy. "I knew I'd heard you right."

His smile grew. "And when you told me that you and Cameron were done, I knew the time was right."

I stared at him, hardly believing that what I'd wanted most—to have him love me—was actually happening. My heart felt so full that I thought it might burst. I glanced at Natalie, who was still working on her roll and watching a child at a nearby table, then looked back at Marcus, whose eyes were locked on me.

"Lily," he said, holding my hand with both of his. "I want us to be a family. You, me, and Natalie."

I went completely still and held my breath, scarcely able to believe the words coming from his mouth. *Was he about to say what I had only dreamed?*

His eyes bored into mine as he spoke. "Lily, will you marry me?"

Chapter Thirty-One

My breath came out in a rush, and a million thoughts raced through my head. Chief among them was that I wanted nothing more than to be his wife, and for him to be Natalie's father. *He loves me! He wants to marry me!* Joy suffused every fiber of my being.

I opened my mouth, ready to accept unequivocally, but then my earlier realization that his mother, Trish, evidently hated the idea of me dating her son so much that she'd lied to me and tried to manipulate me, came into my mind as a bold, clear statement. *She doesn't want you to be with her son.*

Though I desperately wanted to tell him yes, I hesitated, worried now about driving a wedge between mother and son. If I accepted, he'd want to tell his parents right away, and I was certain Trish would not be happy. I didn't want to shatter our good news with the disappointment of his family.

The other option would be to accept, and then to ask him not to tell his parents yet, but understandably, he'd want to know why. I couldn't tell him that his mother had lied to me, as I was sure he'd go straight to her and then maybe they'd end up estranged. I had no family. I wanted my husband's family to love me like their own. Driving a wedge into what could already be a fragile relationship was not a good way to start a marriage.

No, I could not accept his proposal until I'd talked to Trish.

"Lily?" he said, his face full of earnestness.

"Oh, Marcus, I love you so much."

He grinned. "Is that a yes?"

How to do this? I wondered, my mind working frantically. "I want to say yes, but . . ."

"But what?" His face showed sudden distress. "What's wrong?"

I smiled, trying to reassure him. "Please. Just give me a few days, and then I can give you a resounding yes."

He looked confused, but he nodded. "I don't understand, but I know I kind of sprung this on you without any warning." His look of distress was replaced by a tentative smile. "I trust you, Lily. I'm trusting you with my heart." The earnestness returned. "Please don't break it."

"Oh, Marcus. I would never do that. I *love* you."

He smiled, and I felt my heart expand to proportions I didn't think possible. *We're going to be married!*

The rest of the meal went by in a blur, my mind on my dreams coming true, as well as what I would say to Trish when I spoke to her.

After Marcus paid for the meal, he lifted Natalie from her high chair and held her against his chest, then took my hand as we left the restaurant. I was on a high like I'd never been before, and I felt like I was floating as Marcus opened my car door for me, then put Natalie in her car seat, and drove us home.

When we got to my house, he hurried to my side of the car and opened the door and held out his hand. I took it and he held on as I climbed out, then he said, "Let's get Natalie and go in the house."

A thrill of anticipation raced through me as we walked around to Natalie's door, hand in hand, then he released me as he took her out of her car seat and carried her to the front door.

I fished the keys from my purse and let us in, then I smiled. "Let me put her to bed."

He nodded. "I'll be here."

Those three simple words filled me with an inexpressible bliss. Soon he would be there with me every single day, and I could hardly wait. After putting Natalie in her pajamas, I tucked her in and closed her door, then I went back into the family room. Marcus was bent over the tile, pulling out the spacers.

He stood and turned as I entered the room. "They're already pretty dry. Maybe we can grout tomorrow."

"That would be great." Tile was the last thing on my mind, and I stopped at the transition from the family room to the kitchen.

He set the spacers on the kitchen counter and walked toward me, his eyes dancing, then he held out one hand and I eagerly placed my hand in his. He stepped toward me, then with his other hand he tucked a stray hair behind my ear. He ran a finger down my face, leaving a trail of fire, and his finger ended under my chin. He lifted it so that our eyes met, and my gaze locked on his.

This all felt like a dream—a dream I never wanted to end.

"I've wanted to do this for a long time," he murmured, his voice husky. Then his eyelashes fluttered closed, and his face descended toward mine.

I kept my eyes open, wanting to take in the moment and lock it away for safekeeping, but when his lips touched mine, desire like I'd never felt before coursed through my body and I had to close my eyes to stay anchored in the here and now. My arms slid around his neck, and his arms went around my waist, pulling me against him.

I melted into him, wanting more, so much more, but I knew the limits I'd set for myself. I'd made Trevor wait until our wedding night to be intimate, and I had no intention of changing that now. Marcus and I would be married—the sooner the better—and we could wait that much longer to fulfill the desire we both so obviously wanted.

He pulled away slightly and whispered my name against my lips, which nearly swept me away. This was something I'd wanted for so long. Even as I'd kissed Cameron, my thoughts had been on Marcus, hoping, ever hoping, that somehow this day would arrive.

Just when I felt my resolve slipping, the doorbell rang, followed by three brisk knocks.

Marcus pulled away, his eyes filled with desire. "Are you expecting anyone?"

I shook my head. "No." My lips felt swollen from his ardent kissing, and I smiled.

"Probably just a sales person," he said as he leaned toward me for another kiss.

The door bell rang again.

"On a Saturday night?" I said. "Let me just see who it is."

With seeming reluctance he released me, and I walked to the door, secretly glad for a moment to cool off. I didn't have a peephole, but I felt safe with Marcus there, and I opened the door.

Two teenaged girls stood on my porch, a plate of cookies in the hands of the younger of the two. "Hi," the taller girl said. "We live next door and wanted to welcome you to our neighborhood." The younger girl held out the plate.

"Thank you." I took the plate and the scent of warm oatmeal cookies wafted toward my nose. "These smell delicious."

"I'm Emily," the taller girl said. "And this is Rachel."

"I'm Lily. And I have a baby named Natalie."

Rachel smiled. "I know. We saw her. She's so cute."

"Thank you."

"We can babysit," Emily said. "I'm fourteen and I have a lot of experience."

"Oh. Well, that's good to know." I wondered if I'd be willing to leave Natalie with a sitter. On the cruise it had been different—Haley was Ty's sister, and we were on the ship. But I didn't know these girls at all.

"Well, see you later," Emily said, smiling.

"Okay. Thanks for the cookies." A moment later they were gone, and I carried the plate into the kitchen and set them on the counter. "Hungry?" I asked Marcus.

He grinned. "Hungry for you."

I blushed, but smiled, still feeling euphoric about the sudden turn of events the afternoon had brought.

He lifted a cookie from the plate and held it out for me to bite. After I took a small nibble, he took a bite, then set the remaining cookie on the plate. He pulled me into his arms, and I rested my head against his chest and listened to the rhythm of his heartbeat.

With his arms wrapped around me, I felt safe, secure, and most importantly, loved, and I wanted to stay there forever. I smiled, exhilarated to know that now I could count on being held by him whenever I wanted. As we stood together, I snuggled against him, and after a moment he pulled back slightly and I looked at his face.

Desire was etched in his features, and I realized I needed to make my limits known before his expectations went too far in the wrong direction.

I stepped back and took his hand. "Marcus, can we talk for a minute?" I gently tugged him toward the couch and he followed without protest.

We sat close together, our hands still clasped.

A look of concern crossed his face. "What is it?"

I sighed, wondering how to explain my old-fashioned beliefs. "I just wanted to talk about something that's important to me."

He watched me closely. "Okay."

"I'm not sure what your expectations are when it comes to . . . well, to sex . . . but I believe a man and a woman should be married before . . . well, before they . . . you know."

"Make love?"

I nodded, glad my words hadn't been too muddled.

"I see."

I grimaced. "I hope that's not a problem."

He was quiet for a moment. "I suppose not." He laughed. "I'm just surprised." He paused, a look of curiosity filling his face. "Does that mean you've only ever been with . . ?"

"Trevor? Yes."

"And you waited until you were married?"

I nodded.

"Wow. I'm impressed."

"Why?"

"It's just kind of unusual nowadays."

"I know. But it's the way I was raised."

He nodded. "Okay."

I smiled, relieved he understood.

"I'm glad you told me before things went too far."

"That's why I thought I'd better tell you."

"I have to admit, it will be difficult to wait." He paused, then smiled. "Hold on. Does that mean you're saying yes?"

Oh boy. "Like I said at the restaurant, give me a few days and then I'll give you a resounding yes." My brow creased. "Is that okay?"

"I still don't understand what the wait is all about."

"I can't explain, but I just don't want to make it official yet."

"Okay. I guess I don't have a choice in the matter." He didn't seem happy about it.

I gave his hand a gentle squeeze. "Thank you. And I'm sorry to make things difficult."

He smiled. "I think you just like to keep me guessing."

I laughed. "Yes. Now you've figured me out."

After a moment he said, "It's been a busy day. I think I'll get going and then I'll come over tomorrow to do the grout. If that's okay with you."

"Yes. I think that would be great."

He pulled me against him and we sat like that for a moment, until I heard Greta whining to be let in. Marcus must have heard it too, because he said, "I think we need to create a dog door for her."

I went to the sliding glass door and let her in. "Yes. The sooner the better."

He came over to where I stood. "Do you want to put it as part of this door?"

I thought about it for a moment. "No. I think I'd rather have her come in through the garage."

He nodded. "I'll pick up a dog door on my way over tomorrow, and we'll get it put in."

"You're wonderful," I said, smiling at him. "Did you know that?"

He leaned toward me and kissed me. "So are you." Then he took my hand and we walked to the front door.

"Thanks for dinner," I said, grinning.

He smiled. "It was my pleasure."

After he left, I sank onto the couch and replayed the evening, my happiness growing with every passing moment.

The next morning, as soon as he set down the tools and dog door, I threw my arms around him, wanting to prove to myself that the evening before had really happened. He slid his arms around me and held me close, and I couldn't get the smile off of my face.

"Good morning, my beautiful Lily," he murmured.

"Hi." I relished the feel of his arms around me, and only let go when I felt Natalie pulling on my leg. Laughing, I picked her up and held her on my hip.

"Hi there, sweet Natalie," Marcus said, touching her tiny hand.

She smiled at him with her two-tooth smile, then she reached out to him. He took her from me and gently swung her around, making her giggle. After a few minutes he set her down and we got to work.

It took less than an hour to push the grout into the spaces between the tiles, although it took some time to clean the tiles afterwards.

"You're right," I said. "It looks so much better now."

"Are you happy with the way it turned out?"

"Oh yeah. I love it."

He smiled. "Good. That's what I like to hear." He paused. "When you're ready, we can install the backsplash and put in the dog door."

"Let me just give Natalie something to eat and put her down for a nap, then we can get started."

Half an hour later she was in her crib, and we were deciding how to arrange the glass tile backsplash.

"It's going to look so pretty," I said as I touched the blue and gray rectangular pieces of glass.

Marcus looked at me, drawing my attention away from the tile. "We haven't talked about this," he said. "And I don't want to assume. But if we get married," he smiled, and my smile matched his. "Are we going to live here?"

"Yes. I'd like that. I mean, you were with me when I picked this place out, and you've put in more work than me in these projects." My smile grew. "This place is yours as much as mine."

He smirked. "Except for the money you spent."

I laughed. "Well, there is that. But I'm sure we can work that out."

"Okay."

We spent the next several hours installing the backsplash, then putting in the dog door.

"I can come over tomorrow night to grout the backsplash," he said. "And then we can move on to the bathrooms. They won't take nearly as long since they're so much smaller than the kitchen."

He cleaned up the mess we'd made, then said, "I promised my

parents I'd come over for dinner tonight." His face brightened. "Hey, maybe you can come with me."

I shook my head, and he looked surprised by my reaction.

"Why not? I'm sure they'd be fine with it."

I could only imagine Trish's reaction if I were to show up with Marcus at a family dinner. "I'm just not sure. I mean, we're not actually engaged yet."

"So what? We can at least make it clear we're dating."

That was the worst idea ever, but I couldn't tell him that. I decided I needed to hint at the dilemma I was having. "Won't your mom be disappointed that you're not dating Chelsea?"

"Look, my mom can't choose who I love." He put his hands on my shoulders and gazed into my eyes. "And that person is you, Lily."

My heart rejoiced at his words, but I was still worried about Trish's reaction. I really wanted her to accept me, and springing this on her at a family dinner didn't seem like the best approach. I gazed at him, at a loss at how to explain why I didn't think it was a good idea for me to go.

Without warning, he pulled me against him and kissed me, dragging my thoughts away from Trish and back to him. Always him. The man I loved.

"Please, Lily. For me."

How could I refuse him? "Okay. I'll go."

He grinned. "Great. I'll pick you and Natalie up in two hours."

Chapter Thirty-Two

As we pulled into his parents' driveway, I felt a bead of sweat forming on my upper lip. I wiped it away with the back of my hand.

"Ready?" Marcus said from the driver's seat.

I nodded, and my stomach churned.

"I'll get Natalie," he said, then smiled at me. "Wait there."

I smoothed down my skirt as I waited for him to unbuckle Natalie, then come to my side of the car and open the door. After I got out, I took Natalie from him, wrapping both of my arms around her so that Marcus wouldn't be able to hold my hand—what if Trish looked out the window and saw?

As we walked up the steps to the porch, I asked, "Did you tell your parents you were bringing me?"

He shook his head. "No. I didn't think about that." He frowned. "Sorry. But I'm sure it's no big deal."

I was less certain—much less—but I just nodded. It was too late to do anything about it now.

Marcus knocked, then opened the door and called out, "We're here."

"I'm in the kitchen," Trish called back, and I wondered if she'd caught the 'we're' part of Marcus's announcement.

As we walked toward the kitchen, we passed the formal dining room and I noticed that four places had been set at the table. My forehead creased. Who, besides Marcus, Jeff and herself, was Trish planning on?

Marcus rounded the corner into the kitchen first, and I paused, gathering my courage before following.

"So you came together?" I heard Trish ask.

"What?" Marcus said, clearly confused.

I took a deep breath and released it, then, putting a smile on my face, walked into the kitchen.

"Oh," Trish said, her eyebrows rising. "Lily." The surprise on her face quickly smoothed out as she pasted a smile on her face. "What an unexpected pleasure."

"Hi, Trish."

"Sorry I didn't warn you, Mom," Marcus said. "I didn't think you'd mind."

She seemed a bit flustered. "No, it's fine."

The doorbell rang.

"Can you get that, Marcus?" Trish asked, then looked at me. "Would you like something to drink, Lily?"

"No, I'm fine." I wanted to see who had arrived, but Trish linked arms with me and tugged me toward the kitchen.

"Let's see if I have something for Natalie to snack on," she said.

Not wanting to be rude, I let her drag me into the kitchen. Jeff was out back, grilling something, and Trish went into the pantry and began digging around.

"Can she eat this?" she asked, turning to me with a box of crackers in one hand.

"I fed her before we came, so she's probably fine."

"Oh." Trish set the box back on the shelf and shut the door. Then she faced me, a look of concern on her face. "Can I be perfectly honest with you?"

I nodded, wondering if she really would be. "Of course."

"I invited Chelsea to join us."

Oh boy.

"I know you and Marcus are good friends," she went on. "So I know you want what's best for him." She laughed in what seemed a self-conscious manner. "I told you the two of them were dating, and it's true that they've been on a few dates, but he doesn't seem as interested in her as she is in him."

In a way I felt sorry for Chelsea because I knew exactly how that felt. "So they're not dating?"

Her face flushed. "Unfortunately, no. But I think she would be so good for him, if I could just get him to see it."

I smiled with what I hoped was warmth. "Don't you think he's old enough to figure out his love life for himself?"

Her lips pressed together, then, "I warned him away from that Marissa, and he didn't listen. And then she broke his heart."

Ah ha. Marissa strikes again. Out loud I said, "He's probably learned from his mistakes, don't you think?"

One of her perfectly shaped eyebrows lifted. "Hard to say." Then her expression calmed. "But that's where you can help, Lily."

What? "I don't understand." Even though I had no intention of doing anything to help Chelsea with Marcus, I was curious to hear what she would say.

"I suppose I'm asking you to encourage him to spend time with her. I'm sure once he gets to know her better, they'll click."

I hesitated before speaking, but finally said, "What if he's seeing someone else? Someone he really cares about?"

She recoiled slightly. "Like who?"

Her reaction was like a slap in the face, but I plastered a smile on my mouth. "It's just a hypothetical."

"Then it doesn't matter, does it? Anyway, I'm sure I'd know if he was seeing someone else."

I didn't know why she would think that, but I let it go.

She smiled at me with encouragement. "So will you do this?"

"I don't think I . . ."

"Please, Lily."

Just then, Marcus and Chelsea came into the kitchen.

"Hello, dear," Trish said, walking over to Chelsea and giving her a warm hug. "How are you?"

I bit my lip to hold back a smile at the look of discomfort on Marcus's face. He caught my eye and clenched his jaw, obviously irritated with his mother's matchmaking attempt.

"You remember Lily," Trish was saying to Chelsea.

"Of course," she said. "And your adorable baby."

I smiled. "Thanks."

"Dinner's almost ready," Trish said. "Marcus, would you add another place setting, please?"

"Sure, Mom." He pulled a plate out of the cupboard, along with a glass, and carried them into the dining room.

"Let me help," Chelsea offered, taking some silverware out of a drawer and following him into the dining room.

Even though I knew Marcus wasn't interested in Chelsea, and in fact wanted to marry me, I felt a stab of jealousy as I watched the two of them disappear around the corner.

"How is the move going?" Trish asked me. "Have you gotten settled in?"

I turned to face her, straining to listen for any conversation between Marcus and Chelsea. "Pretty much. It's feeling like home already." I needed to have a conversation with her about me and Marcus, and soon.

"In fact, why don't you come over and see the place tomorrow? I can make us lunch."

"Sure. That would be lovely."

I heard Chelsea's laughter from the adjoining room, and inwardly I cringed. Was Marcus flirting with her?

"Sounds like it's going well in there," Trish whispered.

I bristled at the implication. *That was my almost-fiancé in there.* Of course, Trish had no idea that Marcus had proposed to me, but *I* knew, and *he* knew. I hoped he wasn't doing anything to lead Chelsea on, even unintentionally.

The two of them came back in the kitchen a moment later and Chelsea walked over to Trish and asked what she could do to help.

I looked at Marcus, and he was smiling, which made me frown. His gaze met mine, and when I narrowed my eyes, his lips quirked up into a knowing smile. I smiled back, knowing that even if he was friendly to Chelsea, in the end, he was mine. I vividly recalled the feel of his arms wrapped around me earlier that day and a shiver of longing raced through me.

"The meat's ready," Jeff said, poking his head into the kitchen.

"Thank you, honey," Trish said. "I just need to put the rest of the food on the table."

A moment later we all trooped into the dining room. The table was set for five, with two chairs on each end, two chairs on one side of the table, with one chair across from that.

"Chelsea and Marcus, why don't you sit over here?" Trish asked, her hands on the backs of the two chairs that sat adjacent to each other. "And Lily can sit across from you."

I felt like the third wheel in Trish's little matchmaking attempt, but rather than protest that Marcus was with me, I gamely walked toward the side I'd been assigned.

"I think it would be better if I sat next to Lily," Marcus said.

Everyone looked at him, and Trish's expression of irritation was unmistakable.

"That way I can help with Natalie," he said, smiling sweetly.

Everyone was silent for a minute, but how could Trish object to that? Chelsea nodded, but her smile dimmed noticeably.

"Lily?" Marcus said, holding out the chair he wanted me to sit in.

Holding back a triumphant smile, and with Natalie in my arms, I walked over to the chair. Marcus helped me get seated and I murmured my thanks. Then he sat next to me, leaving Chelsea stranded in the lone chair across from us.

Dinner was delicious and the conversation was pleasant, though knowing Trish's plans, I thought she seemed subdued. When it was time to leave, I walked over to Trish and thanked her for dinner.

"You're welcome," she said, then she leaned toward me and whispered, "Next time we'll have to have a better plan for you-know-what."

I forced a smile on my face and thought, *Next time Chelsea won't be here*. "So I'll see you tomorrow?" I said.

"Yes."

As Marcus drove us away from his parents' house, he sighed, then said, "Well, that was interesting."

I laughed. "Has that happened before?"

"Yeah. A couple of times. I shouldn't have been surprised." He glanced at me. "I guess I'd kind of forgotten about her over the last couple of days."

I grinned, knowing I'd been the one to make him forget.

A short time later we pulled into my driveway and Marcus walked with me into the house, then helped me put Natalie to bed. After tucking a blanket around her, I gave her a kiss, then stepped back. To my pleasure, Marcus leaned down and gave her a kiss as well.

"Good night, sweet Natalie," he whispered, then he took my hand and led me into the family room.

As we walked, my heart felt so full of love for him, I couldn't imagine being any happier. "I want to get married right away," I blurted out.

He stopped and spun towards me, his face lighting up. "Really?"

I nodded as tears pricked my eyes. "Yes."

He pulled me close. "Oh, Lily. I love you so much."

"I love you, too," I said against his shoulder.

He pulled back and looked at me, his hands on my arms. "We need to tell my parents." He laughed. "Then my mother will stop pushing Chelsea at me."

My smile faded a bit. "I need to tell you something."

Wariness replaced the look of joy on his face, and he released me. "What?"

At that moment I decided I needed to be honest with him. He was going to be my husband. It wasn't right for me to keep anything from him. "I invited your mom over for lunch tomorrow."

"Okay."

"Marcus, a week ago your mother had me over for lunch, and she told me not to tell you that I wasn't seeing Cameron anymore."

His head jerked back. "What? Why would she do that?"

"She told me you were dating Chelsea and that I should discourage you from spending time with me because the time you spent with me was becoming an issue in your relationship with Chelsea." It felt great to get that out into the open. I didn't want to keep any secrets from him.

He looked from side to side, obviously upset by the lies his mother had told me, then he looked at me. "I'm going to go over there right now and set her straight."

I grabbed his arm. "No, Marcus. This is why I didn't tell you before. I don't want you to be angry with your mother."

"Lily, how can you be so forgiving?" His eyes softened, and he reached out and stroked my face. "That's one thing I love about you. One of many."

I pressed my cheek against his hand, loving his touch.

"You shouldn't have to deal with this," he said, moving his hand to my arm and rubbing it with his thumb. "This is between my mother and me."

"I know, but please try to understand. I don't have a mother, and I like your mother." My eyes filled with tears as I spoke. "I want her to be like a mother to me." I took a deep breath, getting myself under control. "Let me talk to her tomorrow first."

He gazed at me. "Okay. But don't let her push you around. She doesn't like it when things don't go her way." He paused. "Are you going to tell her we're getting married?"

I shook my head. "I'll just tell her we're dating. If I tell her we're getting married, I think that might be too much, don't you?"

He laughed. "We'll have to tell her sooner or later."

"I know." I smiled. "Baby steps."

He drew me into his arms, and as I tilted my face to his, his lips sank toward mine. Our kiss became more passionate and I felt myself getting lost in the sensations swirling through my body. Gently, I pushed away from him, and gazed into his eyes.

"I think we need to get married soon," he said, his voice husky.

It was the same thing Trevor had told me, but this time I nodded, wanting nothing more than to make him my husband.

"I think I'd better go now," he said. "I'll come over after work tomorrow and you can give me a full report on your meeting with my mother."

"Yes." I smiled. "And then we can grout the backsplash."

He laughed. "Yes, that too."

I walked him to the door, and after he gave me a quick kiss on the lips, he left.

The next day I worked all morning to make a lunch that rivaled the meals Trish had served, and when she arrived, I felt a mixture of pride in the lunch I'd prepared, and nervousness about the conversation I was about to have with her.

"Hello, Trish," I said, inviting her in.

"Your house looks great, Lily."

"Thanks. Come see the tile that Marcus and I put in."

She followed me into the kitchen. "It looks wonderful."

"We put the backsplash in yesterday, and this evening we'll grout it."

"I like the colors you picked."

"Thanks."

"Is Natalie sleeping?"

"Yes." I paused. "Do you want to sit down?"

"Sure."

We sat on the couch in the family room. "Dinner was delicious last night," I said. "You're a really good cook."

She smiled under the compliment. "Thank you."

We sat down to lunch and we talked about random things, but in the back of my mind, I wondered how to bring up the real reason for inviting her over. The opportunity presented itself at the end of the meal when Trish said, "I hope it wasn't awkward for you when Marcus insisted on sitting next to you at dinner last night. I know you want to help him get to know Chelsea."

Chapter Thirty-Three

I chewed the inside of my lip, and my heart raced. *This is it.* "That's actually one reason I invited you over. To talk about Chelsea."

Her eyebrows rose in question.

"You see," I began, "Marcus told me he isn't interested in Chelsea."

"He just needs to get to know her better," she said, interrupting me.

I shook my head. "It's more than that. He's seeing someone else."

Her forehead creased. "No. I don't think that's true. Did he tell you that?"

I couldn't hold back a smile. "He didn't have to."

"Then you're imagining things, Lily." She picked a piece of lint off of her slacks, then looked at me. "I hope you're not pining after something that's out of your reach."

My mouth fell open at the bold insult.

"I'm sorry to be so blunt," she said. "But you need to know the truth.

I know you've had a hard time of it, but I don't think you're the best fit for Marcus. He has a great future ahead of him, and you, well, you're a single mother and you're only, what, twenty-one? You've already been married, for heaven's sake."

The things she said about me were true—except about not being a good fit for Marcus. Or was she right about that too? Flustered now, I said the only thing that came to mind. "We're getting married." My hand flew to my mouth as I realized what I'd said, and I wished I could suck the words back in.

She recoiled. "What?" After only a second, her expression smoothed out, and her smile held pity. "I know he's a wonderful man, but you need to accept that he is just not the man for you." She frowned, but the look held compassion. "I know it's hard to be alone, but that's just the way things are for you. It's not fair to Marcus to drag him into your drama." Her voice softened. "Let your fantasy go, Lily. You'll be happier in the end if you just accept reality."

I shook my head. The conversation wasn't going the way I'd planned at all. "Trish, it's you who doesn't understand. Marcus *proposed* to me." I smiled. "And I accepted."

She shook her head, obviously in complete denial. "I don't believe it. He would have talked to Jeff and me about it first." She laughed, but it sounded forced. "I mean, he's never even told us that he's interested in you."

"Well, we love each other. And we're going to be married."

"I don't believe this," she murmured, almost to herself.

I frowned as I watched her.

She looked at me, plainly upset. "Thank you for lunch, Lily." Then she stood, grabbed her purse from the couch, and rushed out the front door.

"Great," I said out loud. I called Marcus's cell phone, but got his voice mail. "Your mother just left," I said. "I'm sorry, but I let it slip that we're getting married." I paused. "She didn't take it well. Call me when you can."

I put the phone in my back pocket and began cleaning up the kitchen, wondering what Trish was going to do now.

I didn't hear back from Marcus until late that afternoon, and when he called, it was obvious that he was feeling stressed.

"I hate to say it, but I wish you hadn't told my mother that we're getting married."

"I'm really sorry, Marcus, but it just slipped out." I didn't want to tell him the rude things his mother had said to me, so I left it at that.

He sighed. "She came to see me here at the office, and she was all worked up. Went on and on about me not rushing into anything. I finally got her to calm down, and I had to call my dad to have him come and get her." He paused. "It's kind of a mess right now."

Alarm bells rang in my mind. "What do you mean?"

"I just got off the phone with my dad. After he brought her home he went back to work, and apparently he came home to check on her, and when she saw him she started getting worked up again. Then she fainted and hit her head and he brought her to the hospital to have her head looked at. I'm on my way over there now." He laughed. "I guess we won't be grouting tonight."

"Oh, Marcus. I'm so sorry. If I'd had any idea she would react like this, I never would have told her."

"It's not your fault. My mother can be a little . . . high strung." He paused. "I'm just pulling into the parking lot now. I'll call you later."

"Okay."

I set the phone on the counter, then sat on the floor in front of Natalie. She was playing with some toys I'd set out, and I looked at her sadly. "No Marcus tonight, baby girl."

She smiled up at me, her blue eyes shining.

I spent the rest of the evening going back and forth between playing with Natalie and worrying about Trish. After I put Natalie to bed, I sat on the couch and thought about Trish and her reaction. Did she really think I was so beneath him that the news of us marrying would make her faint? Was she right? Did all the mistakes I'd made and the things I'd been through make me a poor choice of wife for Marcus?

Was I not good enough for him? My heart sank at the thought. I loved him so much, how could I even consider pushing him away? But if I truly loved him, shouldn't I do what was best for him, regardless of what I wanted, and make sure he was with a woman who was worthy of him?

The thought of letting him go made me breathless, and as I imagined telling him good-bye for the last time, a wave of dizziness swept over me and I had to lie down. Greta pressed her nose against my hand, urging me to come and play, but I pushed her away. Insistently, she licked my hand, then moved up to my face.

"Stop it," I said listlessly, my heart already breaking as I contemplated what it would be like if Marcus was no longer in my life. I contrasted the way I felt then with the way I'd felt only the day before. Then, life had held so much promise—Marcus and I wanted to get married as soon as we could. Now, it all seemed in jeopardy. Not because of Trish, exactly, but because of the doubts she now placed in my mind.

I stayed up later than normal, waiting to hear from Marcus, but he never called. Dejected, I finally went to bed.

He called during his lunch break the next day.

"How's your mom?" I immediately asked.

"She needed some stitches, but that's not the problem."

I tensed, waiting for the other shoe to drop.

"When we got her home, she became hysterical again. She went on and on, trying to make me promise to wait at least six months before I made any final decisions, and trying to get me to commit to dating other women for a while." He sighed. "Lily, I don't know what her problem is, but she is really upset."

I know what it is, I thought. It's me. I'm not good enough for you. Out loud, I said, "What now?"

"I think I need to spend time with her. Calm her down." He sighed again. "I don't think I'll be stopping by for a few days."

My shoulders slumped with disappointment. "Okay." I paused, then in a small voice, "I love you."

"I love you too, Lily."

I wandered around the house, not knowing what to do about this. "I need some advice," I said to the walls of my bedroom. At first I thought of calling Alyssa, but she would most likely just advise me to forget about Marcus and go back to Cameron.

Then I thought of Marcy. I needed someone with a more mature outlook. But then I shook my head. She had dissolved into tears at the mere idea of me being friends with Marcus. She couldn't be objective about him.

But I couldn't go on like this. I needed to get away.

I can go to Marcy's house for a visit, I decided. I don't have to tell her what's going on, but maybe putting a little space between myself and my situation will give me perspective.

Feeling better now that I had a concrete idea, I called her right away.

"I'd love for you to come for a visit," she said after I made the suggestion. "When did you want to come?"

"Today," I said without hesitation.

"Oh." She paused. "Okay."

"Are you sure?"

"Of course. You know you're welcome anytime."

"Thank you so much. I'll be there this evening."

"Wonderful."

As soon as I hung up, I packed the things Natalie and I would need, then loaded them into the car, then I changed Natalie, gave her a snack, and headed out. I took Greta to a local kennel that had space—Marcus had too much going on for me to ask him to care for her. And as I put more distance between myself and Marcus, I felt bereft, but I also felt the weight of Trish's disappointment lifting.

Late that evening I pulled up to Marcy and John's house. As I carried Natalie to the front door, I smiled, remembering the last visit. It had been emotional in a lot of ways, but I felt the air was slowly clearing between me and Trevor's family.

"Hello," Marcy said, pulling me into a warm hug, and I burst into tears. She pulled back and looked at me. "What's wrong?"

I just shook my head and sniffled.

She took a sleepy Natalie from me and we went inside. "Go sit down, Lily. I'll put Natalie on a blanket on the floor of your room." She smiled. "I don't want her rolling off of your bed."

I just nodded, grateful to have her take care of Natalie for me. She left the room and I sat on the couch, then pulled out a packet of tissues from my purse. I blew my nose and dabbed at my eyes until I'd gotten myself under control.

A few moments later Marcy was back and she sat next to me on the couch and put her arm around me. "Do you want to talk about it?"

I shook my head. "Not right now," I managed to say between sniffles.

"Okay." She smiled in a motherly way. "You're probably exhausted from your long drive. Why don't you go to bed and I'll see you in the morning?"

I nodded and let her lead me to my room, where I found Natalie sleeping soundly on a thick blanket. She seemed fine, so I left her there and got myself ready for bed, then crawled under the covers and closed my eyes.

The next morning when I went into the kitchen, Marcy had a nice breakfast waiting for me. She and John were retired, so they didn't have to go to work. John smiled at me as I walked in carrying Natalie.

"Good morning," he said.

"Hi. Thanks for letting me come for a visit at the last minute."

"You're family," he said. "And you're welcome anytime."

I smiled at him. "Thank you. You don't know how much that means to me." And I realized that's why I'd burst into tears the moment Marcy had hugged me the night before. In her own way, she had become the closest thing to a mother that I had, and feeling the warmth of her welcome had made me lose it.

"Have something to eat," he said, motioning to the food set out.

"I hope you like pancakes," Marcy said, sliding some hot ones onto the platter on the table.

"Yes." I slid into the seat and held Natalie on my lap, then I took a slice of bacon, and two pancakes. Natalie reached for my plate and I pushed it out of her reach.

"I'm done," John said. "Let me take her." He walked over to me and held out his arms. Natalie let him pick her up and he smiled at her. "You sure are a beauty," he said. He smiled at me. "Just like her mother."

I blushed, but felt myself relaxing under their loving care. "Thank you."

After I fed Natalie, I helped Marcy clean up, then she invited me to come sit in the living room so we could catch up.

"My landlady needed her family to move into the house I was living in," I said. "So I decided to buy a place for me and Natalie."

"I'm disappointed you didn't buy a place here, but I'm excited for you that you were able to buy your first place."

"It needed a little work, but it's shaping up nicely now." I thought of the work Marcus had put in to the place, was still planning on putting into it, and melancholy settled over me.

"I'd love to come see it sometime," Marcy said.

"Oh, that would be nice. I'd like to have you and John come for a visit."

We both watched Natalie as she played with some toys I'd set on the floor.

"Lily," Marcy said, and I looked at her. "Do you want to tell me what's going on? Why were you so upset?"

I sighed. "Honestly, I could use some advice, but I don't want *you* to become upset."

She looked puzzled. "Why would I become upset?"

"It has to do with my . . . friend . . . Marcus."

She nodded. "I see." She leaned forward, resting her forearms on her knees. "I've thought a lot about you and . . . other men . . . since your last visit. You're so young, and I . . . well, it's not fair for me to expect you to be alone." She smiled. "Please, tell me what's happened."

Feeling better about sharing my problems, I tucked my feet underneath me and began talking, telling her how much I'd grown to love Marcus, how much he loved Natalie, and how, after waiting a long time, he finally admitted that he loved me too. "He proposed to me, Marcy."

She smiled, and her happiness seemed genuine. "Well, that's wonderful." Then her brow creased. "Then why the upset?"

"His mother," I said simply.

"What about her?"

I explained all that had been going on. "Maybe she's right. Maybe I'm not right for her son." Tears pricked my eyes and I couldn't stop my voice from shaking as I looked at Natalie. "Why should I saddle him with a child that's not even his?"

"But you said he loves her."

I nodded. "He does, but . . ."

"This is nonsense, Lily," Marcy said, her tone sharp.

I looked at her with surprise.

"This man would be lucky—more than lucky—to have both you and Natalie." Her eyes narrowed. "I'd like to give that woman a piece of my mind for saying those things to you. The nerve of some people."

I smiled at her passion in defending me and was so glad I'd come. "Thank you, Marcy. That's very kind of you."

"Now, have you told Marcus about the things his mother said to you?"

"Well, no. I think his hands are pretty full right now."

"Her attitude is not your problem. You know that, right?"

"But she's his mother. I don't want to be the cause of a family fight."

With sternness, she said, "That's between the two of them."

My self-doubt reared its ugly head again. "I can't help but think that there's someone better for him out there, and that maybe I should encourage him to explore a little more before he settles for me."

"Listen to yourself. You are a beautiful, smart, capable young woman. You're doing a wonderful job with your daughter, and all on your own." She shook her finger at me. "Don't doubt yourself. There's no 'settling' in this equation."

I smiled, but I had to admit, I wasn't completely convinced that she was right.

As the day went on, I enjoyed talking to Marcy more and more and felt like we were getting closer. I considered calling Marcus to touch base with him, but decided he had enough going on, and that if he wanted to talk to me, he would call me—he had my cell phone number, after all.

Marcy had an appointment in the afternoon, and while she was gone I sat quietly in the living room—Natalie was taking her afternoon nap—and thought about what Marcy had said versus what Trish had said. My own self-doubt pushed me to believe Trish over Marcy—after all, Marcy and I hadn't spent a lot of time together. The thought even crossed my mind that maybe I should sell my new house and buy a place down here, closer to John and Marcy. They'd made it clear that they wanted me to live closer, and if things didn't work out with Marcus, I would have them to fall back on. If I stayed up north, I had no one.

My mood bounced between despair at ever finding happiness, and hope that everything would work out. But when my phone finally rang, and I heard the voice of Marcus's dad on the other end, a new problem presented itself.

Chapter Thirty-Four

"We don't know where Marcus is," Jeff said. "His cell phone goes straight to voice mail, and his work said he ran out the door hours ago without saying anything to anyone." He paused. "Have you heard from him?"

I shook my head. "No." I paused, my mind racing. "What about Trish? Has she heard from him?"

"No. She's right here, and she doesn't know anything either."

Frantically trying to think where he could be, I came up blank. I had no idea.

"If you hear anything, will you let us know?" Jeff said.

"Of course. And if you'd do the same for me, I'd appreciate it."

"Sure." He was quiet for a moment. "Lily, I'm sorry about everything that's happened."

All my self-doubt floated back into my mind, and that, coupled with my fresh worry about Marcus and where he could be, made me shrink in on myself. "Okay," I whispered, wanting him to know I heard what he'd said.

"Trish wants to talk to you," he said.

Before I had a chance to object, she was on the phone.

"Lily?"

"I'm here," I said.

"I'm so sorry about the way I reacted." She paused, and I thought I heard the sound of her voice cracking. "Will you forgive me?" Yes, she was definitely crying.

The sting of her words was still fresh in my mind, but I wasn't one to hold a grudge. "Yes, of course," I said.

"I was wrong. You must know that."

But was she? My self-doubt flared within me. Maybe her gut instinct was right and I wasn't the best match for Marcus. *Marcus.* Where was he? I needed to get off the phone with his mother and try calling him myself. "Okay," I said, just wanting to hang up now.

"He told me how much he loves you. I can see it now. I understand."

"He told you that?"

"Yes."

I smiled as tears filled my eyes. *He stood up to her for me. He really does love me.* "Thank you, Trish."

"For what?"

"For raising such a wonderful man."

"Oh, Lily." I could hear the smile in her voice. "I can see why he cares so much for you."

"I'll let you know if I hear anything," I said.

"Okay. Good-bye now."

The moment our connection was broken, I dialed Marcus's phone, but Jeff was right. It went straight to voice mail. *Where could he be? What had happened that had made him leave work in such a hurry, and without a word to anyone?* My worry growing, I didn't know what to do. Marcy wasn't back from her appointment, and Jeff had gone to run errands. I was all alone there, except for Natalie.

Maybe he's on his way to see me, I thought. But I hadn't told him I was coming down here, so he wouldn't even know where to find me. Maybe there was a problem with Greta at the kennel. But no, that wouldn't take hours, and they would have called me, not him. He didn't even know she was there.

At a loss, I paced the living room, anxious for Marcy or Jeff to get home so I could get some advice about what to do. As the afternoon stretched on, I tried to call Marcus several times, and left a voice message when he didn't answer. While I was feeding Natalie, someone rang the door bell. John and Marcy were still gone, so I hurried to answer it. As I began pulling the door open, I expected to see a salesperson, but when I saw who it was, I nearly dropped the jar of baby food I held in my hand.

"Marcus," I said, my voice barely audible.

"Are you okay?" he said, his face serious.

"Of course. Why wouldn't I be? What are you doing here?" I shook my head. "How did you even know I was here?"

He smiled hesitantly. "Can I come in?"

"Yes." I held the door open and he walked in. "I'm just feeding Natalie." I turned and went into the kitchen and he followed me. I set the jar on the table and turned back to him, but after all my thoughts about whether I was good enough, and if we were really meant to be together, I was ambivalent about throwing my arms around him. I ached to be in his arms, but why torture myself if this was the end?

"Marcy called me," he said.

"What?" Confusion washed over me. "When?"

"This morning."

"Why?"

"She told me about the conversation you'd had with her. She said you were on the verge of ending it with me." His voice choked up. "Lily, how could you even consider that? After all it took for us to finally get to this point?"

Stunned that Marcy had called him, and more than that, astounded that he'd raced down here to talk to me, I stared at him in amazement, trying to digest what he'd said. "Your parents are worried sick about you. They said you ran out of work hours ago, without telling anyone where you were going."

"After I talked to Marcy, I knew I had to come see you right away, so I booked a flight and I only had enough time to race to the airport. I almost didn't make it in time, then I took a cab here."

Love and hope blossomed inside me. He loved me so much that he did that, all for me, just to talk to me. "But why didn't you just wait until I came home?"

He shook his head, his expression grave. "I couldn't take a chance on you convincing yourself to end it with me. I know you well enough to know that once you make up your mind, it's hard to change it." He smiled. "I had to intervene." He stepped toward me, and gently ran his finger down my jaw. "Will you marry me, Lily?"

I gazed at him, my love for him filling me up completely, and I nodded. "Yes. I will."

His smile grew. "Today. We have to do it today."

My eyes grew wide. "Today?"

He nodded, then moved closer to me. "Yes. I don't want any more of this nonsense about whether we're right for each other or not. I want to make it official so that no one can get in the way."

A thrill of desire raced through me, and I nodded, helpless under the gaze of his incredible green eyes. This wasn't like with Trevor, who had pressured me to marry him when I was still uncertain if I should. I wanted this as much as, if not more than, Marcus. Yes, there was no doubt that this was the right thing for me to do.

He slid his arms around me and pulled me close, and my arms went around his neck, then our lips met, and I thought I would fly apart with the depth of feeling I had for him.

After a moment Natalie reminded us that she was there, and we reluctantly separated. I turned to take care of her, then I remembered my promise to Jeff that I would let him know if I heard from Marcus. "You need to call your parents," I said as I spooned some food into Natalie's mouth.

He sighed. "Yes, I do."

"What are you going to tell them? About us, I mean."

"I'm going to tell them that I'm going to make you my wife today."

I frowned. "Won't they be upset not to be here?"

"We can have a more formal wedding later, but I won't let them talk me out of making you my wife. Today."

I smiled, loving the determination he had to make me his wife. *His wife.* The phrase I'd dreamt of, but had lost hope of ever having come true. I nodded, leaving his family issues in his capable hands, as Marcy had said I should. It felt good to not worry about it. I wanted to make his family my family also, but after Trish's apology, I was confident it would happen in time.

I listened to his side of the conversation, but focused on caring for Natalie. When he ended his call, I asked how it went.

He grimaced. "You were right that they aren't thrilled about this, but as you heard, I made it clear that this is what I want, and in the end, they supported me." His grimace turned to a smile. "And I promised my mother that we'd have a more formal wedding soon." His eyebrows rose. "She'll probably want to be involved in the planning."

"That's fine with me." I put Natalie on the floor to crawl around, then put my arms around him. "As far as I'm concerned, she can plan the whole thing. The only thing that matters to me is that I'll be your wife."

He held me close, and a few minutes later I heard the front door open.

"Oh," Marcy said as she walked into the room where we stood.

We turned to face her. "Marcy, this is Marcus." I grinned at her. "I believe you've talked to him on the phone before."

Her face flushed, and she stepped forward and gave Marcus a hug. "I didn't know you'd be coming down." Then she looked at me. "I'm sorry, Lily. After you told me how you were feeling, I just thought I needed to call him and let him know what was happening." With a look of chagrin, she said, "I borrowed your phone when you were taking care of Natalie this morning."

I smiled. "It's okay. I'm glad you did."

She looked relieved. "It's not something I would normally do, but I just felt like it was the right thing to do."

I nodded. "I understand." I paused. "We have some news."

A look of expectation swept over her. "Yes?"

"We're getting married."

She chuckled. "You kind of mentioned that this morning."

I laughed. "What I mean is, we're going to get married *today*."

"Oh! That is news. Congratulations." Then she laughed. "This is Las Vegas. Lots of places to get married here." She looked at Marcus. "But what about your parents? Surely they'd want to be here."

"I talked to them and let them know this is what we've decided to do. They weren't thrilled, but we'll have another ceremony later." He paused. "And I hope you and your family will come to that one."

Marcy put her arm around my shoulder. "Of course we will."

It felt great to have this support from her, and impulsively, I hugged her close. "Thank you, Marcy. For everything."

"I consider you one of my daughters, sweetie," she said, smiling. "Now, do you know where you're going to go to do this?"

I looked at Marcus, but he just shrugged.

"First of all," Marcy said, "I hope you'll allow John and me to be there."

I nodded. "Yes, I'd like that."

She smiled. "Good. Second, I hope you'll let us babysit Natalie overnight tonight. It will be your wedding night, after all."

I slipped my hand into Marcus's. "Yes. Thank you."

"Good. Finally, let's find a place nearby where you can get married. John should be home soon, and we can go whenever you'd like."

Excitement pulsed through me. Marcus and I would be married in a matter of hours. I didn't care that I wouldn't have the fancy wedding dress, or all the guests, or the flowers and the walk down the aisle—I'd had that once before. All that mattered was that Marcus would make me his.

A short time later John got home. Marcy explained what was going on, and he graciously welcomed Marcus to their home. Then we looked online and found a place where we could be married, and we called and reserved a time slot.

An hour later, the five of us were on our way. I'd put Natalie's car seat in John and Marcy's car so they could bring her home afterwards, so they drove her to the chapel we'd chosen. We arrived a short time later and walked in together. John, Marcy, and Natalie sat on the front row of the chapel to witness the ceremony.

As Marcus took my hands in his, and promised to love and cherish me forever, tears filled my eyes. We'd only had time to buy a pair of cheap rings on our way to the chapel, but that didn't matter—they were only a symbol. The only thing that mattered was the officiant pronouncing us husband and wife.

"You may kiss your bride," he said.

Marcus pulled me into his arms and kissed me passionately, and I allowed myself to be enveloped by the feelings that poured through me. When he released me, I was breathless, and we gazed at each other, love flowing between us.

Marcy and John hugged us, and we took pictures of us holding Natalie. A short time later John and Marcy took Natalie home, and Marcus drove me to one of the fancy hotels. After checking in, we walked hand in hand to the elevator, and rode up to our floor. We walked to our room, and I waited while Marcus unlocked the door.

"Allow me to carry you across the threshold, Mrs. Oliver," he said, grinning.

My smile matched his as he scooped me into his strong arms and carried me into our room, then set me on the floor. He put a *Do Not Disturb* sign on the door, and locked it from the inside, then turned to me with love in his eyes.

I gazed back, then moved into his arms and reveled in the security of his embrace. His lips met mine, and this time when feelings of desire overwhelmed me, I let them engulf me, and I savored being his wife, hardly able to believe that my dreams had come true, and I'd found love at last.

Epilogue

One Year Later

Holding Natalie's hand, Marcus walked into my hospital room. "Look there, Natalie," he said. "You're a big sister now."

She raced over to me and jumped onto my bed. She was nearly two years old and had been excited for this baby to come. As she gazed at our new baby boy, she tenderly touched his head, then she turned to Marcus. "Look, Daddy."

"Yes, sweetheart, I see." Marcus leaned over and kissed me on the lips. "You are amazing, Lily."

I smiled at him, feeling like I was lit from within with love and happiness. He'd been so good to me ever since the day I'd met him, and he'd never let me down. I knew he loved me with all his heart, and he always put me and my needs first. "And you're wonderful," I said, touching his face.

After our wedding in Vegas, we'd come home to a warm welcome from Trish and Jeff, and as Trish and I had planned the more formal wedding, she and I had actually become good friends. Once we'd gotten to know each other better, she'd broken down in tears, expressing how sorry she was that she'd pushed me away from Marcus when it turned out I was so good for him.

She'd explained that she'd always had a picture in her mind of what Marcus's life would be like, and it didn't involve a widowed woman with a baby. But she'd come to realize that things didn't always turn out the way she'd planned, which was probably a good thing, as she knew now that maybe she didn't always know what was best for everyone.

As promised, John and Marcy attended the formal wedding, as did Chris, Scott, and their families. Chris was polite, and seemed to be warming to me, and I felt confident that we'd be friends one day, although I suspected his attendance was due to John and Marcy's urging. His wife, Melody, pulled me aside after the wedding and confided to me that after she'd learned the details of Trevor's actions, she'd had a long conversation with Chris, which seemed to help him soften towards me.

Alyssa and Ty had come to the wedding as well, and after having a chance to get to know Marcus, Alyssa had finally discovered for herself why I was so in love with my husband, and she'd told me that she believed I'd made the right choice. She told me she'd talked to Cameron before coming to the wedding and not only was he happy for me that I'd finally found happiness, but he'd found a wonderful woman who he was getting serious with. In the short time I'd known him, he'd been really sweet to me and I was glad to know he was finding his own happiness.

With John and Marcy's blessing, Marcus had formally adopted Natalie, which thrilled me to no end. And now we'd added a baby boy to our growing family. Even though Marcus was officially Natalie's father, I planned on Natalie spending plenty of time with John and Marcy. I wanted her to know her grandparents. I'd expressed as much to John and Marcy, which I'm certain was instrumental in them feeling good about Marcus adopting Natalie.

Now, as I looked at my husband and two children, I knew my life couldn't be any better. I'd been through extremely difficult times, but I'd persevered, and now it seemed my joy knew no bounds. I knew there would be challenges ahead—who didn't have challenges? But with Marcus by my side, I knew I could get through anything.

Lily's Story concludes in *Life Imperfect (Lily's Story, Book 4).*

Christine has always loved to read, but enjoys writing suspenseful novels as well. She has her own eReader and is not embarrassed to admit that she is a book hoarder. One of Christine's favorite activities is to go camping with her family and read, read, read while enjoying the beauty of nature.

Please visit Christine's website: christinekersey.com

23024049R00209

Made in the USA
Middletown, DE
14 August 2015